A Sense of Duty

A Medieval Romance

Lisa Shea

Lisa Shea
Visit my website at www.LisaShea.com

Printed in the United States of America

First Printing: December 2011
Minerva Webworks LLC

ISBN-13 978-0-9798377-4-6

3

At first, a dream can seem out of reach.
Then, step by step,
Day by day,
You make progress towards your goal.
Suddenly, it is all around you!

A Sense of Duty

Prologue

England, 1189

I wish I had been the wife of a better man,
someone alive to outrage the withering scorn of men.
-- Helen in the Illiad by Homer

Constance stood motionless on the rocky beach, gazing out at the rolling ocean waves with slowly growing acceptance. Today had been the most joyful day of her life … now it would become the most painful. She spared one last glance for the parchment scroll held in her hand, then deftly rolled it up and tucked it into a small leather bag at her belt. A seabird soared far above, wingtips outstretched, drifting easily on the wind currents, but otherwise she was alone. She had walked a distance from town before reading the missive from her parents. She'd had a foreboding of what the note would say; she had wanted time to absorb the message alone, unwatched.

Footsteps sounded on the gravel, and her heart leapt with welcome recognition. Gabriel, her personal guard for the past five years, strode steadily down the beach towards her. His short blond hair, chiseled face, and muscular, lean build were all as familiar to her as the sharp tang of salt in the brisk air. She had seen those dark blue eyes sparkle with laughter at a shared joke, had watched them narrow with displeasure at any perceived slight to his lady.

Constance had grown up around guards, spent her childhood with swords and shields a part of her daily life. Even so, when Gabriel had been hired by her protective parents, her world had changed instantly. Where others had treated her as a porcelain vase, working to keep her safe from all dangers, Gabriel had insisted she learn how to face and conquer threats. She had gone from a cautious girl of fourteen to a self-assured, confident adult. She knew she owed much of that transformation to his diligent efforts.

Gabriel smiled as he came up behind her, drawing his long, woolen, full-circle cloak around her snugly to shield her from the brisk autumn wind. An absolute sense of peace and calm filled her as the folds enveloped her. She was in the most beautiful place on earth. The man she loved cradled her in a protective embrace. If only she could stop time, preserving this moment for an eternity.

A tear slipped down her cheek, and she turned her head to nestle against his chest. The wind blew her long, tawny hair across her face in waves, and he gently lowered a hand to brush them aside. Glancing more closely, he cupped his fingers beneath her chin, raising her eyes to his.

"My darling, what is it?" he asked quietly.

Constance smiled wryly. She would not spoil this moment for the world. "I am just so happy," she replied, admitting only half the truth.

His arms wrapped more tightly around her, and she sighed as he lowered his head, pressing his lips gently to her forehead. The cloak sheltered them there for over an hour, the waves on the beach flowing and ebbing in quiet harmony.

Finally the setting sun caused the sky to redden and mist. Reluctantly, Constance slipped free from Gabriel's cocoon and walked alongside him back towards the village, her protector's hand resting lightly on his sword's hilt. They climbed a short, grassy hill, then moved across a heather-thatched meadow. There was no need for words; over the years they had become comfortable with silence, with simply being together. He took her hand in his as she passed over a stile in the fence, and the touch was familiar, natural. Even so, every time her fingers met his it sent a new thrill through her body.

She shook the grass and sand from the bottom of her sea-blue dress as they moved on to the packed dirt roads of the village proper, heading towards the small tavern at the town's edge. The building was well kept and neat, with a wooden sign shaped like a copper kettle hanging above the entrance. Gabriel pushed the sturdy door open for her, standing aside to let her in before following behind.

"Gabe! Constance! Welcome back!" called out the portly innkeeper with delight, coming over to clasp Gabriel's hand firmly.

"Pete, always a pleasure," greeted Gabriel with a grin.

"Here, let me bring you to your table." The owner led the pair through the half-empty room over to a small oak round, tucked in a back corner, flanked by a pair of simple wooden chairs. He gave the table a once-over with the cloth from his waist, then went to fetch a pair of tankards of ale for the couple. Pete was back in moments with the fare, then moved on to help another patron.

Constance chuckled as she sipped the proffered drink, looking at the back of the friendly owner. "I swear, you must know every tavern keeper from London to Portsmouth," she offered with a shake of the head. "However do you do it?"

Gabriel gave her a wry smile. "You know I do not reveal my secrets," he rebuffed her with a wink. "Still, keep it in mind if you are ever in trouble. Just leave word at the nearest pub and the news will get to me in a flash."

Constance did laugh at this. "Good to know," she agreed with a toast in his direction. "I will make sure to remember that."

Gabriel took another sip, scanning the room briefly with a sharp eye, nodding to a pair of men who sat by the fire in matching yellow on white tunics. Satisfied with what he saw, he leant forward and lowered his voice. "So, was there anything interesting in that letter from your parents? I take it they want you to come back home from visiting your aunt, since they sent those two with the note and not simply one of the messengers. You have been out here only two weeks – I thought you meant to stay for longer?"

Constance looked down at the worn table. She evaded the answer deliberately, wondering how long she could delay the revelation. With an effort, she kept the tone of her voice light and playful. "I know being here is a welcome vacation for us both - but also difficult for you since I spend all day with Silvia at the nunnery. Few men are allowed within those walls." Her mouth quirked into a smile. "Still, I do enjoy staying with her, assisting her with her daily tasks. She has always been so good to me, and I am immensely curious about her way of life."

Gabriel chuckled softly. "Maybe your parents thought you were becoming *too* curious, and that is why they are bringing you back," he agreed with a grin.

Constance continued to gaze down at the table, taking one of his hands within her own. She ran a finger over the bronze ring he wore on his little finger. The band's face held an engraved cross. She knew Gabriel had been given this ring in the holy land by his mentor, Sir Templeton, the man who had raised him after his parents had died.

Constance wondered again just what atrocities Gabriel had witnessed during his years of service in the Crusades. There were times she caught him at an unguarded moment, when his look was shadowed and lost. She wished there was a way to keep this fresh pain from him.

She took in a long, deep breath, and then let it out in a smooth rush. She could not dodge the issue any longer. Her voice came out low and flat, lifeless.

"I am to marry Barnard in one week."

There was complete silence, and after a moment Constance glanced up. Gabriel sat in shocked surprise, his drink halfway to his mouth. Slowly, carefully, he lowered his mug to the table.

"You cannot be serious. Your wedding will not be held for another year at least. Barnard had agreed to wait until you turned twenty-one." His eyes searched hers, the color draining from his face. "We have another year ..."

Constance shook her head slowly. "You know what the fighting has been like with the bandits. My father needs Barnard's troops to man the Beadnell lands." Her voice fell into the rhythm of a catechism long recited. "However, to let Barnard's forces move in without legal protection of my family's rights would be suicide. Father needs the marriage to guarantee that our family has some control over that land –

through me." Her voice dropped to a whisper. "Through my children."

Gabriel let out a low growl. "The man is twenty years older than you are," he shot out. "He is a coward, a weakling. How could you go to him?"

Constance lowered her eyes. They had gone over this ground countless times over the years, argued about it, talked about it, and it was a situation they had never found agreement on.

"Barnard has waited these ten years for me, since the engagement was first made," she pointed out quietly. "He has been more than patient. The need is upon us, and I will do what I must to keep our people safe."

"You do not have to do what your father orders!" bit out Gabriel, his voice a plea. "There are other options!"

Constance sat back in her chair. "You know full well that I agree with this marriage," she sighed. "Not for me personally, but for all those innocents in the Beadnell area. As a noble I have a responsibility to keep the people on our holdings safe. It is the legacy I will pass down to future generations." Her eyes grew fierce. "I will not neglect that duty due to cowardice or personal selfishness."

Gabriel's voice was hoarse. "And so you would go to that sickly, grey-haired neighbor of yours …" His knuckles went white on the mug still in his grasp. "Constance, you will wither in that home. I cannot sit back and …"

Constance felt the fear grow within her at the prospect of decades of loneliness. She fought it off with familiar effort. "I can handle any personal pain for the sake of those families and children who are at the bandits' mercy."

Gabriel leant forward. "Yes, of course," he agreed tightly, "it is about safeguarding the innocents. If your aim is to protect the defenseless villagers, surely there is another way. One that does not involve you selling your soul …"

Her gaze did not waver. "You know there is not. Could you protect that large area of land on your own? Even my father's forces cannot manage that. No, we need Barnard and the trained soldiers he has at the ready. This is the path I must take, and I am set on it."

Gabriel's eyes became distant, and long moments passed.

"I am lost," he finally stated. "I shall never love another. I shall wait for you to come to your senses, or for him to leave you a widow."

Constance wavered as all color drained from her world. It was one thing for her to consign herself to a loveless, lifeless marriage. She had long since reconciled herself to that fate, and was determined to make the best of it. Her long talks with Silvia had given her guidance on how to find comfort in quiet routine. After all, many girls and women deliberately entered the far more restrictive walls of the nunnery in order to escape life's troubles.

Still, could she doom Gabriel to a miserable existence? Not Gabriel, not the man whose strong arms had protected her for so long, whose sharp eyes could spot danger from a mile away. Not the man who shared walks along the beach during golden-hued afternoons and held her close when ink-black storms hammered the keep's walls. This man deserved to love, to live, to glory in his strengths. Somewhere out there was a woman free to give him the comforts and consolations she could not. He was only twenty-five. His entire life stretched out before him, full of potential, open to all possibilities.

She loved him far too much to deny him that life.

She began to speak, but her throat closed up. She took in a long, deep breath, then let it out again slowly. A second try, and she still could not say a word.

Finally, she took up her tankard and swallowed the ale down in one long draw, pulling strength from the rich brew. When she was done, she put the empty mug solidly down on the table and looked up at the man she loved. She spewed the words out in a rush, knowing if she stopped she would never get through it.

"I will never go to you, Gabriel. You are my guard, and it has been an amusing few years. Now it is time for me to marry, and I must have a real noble as a husband. I need a title for my children, and a fine house to raise them in. Surely you knew this."

Gabriel stared at her for a long moment, stunned. Constance struggled to keep her face still, to keep even the slightest hint of emotion from her demeanor. She nearly broke from the effort, but she held firm.

Then he was standing, his gaze cold, distant. He straightened, turned, and walked toward the door. He did not look back as he strode through the archway and out of her life.

Chapter 1

Six years later

Constance leant back against the warm stone bench, stretching out her arms to release the ache in her shoulders. The summer sunshine dappled her dress, the roses of her private garden spreading around her like pebbles on a rocky beach. She put down the embroidery she was working on – a new pillow cover for her aunt's upcoming birthday. Bees droned lazily from one flower to the next, and lassitude filled her.

A rounded white rose bush, planted for her son, Enoch, flowered prettily to one edge of the path. She looked on it with sadness, thinking of how tiny the infant had been when she miscarried at five months. Alongside this bush was another holding yellow roses ringed with ruffled petals. This was for Vera, her daughter who had clung tenaciously to her chance at life. After the sixth month the struggle had overwhelmed her frail form, and she too had been stillborn.

Two young lives had been denied their opportunity to sample the world's bounty. After that … nothing.

Constance sighed. Despite her desire to have children, she knew she counted herself lucky that Barnard had stopped intruding on her bedchambers for the past five years. It was clear to all in the keep that he was busy trying his luck with other women. By all accounts he was failing there as well. It eased the burden of blame and guilt on Constance's shoulders, but it did not make her life any smoother.

Constance reached out to gently touch one of the yellow roses, feeling its velvety softness. She could almost feel sorry for Barnard. He had honored her parents' wishes and waited a

long ten years between the initial engagement and final
handfasting. He had assumed her youth would guarantee him
instant heirs. Instead, he found himself fading and without
offspring.

She let out a long breath and picked up her needlework
again. She longed for a ride through the forest, a breath of fresh
air, but she knew it was not safe. The bandit attacks had grown
progressively worse over the past years, and it was all Barnard
and her family could do to maintain the safety of the two keeps.
She had become a virtual prisoner within Barnard's walls.

Even worse, as the icy chill of her personal relations with
Barnard grew, her world had shrunk even smaller – to her
bedchambers, her sewing room, and her personal garden. These
three areas were her inviolate sanctuaries. She found what peace
she could here. After all, where else was there for her to go?

Her heart became melancholy as she sorted through her
dwindling options. Her father had been slain less than a year
after she arrived, taken down by a mace in a heated battle
against the incursions. Her mother, grief stricken, passed away
only a few months later. Now her elder brother ruled her family
keep, and Barnard dissuaded her heavily from visiting. She
wondered if he feared she might try to return to her home, and
take her provinces with her. She knew that was no choice at all.
Without Barnard's protections, her lands would fall quickly to
the bandits. The people who relied on her for their safety would
be mown down without remorse. And so she remained.

Yet, in return for her sacrifices, Constance did insist on one
trip. She went to pay respects to her aunt Silvia on a yearly visit.
Barnard could not deny this pilgrimage of faith. Other than that
one indulgence, her routine was quiet. She knitted and sewed
clothes for the less fortunate. She tended to any who were ill
and brought to the keep's infirmary. It would have to be enough.

A heavy footstep entered her garden, and she looked up with
a smile. "Ah, Ralph, is it time already?" she asked pleasantly.
"Well then, I am prepared."

She put down her needlework and drew a dagger from the
belt at her side. Standing before her was a wiry guard with a

deeply creased face. Ralph had taken on employment here just about when Constance had arrived, the soldier having recently returned from the Crusades. Where most of Barnard's own guards were dismissive of her interests in sword work, Ralph had been understanding, even approving of her efforts. He had worked with her privately over the long years, helping her maintain and expand her skills with sword and knife.

He had slowed only slightly as time had rolled past. His short, dark hair was peppered with grey, yet his decades of service in the Crusades and his calm patience served him well. He was lean, rangy, and fit. Constance found him an excellent teacher and a good friend.

She stood and walked over to face him, settling the dagger more firmly in her grip.

Ralph drew his sword with a gentle salute. First they went through a series of stretches as a pair – circling their arms, leaning into lunges, rotating their wrists. Then Ralph turned to stand before Constance.

"All right, let us take up where we left off," he offered. "Defenses against high attacks. I am a bandit, and I am bringing my sword down at you from above my head. What are your strengths here?"

"Speed, and my small size," responded Constance easily. "He will be weighed down by his armor and used to fighting a larger foe. I can leap back before the blade strikes me and duck beneath his swing."

Ralph nodded in satisfaction. "Correct. He will probably be stronger than you, but perhaps not quicker. You must seek out every advantage you can in order to stay alive." He began to bring the sword over his head in a slow arc. "So what is your defense here?"

Constance dodged to the right, bringing her dagger up to deflect the sword just enough to the side that it missed her body. Then she pivoted sharply, bringing the dagger up against Ralph's neck.

"Exactly!" praised Ralph with a smile. "Deflect – do not try to block. Use his strength against him. Then use your smaller size and agility to move in as quickly as you can." He took a step back. "Again."

Constance repeated the motion, and soon they were taking the swings at full speed, Ralph changing his angle of attack, sweeping in from the right and the left. Constance focused on the small changes in his stance, in the slanting of his shoulders, in the direction his eyes looked to judge which way to leap. She enjoyed this part of her day, enjoyed the testing of her knowledge and muscles against a larger opponent. The minutes flew by in a blur of spinning blades and dancing feet.

"Right then," called Ralph at last, stepping back. "Now let us see if you can use the same mindset to handle me attacking with a dagger." He sheathed his sword, drawing out the smaller blade.

Constance settled down lower into her stance. She knew that daggers often involved grappling, quick movements, and tight quarters. Ralph brought his dagger down in a sweeping arc, and she leapt to the right. Without a pause, Ralph turned to strike again. She spun to defend, but he was quicker, and in a moment he had wrapped an arm across her chest, pulling her in close.

Constance was not sure if it was the warm summer sun or the recent musings about the nunnery at St. Francis. Suddenly it seemed that it was not Ralph who was holding her, but Gabriel. It had been so many years ago, and she could still feel the strength of his arms, hear the rumble of his voice, see the sparkle of his blue eyes when she looked up at him. It all flooded back in an instant, and her eyes filled with tears.

Ralph glanced down at her face and released her instantly, his face filling with concern. "My Lady, are you hurt?"

Constance shook her head, lowering herself to the carven stone bench. "No, I apologize, Ralph," she responded between long breaths, wiping at her face. "I am sorry, I just get this way when it is time to go visit my aunt. It brings up sad memories."

Ralph sheathed his blade, nodding in understanding. "Of course, I am sorry for not remembering. Maybe we should finish for today, then. You are gone for two weeks?"

Constance finished drying her eyes, drawing in deep breaths. "Yes," she agreed, "although Barnard threatens to cut my trip short due to the bandits being so active. He is upset at my taking even two guards along. You know that he refuses to allow you to go. He claims that we need every man we have to defend the keep proper."

"Yes, he talks of the imminent threat frequently," admitted Ralph slowly, looking down at her with grey eyes. "It is hard to know how much of his concern is the continual attacks of our enemy, and how much is his desire to look strong with your brother Charles being so covetous of the land." He hesitated a moment, then added more softly. "Apparently now that Charles' brood has grown to four children, your brother is beginning to think that he, not Barnard, deserves the Beadnell lands."

"My brother was always loathe to let the land go," mused Constance with a sigh. Her father's plan was to have the two keeps mark out the two edges of the land area, all held by his children and jointly protecting the province for future generations. With her lack of children, her brother now had designs on taking the whole area himself.

She shook her head wearily. "Even Charles must see that, for now, we need Barnard's soldiers to keep the large area safe. Charles' children are barely walking!" She took in a long breath. "Still, even if my brother wished it, he could not move against Barnard for now, not with the bandits being so hostile. I am sure when he eventually does muster a large enough force to spread this far, his move will be couched in the language of family protection, of watching out for me."

Ralph's face creased into a frown. "It will not make it easier on you," he commented with concern.

Constance shrugged. "I have barely seen my brother in years. My brother's wife apparently has no love for me. I hear she sees my presence, my ability to someday bear an heir, as a threat to her own children and her goals." She looked down, digging her foot into the rich soil. "Still, for now, I am only a potential stumbling block to them." Her eyes lit up with mischief. "After all, I could always retreat to the nunnery and take shelter there. Maybe the nuns would enjoy the land."

Ralph's eyes flew open with shock. "My lady, you would not! There are people here who depend on you!"

Constance smiled, taking up her embroidery as she stood. "No, I would not," she agreed. "However, my brother does not know that – and my father shrewdly worded the legal agreement to keep the Beadnell lands under my name, to ensure Barnard could not keep them should something happen to me. They go to me or to my issue, not to him. If I went to the church, so would the lands. Would that not create a sticky problem for both my brother and Barnard?"

Ralph escorted his lady back toward the keep. "Aye, it would, lass," he chuckled gently, his voice dropping low as he used the more familiar term. "You just watch out for yourself, all the same."

A tall man in the uniform of a guard strode from the entryway, his dark, curly hair close around his smooth face. "Ralph, there you are," he bit out tersely. "You should have been on duty a half-hour ago. Get up on the wall."

"Yes, Captain," responded Ralph neutrally, giving a fond bow to Constance before turning and heading into the building.

Frank waited a moment until Ralph was out of sight before turning back to the woman before him. He ran his eyes slowly up and down Constance's form, his mouth widening into a grin. "You appear to have had quite a work out, M'Lady," he murmured suggestively.

"No more than any other day, Frank," replied Constance, keeping her tone even. It would do no good to rile Barnard's right-hand man only a few hours before she left.

"You know, Lord Barnard does not like you participating in that training, but I think it is good for you. It keeps your body fit and firm." His grin grew wolfish. "Would you not agree?"

Constance folded her hands before her. "You know that is not my aim, Frank," she responded quietly. "We have many villagers who come to us for alms. I am able to help train those who are alone – the widows, for example – in ways to defend themselves." A smile grew on her face. "Only three weeks ago, Cecily was able to fight off a wolf who came into her barn to go after her new lambs. It is tales like that which keep me going."

Frank took a step closer to her. "I would like to hear what else keeps you going," he leered.

"I am sorry, but I am afraid I have some packing to do," demurred Constance, moving her way past him. "Are the guards almost ready to go?"

Frank gave a short bark. "Do you think we would waste trained guards on a babysitting duty such as this, given the current bandit situation?" He laughed in amusement. "We need them all here, around the keep. No, Barnard has hired a pair of locals to ride with you. They should be more than adequate to protect you on your journey. Your trip is short, and only during daylight hours. You will be fine."

Constance glanced up at that, confused. "Local men from the village? But surely Ralph …"

"No," snapped Frank, his face darkening in jealousy. "That man spends far too much time with you as it is. The locals are ready in the main hall. You will take the coach, as usual, and once they get you to the nunnery, those walls are more than ample defense. No bandit would dream of taking on that challenge."

Constance looked down. Arguing would do little good, and if she made a fuss it was likely Barnard would refuse to allow her to go at all.

"If that is Barnard's request," she conceded quietly.

Frank chuckled without mirth. "That is your husband's *order*," he corrected her deliberately.

Constance flushed, and her left thumb went automatically to rub against the ring on her finger, the golden band engraved with a winding ribbon, not with crosses. She turned quickly, hoping Frank would attribute her discomfort to his tone, not to that word, *husband*. She had never been good at lying, and playing this game for six long years had worn at her. But it was critical for the safety of the villages in the Beadnell lands, the

people who depended on her and on Barnard's troops to keep
them safe.

She was not Barnard's wife, she reminded herself almost in
desperation.

Her thumb spun the band in a slow circle against her finger.
They had been handfasted, an ancient tradition, a trial period to
see how well the couple lived together. She chuckled with an
edge of cynicism. She knew that, in many cases, it was more a
way to test how fertile the pair was without going through the
messy aftermath of an almost obligatory divorce should the
partnership be barren.

Barnard's edict had been stated clearly to her family before
the handfasting ceremony, and her parents had agreed to it
without blinking an eye. Barnard would marry only when
Constance was on the verge of birthing a healthy child, to
guarantee his line would continue. Constance knew her parents
felt they were looking out for her as well, worried that she might
be trapped with a man no longer capable of siring a child.

She shook her head, mounting the long stairs with slow
deliberation. Her parents were long dead; they could not object
that the year of handfasting had stretched into six. Her brother
knew nothing of the reality of the situation. She knew if she told
Charles that he would demand she return to their family home.
He would also insist the Beadnell lands immediately be turned
over to him. Constance did not know if she feared more that the
bandits would instantly overrun his thinly stretched troops, or
that Barnard would refuse to give up the lands and launch into a
war.

And Barnard ... she sighed deeply. Barnard enjoyed his
power over her. He had the best of all possible worlds. He held
the lands he craved without any contestation. He was also free
to attempt to father sons in any way he wished.

Constance shook her head. It seemed whatever he tried, the
chance of Barnard creating a viable son seemed less likely with
each passing month. It was almost too clear that Barnard was
unable to father a child, no matter what partner he chose.

Constance shivered, stepping into her room, pulling the door solidly shut behind her. She glanced around her bedroom. Barnard was nothing if not status conscious – her heavy, ornate bed, elegant wardrobe, and richly carved trunks all attested to the skill of the house craftsmen. But it was the four circular wood carvings on the walls which brought Constance the most pleasure. She walked over to one of the maple circles and gazed at it for a long moment.

The wood carver hailed from Beadnell. His artful, intricately worked landscapes illustrated the four seasons of life in the quiet village. On the other three walls hung the remaining seasons' plaques. One held a snowy winter scene with laughing children playing by a frozen lake. The second portrayed a bountiful harvest day, the onions and turnips overflowing from a rustic wagon while an elderly couple relaxed on a bench in the shade of a sturdy oak. The third revealed a fresh spring morning, a meadow full of flowers, farmers out planting their fields.

But it was this one by her window which always called to her. It presented the summer scene, the hand-crafted wares and mouth-watering delights of the Beadnell fair. A couple walked hand-in-hand between the tables of ribbons and jewelry, a goldfinch singing from a cage to one side.

Constance ran one finger along the smooth edge of the scene, her stomach twisting as she thought of the tenuous safety of those quiet villagers. She could almost feel the half-life purgatory of her existence closing in on her. She had given up so much to protect the innocents for these past six years. So far she had succeeded. The bandits had been kept at bay; there had been no successful raids. But how long could it last? Her limbo could be shattered at any time if one of Barnard's mistresses bore him a child. She knew while Barnard greedily clung to the Beadnell lands, that his desire for a son would trump even that.

Barnard would publicly marry the woman who birthed his child, and Charles, realizing the truth of the situation, would immediately insist the Beadnell lands become his. She knew what horrors would follow. She had heard the stories from further north, where there were not enough soldiers in place to protect the farmers from the bandit raids.

Constance drew her eyes away from the fair scene with an effort. She walked to the large window, staring out at the forest beyond the walls of the keep. She reminded herself forcefully that she had achieved exactly what she set out to do all those years ago. She had kept the men, women, and children in Beadnell safe. Yes, Barnard would continue to try to beget an heir with every new female he found willing to yield to his advances. He would never give up hope, never resign himself to a marriage without issue. The years would roll by. She would live here, trapped, cloaked in eternal chastity.

She was, indeed, in a perpetual purgatory.

A shaft of sunlight came through the clouds, and suddenly she could almost feel the warmth of Gabriel's arms around her, almost smell the richness of his scent, and she pressed her eyes closed against the tears which threatened to overwhelm her. She had chosen this path for herself, and she would not veer from it now. The Beadnell lands would stay safe. Her duty would be fulfilled. By the time she died, Charles' children would be grown and more than capable of offering the necessary protection. Her nephews would carry on the family lineage, and her obligation would be satisfied.

Pushing up her sleeves, Constance took in a deep breath and turned from the window. It was the best she could hope for, and it would have to do.

She had half-finished packing the small traveling trunk when a sharp series of raps came at her door. There was no pause before it swung open and a sharp-faced woman peered in.

"Oh, M'Lady, here you are," she snapped, her eyes darting to the open trunk. "Your dinner is getting cold."

"I am sorry, I am not feeling hungry tonight," apologized Constance. She looked away, her stomach rumbling slightly. The truth was that she was simply not up to dealing with the disdain of the rest of the household, not when she would be gone in the morning. Ralph was her only friend in the keep. The rest looked at her with a mixture of suspicion and contempt. She had failed their master, after all – not produced children for him, forced him into his many dalliances.

She looked back at the middle-aged maid. "Please tell Barnard ..."

"My Lord is not here," interrupted the woman coldly. "He is off to the village for the evening."

Constance knew she should be long past the hurt, but it still had the power to wound her, to know he was so openly parading his mistresses for all to see.

The maid's mouth drew down. "I suppose you would want me to help you with your packing," she offered sourly.

Constance shook her head no. When the maids cleaned her room, she often had to go back and redo the work afterwards, to make up for their spotty efforts. It was far better for her to handle this task herself.

"Thank you, I will be fine," she assured the maid, attempting a small smile.

The woman pursed her lips, then turned without another word, closing the door firmly behind her.

Constance let out her breath, slumping down onto the bed. She had tried numerous times over the years to be friendly. Back when she had been pregnant, during that first year, the servants had almost thawed to her. But when both attempts ended in miscarriages, it was as if she was seen to be cursed.

She pressed her hand to her chest for a moment, feeling the pewter medallion which hung under her chemise by a thin leather line. It was all that kept her sane, at times – this one necklace, this one link to a happier past. She took in several deep breaths, then stood to finish her packing.

Tomorrow she would be free. If only for two short weeks, she would taste the freedom that haunted her in her dreams.

Chapter 2

Constance cantered along the sun-drenched road, her heart soaring in the glorious beauty of the summer afternoon. A pair of middle-aged, rough-hewn men, surly at the thought of their assigned task, rode tightly on either side, their dark faces twisted into gloomy resignation. Constance would not allow their sour moods to bring down her feelings of joy. She had these two weeks each year as her own, and she was going to relish every hoofbeat, every fragrant new scent of the trip.

The woods stretched along either side of the path, the waving branches green and verdant. She spotted a flock of sparrows swooping across the sky, and she thrilled in their flight. The coach she was sent to ride in, under strict orders of Barnard, was lagging miles behind by now, pulled by the one remaining horse. She knew the young coachman would catch up with them when they drew in at the next tavern.

The miles rolled by, and her shoulders relaxed with each passing moment. She loved her elderly aunt and enjoyed the time she was able to spend sitting and talking with her. She wished that she could visit more frequently but she took solace that the nunnery was friendly and pleasant. Her aunt had chosen a good place to live out her life.

The only thoughts that darkened her joy were the memories that the ocean and beach brought up for her. She could not make this trip, could not walk along the ocean's shore, without vividly remembering Gabriel's arms around her, his eyes gazing down at hers.

Her face dropped. Without any bidding she suddenly remembered the look in his eyes when she told him she could never be happy with him. All light had faded, all hope had evaporated, all emotion had dissipated in the blink of an eye. Constance prayed every night that he had found a new love, had moved on and forgotten her. She knew that the same would never be true for her. Her hand moved again to the medallion she wore beneath her dress, and she pressed against it for a long moment.

There was movement in the woods to the left, and she spun her head. It seemed, for a moment, that a pair of eyes looked out at her from between the dark trunks. Then they were gone, and the blur of trees continued to streak past the three riders, dense with oak and brush.

She shook her head. Now she was seeing things, delusional in her daylight hours as well as at night. She could not count the number of dreams she'd had about Gabriel. Sometimes they were playfully sword fighting, ringing dagger on dagger, twisting in blocks and parries with shouted glee. Sometimes they were walking through her gardens, or along the ocean, content with each other's company. However, most of the time they were seated in the tavern, staring across the small, round table, his eyes bereft of all hope …

She actively pushed away the sorrowful memories. Her aunt was looking forward to her visit, and it would not be fair to mope gloomily about for the next fortnight. There were enough other weeks in the year to ponder her sadness, if that was her wish. For now, she needed to maintain her spirits and to bring comfort to an elderly relative.

She glanced again in idle curiosity at the men at her side. From the looks on their faces the hired locals were not being paid well for their efforts. They seemed eager to return to their homes, and undoubtedly to their local tavern.

The miles flowed by in smooth succession and in a slow, steady slide the sun began to hang lower in the sky. The outskirts of the town came into view and the horses slowed to a trot, then to a walk. The trio made their way through the quiet evening streets towards the tavern, the familiar copper kettle sign hanging over the door.

A stable boy ran forward to take their horses and the two men escorted Constance inside. The main room was quiet, only a few patrons sitting at tables with ale or mead. A low fire crackled in the fireplace to one side. Constance glanced at the table in the back, empty, the chairs sitting to either side, looking the same as it always did in her dreams, a physical reminder of what she had lost.

The barkeep came out from the kitchen promptly, smiling as he saw her. "Lady Constance, always a pleasure!" he beamed. "Shall I get you some ale, or a late supper?"

Constance was tempted, and yet she knew she could not stay in this room, not with the wealth of memories it held. "I am sorry, but no," she apologized. "I am exhausted, and would rather just go up to sleep. We will head on to the nunnery in the morning."

"Yes of course, your usual room is ready for you and your guards," agreed the keep with a smile, stepping forward to lead them upstairs. Barnard's frugality insisted that the guards share a room with their charge, although he claimed it was for her better protection, not for want of coin. Over the years the innkeeper had rigged up a sliding curtain to provide Constance with some modesty during her visits.

She walked briskly into the small room, moving immediately to the window. She stood looking out at the small town and the ocean visible beyond. The salt air scent pervaded the town, but this was her first glimpse of the water itself. She remained there for a long while, barely hearing as the guards left her to return to the main tavern hall for some food and drink. She pressed herself against the window's edge, staring out at the ocean, reveling in its grace and power.

The sky above drifted into orange, crimson, and then finally the deepest blue. Her eyes filled with tears, and soon her whole body was racked with sobs. This is how she had stood, all those years ago, after Gabriel had walked out of her life. It was how she had stood, on her return every year since, her heart broken, knowing that she had lost the one person important to her. He was gone … he was gone.

Time seemed to stand still, marked only by falling tears, until eventually there were none remaining to cry, and she was left only with a hollow ache in her core.

There were footsteps on the stairs, and she wiped her face quickly, moving to the far side of the room, behind the shield of the curtains. The door opened and in a moment the two guards were bustling around, laying out the mats which served as their sleeping areas. Without a word they sprawled out on the thin rolls. A minute or two later, deep snores were emanating from both men.

Constance took her time, carefully stripping off her outer dress and removing her shoes. After both had been laid out, she climbed into the narrow bed in her thin, white chemise. She put a dagger beneath her pillow, a lesson drilled into her by Gabriel, one she never forgot. She closed her eyes and waited for sleep to overtake her.

There was no easy release. She lay awake for a long while, a myriad of thoughts drifting through her head. She could almost feel Gabriel's strong hand in her own, feel the warmth that flooded through her when he smiled at her. Sternly, she gave herself a small shake. Her sacrifice had not been in vain. The alliance with Barnard had brought a stronger wall of troops to Beadnell. She had bought time and safety for the people of her homeland. If she thought the bandits were bad now, how much worse would they have been if Barnard's forces had not moved into the area to help keep them at bay?

Other soldiers had helped as well, she admitted. Her brother's marriage and alliance with the Preston family to the south had further strengthened their alliances. Her brother, in essence, had done the same thing she had done – partner up to create a stronger border.

Even the local wool-making guild had played a part in bolstering the area's stability. Feeling threatened by the bandits, the guild had taken action and hired on a highly skilled group of mercenaries – the Angelus. The soldiers reportedly worked out of the guild's main hall in the east. It was certainly due to the Angelus' presence that the bandits had not won more victories.

Still, nothing yet was certain. The infighting between Barnard and her brother seemed to be growing daily. The bandits, usually a fractious stew of factions and short-lived leaders, had become quiet. It was almost as if they were waiting for something, as if the area held its breath. For what, she wondered ...

There was a creaking noise just outside her door. Constance's hand slid immediately beneath her pillow, her fingers wrapping firmly around her dagger's hilt. The innkeeper would never dare enter their room by night, yet who ...?

The door flung open, and three cloaked, muscular men swarmed into the room in a blazingly fast rush. Two of the men went straight for the two guards, cutting their throats with brisk efficiency. Constance bit back a shriek, staying hidden behind the curtains as the third man raced in her direction. As he lowered himself over her, she came up suddenly with the hidden blade, turning it as she had done so many times in practice, driving the dagger hard against his throat. He reached up in shocked surprise, the blood spurting as he fell down across the bed, trapping her legs with his heavy body.

The remaining two men were on her before she could recover, and the weapon was easily stripped out of her hand. The taller of the two loomed over her, his salt and pepper hair standing straight up like a brush. His face mottled with fury, and he drew back his fist to strike. The other man grabbed his arm with a quick shake of the head, a look of warning on his face. The first held back in barely contained rage, hatred shining strongly in his eyes.

He glanced at the blood now sprayed across Constance's chemise, then with a smooth motion reached down to pull the black cloak off his fallen friend and wrap it around her, hiding the blood from view. The shorter, red-headed one placed a knife at her throat. "Not a sound," he warned with a steely hiss.

It had all happened in less than twenty seconds. Constance's heart pounded in her chest as the two pushed her quickly from the room. The men surely must be bandits, taking her for a ransom. Could she escape? She was barefoot, dressed only in the bloody chemise and a dead man's cloak. She had no resources, nobody else to turn to …

They went down the stairs and into the now-dark main room. Even in the pitch black, Constance's eyes went automatically to the table in the corner, to where Gabriel had sat. Oh, Gabriel …

She saw a movement. The men at either side of her froze, and the knife at her throat quickly moved around to press solidly into her back. She did not need a further command to understand what it signified.

A candle flared from the back room, and the stocky innkeep, rubbing his eyes with sleep, took a step into the dining area. "Constance, is that you?" he asked in confusion.

The taller man behind her spoke in a smooth voice. "We are from the nunnery. Her aunt has fallen gravely ill, and we must take Constance to her with all speed. There is not much time."

"Oh, of course, how awful," agreed the innkeep with a groggy fluster. His eyes moved to Constance's, sleep still maintaining a hold on him. "Is there anything I can do, my child?"

The dagger pricked more deeply into her back, and she felt a warm bead of blood trickle down her skin. She took in a deep breath, willing her voice to be even and calm. This poor man would be slain if he attempted to interfere. Even if she tried to get a message to Barnard or her brother, would they care? Would they come? She was without hope …

Her eyes flickered again to the table in the corner, to the man that even now she could imagine sitting in that spot, his arms strong, his eyes focused on achieving any goal he set. She wet her lips, impetuously speaking out.

"Just tell Gabriel I said hello," she asked softly.

The innkeeper's eyes flicked with surprise, but he nodded his head. "As you wish," he replied shortly. "I wish your aunt good health." He turned and left the room in the dark.

The dagger was pulled away from her skin, she was quickly moved through the main door of the tavern, then around to the stables. The taller man put her up onto a large, black horse and immediately climbed up behind her. In another moment the trio was thundering through the night, heading through the blackness to an unknown destination.

A Sense of Duty

Chapter 3

Constance awoke to a grey dreariness. She looked around warily in surprise, trying to get her bearings. She lay in a small room barely eight feet square. Beneath her was a low, dense mat, and she was covered by a rough wool blanket. There was one window, barred, which let in the morning sun, what there was of it. A fireplace lay cold and barren to the forward side of the room. The only other thing visible besides unfinished stone was the solid wooden door to her right. There were no hangings on the wall, not a stick of furniture except a chamber pot in one corner.

She stood shakily, drawing the musty blanket around her thin chemise as she stood. She carefully made her way to the window. Thick iron bars blocked any chance of her dropping the three stories to the ground below. There was a narrow area of grass, and then forest stretched for as far as she could see. The building was apparently in a hollow surrounded by hills. The landscape seemed both generic and unfamiliar. A hawk sailed high above, scouting for a meal. There was no other noise from beyond her room, neither from inside the keep nor without.

She made her way slowly around the room, looking for any indication of where she was. The chamber pot was of the most basic construction, red pottery with no markings. The stone was plain and rough. The door was firmly locked, and there was no answer to her shouts and pounds. Finally after an hour of walking around the room and trying every bar, hinge, and crack, she returned to her mat to sit and think.

This had to be the bandits. Nothing else made any sense. They undoubtedly wanted a ransom for her return, to fund their further attacks. The question now was whether Barnard or her brother would feel the ransom worth the money. What did they lose if she languished? If she died, the province would revert to her brother's control. Barnard would miss the land, she was sure, but he could be much more open in his quest for a fertile woman. On the other hand, if she were kept alive for years, the status quo would remain, but without her presence in the keep. Perhaps they would enjoy that even better …

A noise sounded at the door, and she drew back fearfully on the bed. The door opened a small crack, and a plate of food was pressed in to the room, along with a mug of ale. The door swung shut again, and she heard a thick bolt being laid down.

Eagerly, she ran forward to grab up the bread and cheese, eating it with a fury. She had not consumed anything since early the previous day and found she was ravenous. She gulped down the ale, then returned to her station. Time would tell what the kidnappers wanted. Until then, she would have to wait, and be ready.

The day drew by slowly, and she passed the time by doing exercises against the wall, stretching her arms and legs in regular cycles. There might be a chance for escape, no matter how slim, and she knew she had to keep her strength at its peak in order to take advantage of even the slightest opportunity.

She went around the room once an hour, pulling at the stones, twisting at the bars, peering up the fireplace, diligent in her search for an escape. Twilight began to dim the room, and yet nobody had come to talk with her, to take away the plate. Soon, exhaustion overtook her and she collapsed on her mat, the blanket curled up tightly around her.

The next day dawned in grey turmoil, storm clouds gathering outside her window. Constance tried to shrug off the ill omen, but her heart sank. They obviously knew who she was. Surely the ransom demands would have been sent immediately on her capture; the kidnappers would want their money as soon as possible. Had they really asked for so much that her family could not instantly provide it?

She ate the food when it was brought, did her hourly cycles of exercise, and searched vainly in the forest for any sign of life, any indication of a landmark. The day drifted by in long languor, and she found her hand moving to press at the medallion beneath her thin chemise, drawing hope and strength from it. Someone would come for her. She knew it. Still, it was a long time after dusk before she managed to fall asleep.

When she woke to the grey, misty morning, she felt a moment of panic. Had it been two days since she had been captured, or three? She sat counting out the events in her mind, reassuring herself that it was now the third day. Still, the thought that she could so quickly lose track of time unnerved her greatly. The chamber pot had been emptied sometime in the night, and the food dish removed. There were two protruding handles on the chamber pot. Carefully, gently, she wedged one of the handles into a corner of the room, pressing against the body until the handle came off with a sharp *snap* in her hands. A small thrill of victory coursed through her. She moved over to where her thin mat lay, and lifted up a corner. Carefully she scratched out three long stripes on the stone beneath the mat, and secreted the handle there as well. She pressed her hand against her pendant for a long while, drawing strength from its presence. Then her food was brought, and her daily routine began.

Another dawning of gloom and bleakness. Another line joining the others in her daily count. She found herself standing by the open window for long hours, staring out at the freedom beyond the barred walls. Surely by now Barnard or Charles would have raised the ransom money and would be bringing it here to exchange for her. She tried to visualize it in her mind, tried to will it into being.

A goldfinch called out in the forest, and suddenly it was not Barnard she was visualizing. It was as if the six years had not passed, as if she was still sixteen, and the Beadnell fair had just begun …

Constance smiled, sure she could see her own reflection in the bright eyes of the goldfinch, the dollop of sunlight singing fiercely from within its wicker cage. She turned to Gabriel, and only half jested when she asked, "Should we free the poor thing? Surely she would rather be soaring in the sky on this beautiful day!"

"If that truly is your wish ..." offered Gabriel with a gentle smile, his eyes twinkling. "I would be more than happy to oblige."

The elderly stall owner turned at that, his wrinkled face lighting up. "Ah, not to worry," he reassured them in a creaky voice. "If I were to try to keep her alone for too long, she would die from loneliness. You see up there?" He pointed to the top of a nearby oak tree, and Constance turned to follow his outstretched finger. To her surprise there was a glow of gold in the top branches, and the grizzled man chuckled again. "Yes, he will stay there all fair long, keeping an eye on her, making sure she is all right. When the fair is through, I will release her again, and nature's balance will be restored."

Constance found herself pouting. "But if you are going to release her, why cage her in the first place?"

The shopkeep smiled more broadly, waving his hand with a flourish. "I have far more visitors stop to examine my goods with this pretty thing on the corner of my table," he admitted with a rusty laugh. "And besides, perhaps she appreciates her true love more after they are apart for a while. I could be helping things along!" He gave her a wink. "In any case, lass, the sooner I sell my wares, the sooner I free the little creature. Might you be interested in a ribbon or two?"

Constance laughed out loud at that, and in a moment she had chosen three long ribbons to bring back for the cook's daughter, handing a coin to the shopkeep with a smile.

She turned from the stall, and the tumult of the fair swept over her in a fresh wave. There was so much to see! The music of the singers, the loud laughter of the crowd filled Constance's ears as she pressed merrily through the throng. She loved going to the fair each year, sampling the wares of the vendors, shopping for new fabrics, for jewelry and carvings and clothes. Gabriel strolled along beside her, his face relaxed and content. There was little danger here, and it was a chance for them to be together away from the prying eyes of the keep.

She nudged into him in delight, and his mouth softened into a smile as he looked down at her.

"I am famished!" she cried out as they passed a table sporting an assortment of baked pastries. Gabriel stopped to talk with the rotund woman who manned the counter, picking out a selection of hot cross buns for the two of them. Constance's eyes were caught by a flash of silver – ahead of them a booth provided a selection of necklaces and pendants laid out on a black velvet table. She pressed ahead through the mob to take a look.

There were golden chains, silver crosses, Celtic rounds, French beadwork … her eyes flitted from item to item, enjoying the fresh sunshine of the day. The slick haired man behind the booth smiled but said nothing, content to let her browse at her leisure. Constance looked up and down each row, appreciating the quality of the selection but not quite finding anything which spoke to her.

And then – there it was. At the end of one of the rows, a round pewter pendant, perhaps two inches in diameter. It was a Celtic dragon. She sensed somehow that it was female – perhaps by the curled scales, perhaps by the gentle look to her face. The dragon gazed off to one side, smoke lazily tracing from her nose. The image seemed both protective and peaceful, and Constance wondered what the creature was looking at. She picked up the pendant, turning it over in her hand. On the back was one word in Latin. Amor.

Constance smiled. She knew that word.

Love.

She felt a presence behind her, and turned to find Gabriel standing next to her. He was staring down at the pendant with a sharp focus.

"Oh, Gabe, it is lovely!" Constance cried out, turning it in her fingers. "Have you ever seen anything like it?"

Gabriel shook himself and looked up at the dark-haired merchant. "How much for the necklace?" he asked, his voice low.

The merchant smiled at the couple genially. "That is quite a unique piece, is it not?" he suggested in agreement. "I have not found another pendant like it in all of my years. It looks to be one of a kind, although of the style usually done in pairs. This is a treasure to last a lifetime. I will part with it for only ... five pounds."

Constance's mouth fell open in shock. "Five pounds? I could buy a fine sword, complete with engravings, with that kind of money." She moved to put the pendant back down on the table.

"Done," stated Gabriel firmly, pulling out his pouch.

Constance saw the merchant's eyes light up with avarice. "No," she protested, putting a hand on Gabriel's arm. "It is far too much. Besides, you are supposed to haggle!"

Gabriel did not slow in his motions, drawing out the coins. He handed them over to the merchant, who counted them with delight. In a moment Gabriel had the necklace in his hands, lifting the long, slim leather loop towards her.

Constance was too surprised to speak as Gabriel slowly lowered the pendant over her head, pressing the medallion in place over her chest.

"This is a guardian symbol," he murmured, looking up from where the dragon hung. "She will watch over you when I cannot."

Constance gazed at the image, marveling in its beauty. She noticed with a smile that the dragon was looking to the right – looking to where Gabriel stood at her side. Impulsively, she turned to give him a warm hug in thanks. He glanced around instinctively, then relaxed against her, drawing her in against his body. She felt his head nuzzle down into her hair for a long moment, and then he gently pressed her away again.

"If anyone deserves to wear this, you do," he added hoarsely, looking down at her with tenderness. Then, giving

himself a small shake, he reached into his bag, drawing out the
hot buns, and the two began to walk down the fairground aisle,
the noise and bustle of passers-by surrounding them.

The dragon was hidden beneath her chemise now, but she
knew every corner of her face, every swirl of smoke by heart.
She had never removed the medallion from her neck since he
placed it there that afternoon. It had been beneath her chemise
on her handfasting day, had comforted her on the long nights
after the loss of her children. It would keep her strong here in
her captivity, until she became free again. She knew it was only
a matter of time. She would remain ready.

Day five ... day six. She became thankful for her scratched
lines, for her only link to time passing. Nothing else changed in
her world. There was no sound from the outside, no movement
in the forest, no sense that the world was revolving and
continuing outside her cell. She began to wonder not *when*
someone would pay for her release, but what would happen to
her if *nobody* did. Would her captors keep feeding her forever?
Would the food stop arriving at some point, leaving her to
starve in this room? She could not afford to ponder that
alternative. She needed to keep up her hopes, her strength.
Something would happen to break this monotony.

She had become so accustomed to the silence by the end of a
week that she began hearing things. She was convinced she saw
shadowy figures in the trees, heard horses rustling through the
dense leaves. She called out until she was hoarse, until her
throat ached with raw pain. There was no change, no alteration
of the sun's slow progress across her worn floor, the absence of
voice, of humanity ...

Constance was jolted from a deep, dreamless sleep. It was
pitch black, and she found herself being roughly dragged across
rocky dirt. There was a sharp pain in her hand, and she realized
she held the pottery shard in a tight grip. She looked up to see a
starry sky, and she cried out in surprise. A fist landed hard
across her face, and she shrunk back, dazed with pain. In a

moment she was roughly flung into a wooden wagon. Two men climbed in after her, pressing her down into a bed of hay, pulling a grimy rag of fabric across her mouth to muffle her voice. One man drew out a sharp dagger and pressed it against her neck. She froze at once. Gabriel and Ralph had both taught her evasions from a hold, but she was far too weak, far too outnumbered to try. It was best to bide her time, to wait for a better opportunity.

The miles rolled by at a quick pace. Constance did her utmost to watch the passing road, to glance at the stars to get a bearing of where she was going. It seemed that they were moving north, but beyond that nothing looked even remotely familiar.

At least they were on the move. Perhaps her ransom had been paid! The kidnappers could be bringing her to safety! She clung to that hope with all her might, bringing a hand up to press against the dragon for good luck. Her ordeal would soon be coming to an end.

It seemed several long, dark hours later before she was wheeled towards a large stone structure. It appeared to be a ruined tower. She had never seen it before, and wondered where they could possibly be. The two men grabbed her roughly by the arms and began dragging her towards the building.

The main hall was small by her standards, and poorly kept. A rotting pile of kitchen scraps moldered in one corner, and the few tapestries which hung on the walls were frayed and threadbare. Several lit torches flickered in sconces on the walls. For the first time, she was able to see something of the men who were holding her. They were rough cut and dressed in grungy clothes. The taller of the pair had salt and pepper bristly hair. She realized with a start that he was one of the men who had dragged her from bed at the tavern – who had slain her guards. Constance gave a shiver at the thought.

He spoke in a low, surly growl. "Where do you want her, Mark?" he asked, maintaining a tight grasp on her arm.

Constance glanced up. A man was coming towards them, his red hair gathered in tight curls around his head. It was the other partner in the kidnapping. In the light of the room she could see a thin scar tracing its way down his cheek. His body was layered in black leather. He ran his eyes up and down Constance's body in slow appreciation.

Constance blushed at the appraisal, but the men at her side held her arms fast, preventing her from covering herself. She wore only the thin chemise she had been captured in, and she knew it did little to hide her shape from view.

"There is no need to rush," murmured Mark with a grin, stepping toward her slowly. He reached out a hand, and Constance reacted on instinct. She tore a hand free and slapped Mark across the face.

His response was immediate – he hit her a resounding blow on the temple which dropped her to her knees and sent her head ringing. She was hauled back up by the two men at her side.

"Careful there, lass," warned Mark with heat. "The rules have changed. You will be with us for a long time. You had best learn to behave."

Constance's head was throbbing with pain, but worse was the stab in her heart as she heard these words. How long could she last in the grasp of men such as these? Her pride burned bright within her and she pulled herself upright. She would hold out as long as she could. She threw her head back and looked to meet Mark's gaze, not willing to show her fear before these men.

Mark reached out a hand towards her face, then his eyes lit up and he slowly traced his hand down her cheek to her neck. Constance held herself rigid beneath his touch. If he thought he would have a docile victim because of one blow, he would learn his lesson soon enough. She'd had far more bruising in her workouts with Gabriel or Ralph. She held her knee at the ready

…

All of a sudden Mark's fingers tightened, then yanked, and Constance felt a searing pain along both sides of her neck. She fell back, gasping, feeling the blood begin to drip down from the wounds. It did not matter – the only thing that mattered was that Mark now held her pendant in his hands, his eyes alight with interest.

"No!" pleaded Constance, her heart shattering in unbelieving shock. She had worn her guardian dragon for years – it could not leave her now! Not when she needed it most!

Mark smiled with greed, spinning the pendant around in his fingers. "Oh, our master will be very pleased with this prize," he chuckled to the other guards. Glancing up, he nodded off-handedly to the men. "Put her downstairs in one of the cells, Jacob" he added dismissively. "I will get to her later." Still staring at the pewter pendant he turned on his heel and left the room.

Constance almost did not feel the ground beneath her feet, did not sense the ever dimming surroundings as the men half carried, half dragged her down a set of stairs into a damp, mold-smelling area. She was flung against a pile of musty hay, into a room which was completely dark, and a door was slammed shut on her. She curled up into a ball in the blackness, holding her hand firmly against the empty place at her chest, finally allowing herself to weep in despair.

***

Constance woke with a start, her body curled in a tight ball on the corner of her mat. It had been four days – or was it five … six … since arriving at this dark prison. A lone torch flickered outside her room, giving no sense of day or night. Food was brought at seemingly random intervals, the greasy fare nauseating. Was it feeding time again? She felt torn between gnawing hunger and a sense that she could not down another mouthful of the sickening gruel.

There was no sound at all coming from outside her cell door. No guard moved down the stairs at a slow, regular pace, no creaking told of a door opening slightly to admit food. There was not even the scurrying of mice from nearby grain stores. It was as if the world held its breath.

Constance remained perfectly still, every sense stretched to its limit. Something had pulled her from her haven of sleep. Her ears ached from the absolute silence. It was as if nothing existed outside of her four stone walls. It was as if she did not exist.

Still ... there was a sound. A faint scratching. Sharp, distant ... the sound of metal on metal. No, not a scratching. More of a clanging. The noise began to grow louder ...

Constance struggled to a sitting position, putting her back against the corner of the room, pulling her knees in tightly against her. That was sword fighting she was hearing, coming from the far reaches of the keep. She swept her hand beneath the mat to come up with the handle of the pot, worn to sharpness from her hours of rubbing it against the stone floor. This could be friend or foe who approached. If it was a rival within the bandit group, she might remember her times in this cell with fondness.

She wrapped both arms around her knees, clenching the weapon in her right hand, and waited. She could see nothing, but with her ears she traced the progress of the invaders as they slowly, inexorably worked their way in past the outer walls. She heard men's shouts, calling for reinforcements, cursing their opponents. No footsteps came running in her direction to move her. So it was not Barnard's forces, then, launching this assault. If it had been, she had no doubt that she would be brought out instantly by the bandits as a bargaining tool. Her blood ran cold. There was nobody to protect her now from the rival bandits that approached. She remained alone, tensely curled up, waiting ...

There was a long, low creak from above her, and she knew that the basement's main door had been breached. She held her breath, her heart pounding. There was no answering clang, no sound of resistance. She had been left unguarded, and now her fate was entirely in her own hands. Taking in a deep breath, she slowly stood, rotating her weapon in her hand. She dropped down slightly into a fighting stance. If they thought they were going to take her without a struggle, they would be sorely mistaken. Better to die here, fighting, than to become the whore for a nest of thieves.

Footsteps came quickly down the stone stairs, and it seemed only seconds before they stopped at her cell. The light of a torch moved around beneath the crack of the door. She stared with focused intent at the edge of the door jam, waiting ... She felt as if a sharp tingling were humming along her skin, making her aware of every movement.

There was a noise, and a creak, and the door slowly swung inward, pressed forward by a sword. In a moment a large shape filled the doorway, a black figure against an ebony background.

Constance had had enough. Her voice came out rough and full of fury. "Be warned," she grated out, her voice cold as steel. "If you lay one hand on me, I vow I will cause you as much damage as I am capable of before I die. I swear it on my life." She did not move an inch, keeping her back pressed against the corner of the cell.

The figure before her froze, and after a long moment he uttered a shocked oath. He took one cautious step into the room, then two.

Constance raked her eyes across his body. The man could be from a rival bandit group, or even a retreating member of the guards who fought above. Which side was he aligned with?

He was dressed in dark, well-worn leather from head to toe, its matte color blending in with the deep shadows of the night. He wore a full helmet with face shield, a tracery of cloud-like etchings glimmering on each cheek. He held his sword at the ready in one hand.

There was a symbol on the leather at his chest, barely visible in the gloom. Her eyes strained to make it out. It was a sword ... a flaming sword. Her eyes flew up to meet his, the shine of them glowing sharply in the torchlight. He was one of the Angelus. Why would the Angelus be brought in to rescue her? Had Barnard or her brother not trusted their own troops for the task?

She did not care. The Angelus were definitely not associated with the bandits. Exhaustion and fear threatened to overcome her, and she fought to stay on her feet.

A clanging sounded from far above and he tensed immediately. His voice came in a low rumble, urgent and short. "Can you walk?"

"I will hobble on stumps to get out of this hell hole," vowed Constance with heat. She pushed herself off the wall and made her way across the cell. She had dreamt for so long of crossing that threshold ... she paused for a moment when she reached it, then stepped deliberately across. She would be free. She repeated the vow to herself with fierce passion. Whatever it took, she would be free.

The mercenary was behind her in a second, then pressed himself past her to take the lead. He escorted her carefully down the grimy hallway, up the stairs, and through the winding corridors of the complex, his head always turning, watching for danger.

Constance stayed pressed as closely behind the Angelus as she dared, unwilling to risk the slightest chance of losing her savior. As they went, men fell in with them, forming a protective shield around them, a moving wall of metal and leather. Not a word was spoken as the troops gathered up and headed out toward the main gate. Constance did not see any remnants of the bandit force alive. Had they all been slain? Had they fled when the attack went poorly for them? She neither knew, nor cared. All that mattered is that she might at long last be free.

Then they were through the main gates of the curtain wall, the ink-black sky stretched out above them, the forests extended into dense dark. A herd of horses stood waiting, a few guards alertly watching over them. Constance drew to a stop, overwhelmed by the enormity of it. This was when the dream would end. This is when she would wake up to the cold stone floor, to the paltry gruel, to the gleeful laughter of her captors. She waited for the dissolve, for the loss of her freedom ...

The mercenary turned as he felt her stop moving, and met her eyes. His face went pale for a moment, then hardened again. Without a word he swept her up in his arms, carried her effortlessly along to a large, black steed, and then put her up on it. In a moment he was astride behind her, and the group was moving at a fast gallop through the moonlit wood.

Constance struggled to stay conscious, to spend every last second with her savior, no matter if he was a phantasm of the night. Even a brief dream was better than her reality. Despite her best efforts, her body became overcome with exhaustion, and at last she collapsed against him, lost in an endless night.

Chapter 4

Constance heard the quiet creak of a door opening, and instantly her body was alert. She kept her eyes closed as she slowly moved her hand beneath her pillow, searching for her weapon. A second passed ... two ... it was gone! Her eyes flew open in panic, and she threw herself back against the wall, drawing herself into as small a ball as she could.

The door stopped moving, and a shadow passed before it. Then, in another moment, a young girl pressed her way into the room, smiling gently at Constance. The girl carried in her arms a well-crafted wooden tray holding a half loaf of bread, a wedge of cheese, and a mug of mead. Constance barely saw her glossy, long black hair, or her neatly tailored green-blue dress. Her eyes were focused on the food, and her body became consumed with ravenous hunger.

The girl had barely placed the tray across her lap before Constance's fingers were flying, moving, bringing the food to her mouth as quickly as she could. It was several long minutes before she could even savor the flavors, enjoy the long drinks of mead in between gulps of food.

"Slowly," offered the girl gently, standing patiently besides the bed, her eyes sparkling. "You will give yourself a stomachache if you eat too quickly. We have plenty more."

Constance knew the girl was right, and tried to slow down. After so many days ... she finally began to feel her stomach fill, to feel satiated. She had never thought to enjoy this sensation again. When the meal was gone, she licked her fingers, taking in a long, deep, shuddering breath. She almost felt like crying in relief that her long captivity was finally over.

The girl retrieved the tray, then nodded down at her. "You rest now," she advised. "Nobody will bother you in here. If you need me, my name is Audrey." Before Constance could say anything further, she turned and went out the door, closing it firmly behind her. Constance listened with a tense ear, but there was no final click of a lock, no soft thud of a sealing bolt. She gave herself a gentle shake. Of course she was not locked in. She was free now ... she was free.

She allowed herself to draw her eyes from the door and finally look around the room. She was in some sort of a keep, apparently. The room was large, with regular grey stones making up the walls, while rich, polished wood lined the ceiling and floor. A low fire crackled in the fireplace across from her bed. A simple but well-made chest stood alongside. A tapestry of rich blues and greens hung to her right, and a chair was pulled close to her bed, a small table next to it showing wear from recent use.

She looked to the other side. A pair of large windows were shielded by blue tapestry curtains, a few steps from the bed. With an effort she pushed off the thick comforter. She was dressed in a clean, fresh white chemise, and she ran her hand in pleasure down the fabric for a moment, luxuriating in its feel. Then, gathering her strength, she swung herself around to sit on the edge of the bed. Exhaustion cascaded over her, the strong desire to simply curl up in the soft bed and sleep ... sleep. She resisted the lure with fierce determination. First she had to get a sense of where she was.

She stood slowly and moved the few steps to the curtains. She paused for a long moment before drawing one back to look beyond.

Her mouth fell open. The keep was perched on a cliff high above the ocean; the crashing waves, the long sweep of blue and glistening gold stretched as far as the eye could see. She flung both curtains wide open, drinking in the view. The beauty of the scene poured into her, refreshing her, renewing her.

Above, seabirds soared easily along the winds, coasting in luxurious abandon across the swells of the air. Below, the sun sparkled with glittering merriment off the rolling crests of the waves. In the distance, a fishing boat bobbed its way toward shore.

Constance stood motionless for what seemed like hours, leaning against the window sill, soaking up the joy of the scene. Tears streamed down her face; she paid them no heed. It was like awakening after a long sleep, welcoming the spring after a brutal winter.

Finally, her strength spent, she reluctantly turned and climbed back into bed. She arranged herself so that she could see a portion of the ocean from where she lay, and easily drifted off to sleep.

* * *

A loud noise awoke Constance, and she blinked in surprise, sitting up quickly and looking around her. It was early morning; the soft light of dawn was just spreading across her room. The curtains were still open, as she had left them, but scanning the room it appeared the chair at her side had been pushed back, as if someone had moved from it quickly.

The noise came again, and Constance realized it was sounding from below her. A heavy thud of some sort, and there was the sharp, angry murmur of men's voices muffled through the stonework. A bolt of fear shot through her. Had the bandits come back for revenge? Was even this keep not safe?

Constance tumbled out of bed and moved quickly to the trunk. She dug through the dresses … chemises … her heart leapt. A simple but good quality dagger was tucked at the bottom of the trunk amongst an assortment of clasps and buckles. She grabbed the weapon, her hand wrapping around the hilt in a firm grasp. A sense of security flowed through her immediately as she did.

Standing, she tossed the weapon from one hand to another, testing its heft. Finely balanced; it would do nicely. She moved to the door and stood there a moment, listening.

There was no sound nearby, only the growling murmur of voices from further away. She pried the door open slowly, carefully, and peered through the opening as she did. A long corridor stretched to either side of her, but there was nobody present in the dawn dimness. *Perfect.* She slipped through the door, pulling it gently shut after her. Then she crept her way down the hall toward the noise.

The corridor opened into a balcony over a great room littered with wooden tables and benches. Blue, green, and gold tapestries decorated many of the walls. A massive fireplace occupied one wall, the marble lintel carved with dragon designs. Several openings and archways gave entrance to other rooms.

Two men were arguing in low tones at the far end of the room, and two sets of men-at-arms milled about behind them, seeming alert but not anxious. One contingent wore tunics of blue and green, while the other wore ...

Constance knew their livery at a glance. It was the yellow and white of her family, of her brother Charles. She scanned the group, picking out a familiar face here and there. They stood near a large, wooden object, a frame of sorts. Looking at it more closely, she realized it was a bed, mounted on poles for carrying. She moved forward towards the balcony rail to get a better look.

Her movement caught the men's eyes, and both turned to look up at her. Her brother stepped forward instantly, his face sharp with displeasure. His voice rang through the hall, high and piercing.

"Constance, what are you doing? Surely you should not be out of your bed!"

Constance's temper flared. She was barely out of a prison cell, and this was the greeting from her brother?

She strode angrily across the top of the balcony, holding his gaze as she descended down the long sweep of stairs. He looked heavier than she remembered; the muscles he had earned during his years of soldiering were now sagging to fat. He wore a gaudy tunic of bright white with gold embroidery highlights, and a jeweled sword hung at his hip. His hair was short and expertly trimmed, his beard elegant and neat.

She stopped before him, aware of the stares of the guards around her, not caring, overwhelmed by anger for the man before her. Her voice came out low and guttural.

"You left me in that … hell hole … for weeks," she snarled, her chest heaving with emotion. "How could you?"

Charles flushed crimson, his mouth pursing. "Things were far more complicated than you can imagine, sister. There will be plenty of time to discuss this all later, when you are more yourself." He waved a hand at the bed standing to one side. "For now, please get into the carrier, so we can take you to our home in North Sunderland."

Constance's world was turning upside down. Would nothing make sense? "Why would I not return to Swinhoe, to Barnard?" she ground out, confused.

Charles made a dismissive motion with one hand. "It makes no sense to trouble Barnard at the moment. Besides, it is too far for you to travel in your state. I will take you home with me. My dear wife Alison can nurse you back to health for a month or two, and then we will see how things go."

Constance did not know if she should argue or give in. Going back to Barnard would be no treat – her "husband" had apparently not bothered to rescue her, had not shown an interest in her welfare for years. Still, her brother was not much of an improvement. What had caused him to finally call in the mercenaries, rather than send his own troops to the rescue?

There was no help for it. Better to go with her brother for now, at least until she healed. Then she could make more certain determinations about her future. She nodded wearily in agreement.

Charles turned to instruct his soldiers to take their positions at the bed's rails, and suddenly Constance could see the man he had been talking with. Her heart froze in shock. His body was more muscular than it had been, perhaps toned by years of service? He wore a deep blue tunic that was well made while simple in design. She knew the calm, blue eyes. In them was ... indifference? Pity?

Constance was suddenly aware of how she must look. She wore only the rumpled chemise, and her body bore the cuts and bruises of her rough capture. Her hair was matted and snarled. This was not how she imagined her first meeting with Gabriel. This was wrong ... all wrong ...

Charles glanced around and saw the direction of her gaze. "Oh, Constance, let me introduce you to Gabriel, the owner of this keep. You might remember him, I imagine; I believe he worked at our home for a few years right after I left."

"Yes, of course," responded Constance faintly, her strength fading. For him to see her like this ...

"My Lady," replied Gabriel with a nod, his voice low. She heard every syllable as a resonant chord through her heart. It had been so long since she had heard him speak, and there he was, before her, only a few steps away ... but so far out of reach.

Arms came to support her, and she did not resist; she docilely let the guards lead her to the bed. When she was settled in it, she felt the bed shift, and then rise. In a moment, they were moving out into the bright sunshine of day, and then she was being placed, bed and all, into the back of a wagon.

She turned her head sideways to look back at the keep. It was stunning. Small and well kept, she could see the sturdy walls which lined the courtyard area, could hear the roar of the glorious sea beyond. Tears welled in her eyes as she was swept away by the rich sound. She brought her view back to the main building, to the large pair of wooden doors which stood open at the keep's center.

Gabriel stood in the center of the archway, his eyes fixed on hers. She watched him for a long moment, then he turned and strode back into his home, swallowed up by the darkness. She closed her eyes, utterly lost.

Chapter 5

Constance faded in and out of consciousness during the hours of the ride, and it seemed like no time at all before the guards were hoisting her bed up to enter the gates of her childhood home. Despite her worries, a sense of relief washed over her as the familiar walls closed in around her.

The bed stopped in the main hall, and she immediately pushed herself into a sitting position, swinging her legs around. A crowd of servants and keep folk murmured with interest from the periphery of the room, but none moved towards her.

"Whoa, lass," called out a familiar voice at her side. Her eyes flew up in surprise.

"Ralph!" she cried, her tone rich with pleasure. "How did you get here?"

The graying soldier moved closer to her, leaning down to put an arm under her shoulder. He helped her to her feet, then began walking her along to the stairs towards the upper chambers. "In a moment," he responded softly as they moved.

She got a glimpse of bright red tapestries as she was helped up the stairs, and then she was being brought into what had been one of the guest rooms while she was growing up. It was a nice size, with a double bed, a pair of windows overlooking the back gardens, a fireplace, and several trunks.

Ralph eased her down into the bed, and gently pulled the covers up over her shoulders. He glanced back at the curious servants who stood in the doorway, dismissing them with a look. "We will call you if we need you," he let them know with a frown. The group pulled back, and the door was closed with a soft thud.

"Oh, Ralph," sighed Constance, finally beginning to feel safe for the first time in weeks. She leant back against the pillow, all strength draining out of her. "What is going on?"

Ralph picked up a mug of mead sitting on the small table by her bed, handing it over to her. "First, tell me how you are. You look …" he shook his head in confusion as he glanced down the length of her form. "You look both thinner than I have ever seen you, and stronger as well. What did they do to you?"

Constance took in a long drink of the mead, the welcoming warmth of it pouring down her throat. "They did not beat me, or torture me," she mused. "They did not make any demands for answers – or for anything at all. They fed me little, and I was locked away in a cell. That solitude and uncertainty was my only torment."

Ralph sat wearily by her side, looking down at her face. "Men have been driven mad by such situations," he cautioned with concern.

Constance shook her head. "It did not make me lose my mind," she promised in a low voice. "It strengthened my resolve. I will never allow myself – or another – to be caught in that position again." She looked up to meet his gaze. "I had long hours available to me and nothing to fill the time with. I did exercises with my arms, with my legs, throwing, dodging. Anything I could do, I did do. With your help, I wish to do more."

Ralph's gaze was firm. "Whatever you need, my Lady, I am here to help."

Constance glanced around her. "Still, why are you *here*?" she asked in confusion. "Tell me what is going on."

Ralph settled back into his chair. "It is complicated," he sighed.

"That is what Charles said," snapped Constance tersely.

Ralph nodded. "For once, he was telling the truth," he agreed. "Let me try to explain."

He drew in a long, deep breath. "When you were kidnapped from the tavern, the first Barnard heard of it was the following day, when a message arrived at the main keep. In it, a demand was made for two hundred pounds for your safe return. An uproar ensued. Barnard had long discussions with his top soldiers, judging the chance of you being held or slain. If you were simply held, then he would retain rights to Beadnell. If you were slain, then because you leave no issue, your brother would move in and take over."

Constance winced slightly at the thought of the cold, calculated debate about her life and death.

Ralph glanced towards the door. "Charles got wind of the problem within hours, and came quickly. He promised Barnard that if you died due to any lack of action on his part, he would petition the King to regain control of not only the province but additional lands in penalty, as Barnard's inaction would be tantamount to murder. The argument went on for three days."

Constance's stomach twisted. Her long days of isolation had been caused by a group of men arguing over coins.

"In the end, Barnard was unwilling to spend the money, and was willing to take his chances on the bandits not killing you. He figured that they would keep you alive, hoping you would come in useful at some point."

Ralph glanced at Constance somberly, then continued. "The bandit's messengers next arrived at Charles' home. The amount was reduced, but the message was the same. From all accounts, Charles was gleeful. He was now in charge of the negotiations. He would either end up with you dead, or with you in his control. To be fair, I think he preferred the second. He does seem to have some familial care left. In any case, he was in no rush to complete the deal. He wanted to get the lowest price possible, and to drag the proceedings on to give a long break to the fighting. That would let him rebuild his own forces and perhaps gain the upper hand."

Constance nodded. "So finally he decided not to pay at all, and sent in the mercenaries?"

Ralph looked away for a moment. "No," he responded shortly.

Constance glanced up in surprise. "Then who sent the forces in to rescue me?" she asked in confusion.

Ralph shrugged and spread his arms wide. "The Angelus were apparently raiding a local bandit stronghold when they just happened to come across you. Realizing at once who you were, they brought you to the nearest safe stronghold – that of Gabriel. He contacted your brother and husband." He chuckled softly. "Your brother got to you first."

At the mention of Gabriel's name, Constance shivered. He had looked so strong, so sure of himself ... so disinterested in her. "He lives in the area, then?"

Ralph nodded. "He has inherited the keep at High Newton by-the-Sea."

Constance looked over in confusion. "I thought he was an orphan?"

"Yes," Ralph agreed, "but he had spent a great deal of time with Sir Templeton during the crusades, both before and after his time with your family. The knight fell ill, and petitioned the king to allow the transfer, as he had no kin of his own and no close family. Because of Gabriel's valuable service, the king agreed. The knight died a short while ago, I believe, and Gabriel is now in charge of that household and the troops."

Constance sat back, her mind awhirl. She could see Gabriel's eyes before her, see the broad build of his shoulders, the sturdiness of his hands. She could see the shape of his lips, so quick to laugh.

She closed her eyes, turning on her side. He was gone to her.

She heard Ralph get up and slowly walk from the room. In a moment the door opened and shut. She waited another minute, then two, then she let the tears flow.

Chapter 6

A slim girl of perhaps thirteen was pushing her way quietly into the room when Constance awoke the next morning. The girl seemed familiar to her, and she sat staring at the apparition in green for several long moments, trying to place her. A name floated around in her head, finally connecting itself to the girl's face.

"Audrey?" she asked with curiosity.

The dark haired face beamed with pleasure. "You remember my name!" she called with cheerful glee. "Yes, it is me. I have brought you breakfast, and we can see about getting you back to full health." She came fully through the door with a tray, bringing it over to rest on Constance's lap. She helped Constance up to a seated position, then moved over to the fire to stoke it to life.

The smell of the food woke an appetite in Constance, and she dove into the oatmeal with vigor. It was only after the third or fourth bite that she remembered where she had seen Audrey. It was in Gabriel's keep. She looked up in surprise, meeting the girl's eyes.

"Why are you here?" she asked in confusion.

The girl smiled widely. "My mother is a healer," she explained. "When you were sent from my lord's house, he had me go along with you, to keep an eye on you during the trip." She glanced towards the door. "When we arrived, the lady of the keep was complaining that she could not spare any of her own maids to care for you. Once I heard this I volunteered to stay until you felt better. I told them that my lord had said as much when he sent me along. That was that, and here I am."

Constance was at a loss for words. Gabriel had sent one of his own servants to care for her? She took in a few more spoonfuls to cover her confusion. "Thank you for staying," she finally offered.

"That is why I was sent," responded Audrey with a smile. "My lord has always been quite kind to me, and I am glad to repay him in any way I can."

Constance finished up the rest of the meal, and Audrey removed the tray with a nod of approval. "I will have a bath sent up for you in the evening, but first, it looks like you could use some more rest." Constance was too weary to resist; she allowed Audrey to tuck the comforter back around her shoulders. She drew in a long, deep breath, relishing her newfound safety. In a few moments she fell into a deep sleep.

***

The next morning she felt far more alert, and found herself free enough of pain to contemplate an exploration of the keep. The room still seemed too much like a cell, and she wanted to be around people. She found a few outfits laid out neatly in the dresser, all in the family colors. She dressed herself in a long yellow tunic over a white chemise, then headed down to the main hall, following the rich smells of bacon and sausage.

"Connie!" called out her brother with mild warmth as she came into the room. He moved around the head table, wending through the many other tables and people to come to her side. "Are you feeling better, then? I am so pleased! Come, join us!"

He guided her through to the main table, settling her on one side of him. From his other side, Alison watched her with a mix of wariness and cautious welcome. Charles' wife was perhaps twenty years old, with a slim figure and long, stunning blonde hair.

"The guest room is to your satisfaction, I hope?" she asked with brittle crispness.

Constance blushed. This had, after all, been her home at one time. She nodded and smiled her thanks. "I am quite comfortable, thank you," she responded agreeably.

Another trencher was brought for her, and she dove into the delicious chicken and turnip stew with abandon. It had been years since she had eaten food this rich and flavorful.

Alison's voice suddenly snapped across the table. "So, what was it like, your captivity? Was the cell dark? Moldy?"

Constance knife stilled mid-cut. She looked up with fear, the words vividly bringing back the memories of the pitch-black cell, the cold walls layered with slime, the intense loneliness ...

Charles saw the look at once and shot a scolding glance at his young wife. "You do not need to think on any of that now," he said gently to his sister, his face softening into a semblance of familial concern, patting her hand. "Put it out of your mind. You are safe here."

"Yes, of course," mumbled Constance absently, trying to shake off the feeling. She focused on the food before her and avoided saying anything for the rest of the meal. She found her center slowly returning, and felt restored as she finished the last bite.

"Your table is set far better than any I can remember," she praised her brother and sister-in-law.

Alison looked up in surprise, then hesitantly smiled at the compliment. Suddenly a bevy of children swarmed around her, and she turned, sighing. "Not now, kids, Mother is busy, there is a lot still to be done before tonight," she protested distractedly, pushing them off, looking around absently. "Just where is that nanny of yours?"

Constance gazed down at the cherubic toddlers. Alison had begun having children the moment she married Charles. She had been sixteen then, and they had borne four children in as many years. All of the youngsters were fresh and healthy, their tufts of blonde hair matched with broad smiles.

She had no desire to return to her cell of a room, and knew that being left alone would result in her mind wandering where she did not wish it to go. Here was the perfect solution. "Let me take them for a while," she offered with a soft smile. "It is the least I can do in exchange for your hospitality."

Alison looked doubtful. "Are you sure? I know their nanny is around here somewhere …"

Constance stood, nodding. "It would be my pleasure," she insisted. She swept up the youngest – Ava, two years old with a bright shock of golden curls – and led the troupe over into a corner of the hall. The twin boys, Alond and Alain, curled up immediately at her feet, while Lucia, the eldest at four, sat herself primly on the bench at Constance's side.

The morning passed in quiet contentment for the group, with Constance spinning tales for the children sitting spellbound at her feet. She found herself finally relaxing, finally loosening her shoulder muscles, finally feeling safe. The hubbub of the keep moved around her as a blur. She was perfectly content in her back corner, the four children looking up with their round, eager eyes as she told them about pirates and pixies, knights and ladies fair.

A bubble of amused laughter sounded above her. Alison stood there looking at her brood in amazement. "I swear, you have quite the touch, Constance! I have never seen them this quiet for this long before. You have done a world of good!"

Constance stood up, her muscles aching slightly. She pushed the feeling off and waved to the little ones as their nanny bundled them off to lunch.

Alison came over closer to Constance, looking her over with a fresh eye. "My sister Gaynor is coming to visit, and thanks to your help I am nearly ready for her." She paused for a moment, then admitted in a more quiet voice, "Having your maidservant here has been an assistance as well; my own staff was becoming overwhelmed with the work."

"Whatever I can do while I am here, you have but to ask," quietly offered Constance. "I am happy to help."

Alison flushed with embarrassment, but nodded. "Well, then, come to lunch," she offered. The two women moved to the main table to eat.

Alison looked around with a sharp eye. "You there, bring the mead!" she called out imperiously, and the maid ran to do her mistress' bidding. Constance bit her tongue at the preemptory tone; her mother would never have snapped at the maids in such a manner. This was no longer her home, however, and she had no right to dictate how servants were treated.

In a moment Charles came to join them, and Alison's attention was absorbed by his discussion about the upcoming plans for their guest. Constance ate in silence, allowing the conversation to flow around her. The time flew by quickly, and soon she was on her own again.

She sought out the children for the afternoon, nestling again in their corner of the hall, finding a safe refuge in playing quietly with the foursome. The twin boys were building a castle with wooden blocks, while Lucia and Ava played at cloth dolls. Constance enjoyed the gentle babble, their simple joy, the closeness of their small bodies, the safety of the serene nook.

She was still curled up there, her yellow dress dusty and stained, when there was a commotion in the front archway. Alison let out a squeal of joy and came running from a side room to embrace a younger, red-headed version of herself. The newcomer had a lush, full figure, and was wearing a captivating dress of red and gold. The two sisters hugged in warm welcome for several long minutes before pulling apart.

"Gaynor, you are here early!" cried out Alison in surprise. "I had not expected you for many hours yet! You remember my husband, Charles?" She turned to loop an arm possessively through Charles', drawing him near. "Charles, my younger sister."

"Of course," agreed Charles, bending to give the girl a courtly kiss on the hand. "You have grown since the last time I saw you."

"I am a full sixteen years old now," boasted the lass with pride, "I am a woman now, no longer a girl!"

Charles chuckled, looking over her bright smile and buxom figure. "I can see that for myself," he agreed with a wink. "You are welcome to our home."

Gaynor turned to look over the pile of children who had pulled themselves into some order behind their parents. "These must be the tykes themselves! Look at them all. My, you *have* been busy, Alison!"

Alison waved her hand down the line. "Here is Lucia, the eldest. Then Alond and Alain, the twins, and finally Ava, our youngest. They are an inseparable mob, much like we were."

Gaynor glanced at Constance dismissively. "This is their nanny, I assume?"

Alison's mouth quirked into an amused smile. "You would be addressing Lady Constance, oh sister of mine."

Gaynor's ready smile vanished in an instant, replaced by a look of shocked consternation. She drew her eyes down Constance's disheveled hair and dust-smeared outfit in one long scan, then immediately dropped into a curtsy. "I am so sorry, My Lady," she whispered, her face turning flame red. "I just thought ..."

Constance had been watching the family reunion with mild amusement, and stepped forward to release the girl from her self-flagellation. "I do not mind, really," she offered quietly. "I *have* been playing nanny to my nieces and nephews, and I am quite content in that role. They are darling children."

Gaynor stood slowly, her eyes going round. "So you are the one who got stuck with Lord Barnard," she whispered in excitement, glancing at her sister. "Alison always prayed her thanks that another woman had been sent his way, saving her from that fate. We used to call him ..."

Alison's face went bright with mortification. "Gaynor, hush!" she called sharply. "This is his wife you are speaking to!"

Constance glanced between the two sisters with a chuckle. It appeared that her time at her childhood home might be more entertaining than she would have thought. It had never occurred to her that other women in the area might see her as a savior of sorts, sparing them a fate they did not desire.

"I would be interested in hearing what you called him," offered a low voice from behind Gaynor's shoulder. Constance knew that voice; she heard it in her sleep, heard its whispers when she lay awake at night. Her gaze moved up in one long sweep, meeting Gabriel's eyes.

Gaynor gave a laugh. "Oh, I forgot to mention," she bubbled cheerfully. "Gabriel here was visiting our house this morning and offered to escort me along for the day, to keep me company. We have had a delightful ride. I believe you know him?"

Alison nodded. "Yes, of course," she agreed, stepping forward to offer her hand.

Gabriel gave a warm smile. "My Lady, you look as beautiful as always," he praised, bringing his head down to kiss her fingers. He then turned to shake hands with Charles, the men's eyes wary but accepting.

Constance felt keenly the disheveled state of her hair, the dusty aspect of her clothes. She saw the dismissive look in Gabriel's eyes as he swept them along to hers. His voice was cool. "Lady Barnard."

Constance winced at the bite of his greeting, that he would refer to her only as Barnard's wife. She hid the pain by dropping her eyes to the floor, holding a curtsy. "My Lord," she murmured in return, her throat tight. By the time she had looked up again, he had taken Gaynor by the arm, and the two were walking over to the main table, laughing together at some jest.

Alison moved up alongside her husband and nudged him in the ribs. "They make quite a pair, do they not?" she asked quietly, her voice full of approval.

"Indeed, that would not be a bad thing at all," agreed Charles with a nod. "We will have to see how we can assist this along."

The two walked behind Gaynor and Gabriel, arm in arm. Constance stood still, watching them go, the world closing in around her.

Dinner passed slowly for Constance. She tried not to watch, tried not to see every glance between Gabriel and Gaynor. Gaynor had the bright beauty of youth, her red hair tumbling down around her shoulders, her lips full and lush. Gabriel was as handsome as always, the rugged set of his jaw, his short blond hair just perfect for running one's fingers through.

Constance could remember doing that, could remember the
feeling of his arms around her, could remember the look in his
eyes when he gazed down into hers. Now he was gone, he was
right there in front of her, but he was gone.

Gaynor's voice burst from the far end of the table. "Surely
you must settle down and get married, Gabriel!" she challenged,
her voice high and light. "Just see how happy Charles and
Alison are together, and how many children flock at their feet.
We girls of Preston are fine breeders. There are four more
brothers at home yet, all younger than us."

Gabriel smiled. "It does sound like a wonderful idea," he
agreed. "I had always hoped to marry a woman of this region,
someone who appreciated the lands."

Constance blushed at this, keeping her face down, her focus
away from his eyes.

Gaynor laughed out loud. "Well, that is me!" she cried out
with pleasure. "I adore the streams and valleys around here. I
have ridden the length and breadth of the region, and I know
every hill and dale."

Gabriel drew his eyes down the form of the woman by his
side. "Surely now that you are a grown lady your father has
plans for you," he jested with a twinkle in his eye.

Gaynor drew herself up proudly. "We northern women are
no chattel!" she boasted. "My sister was truly fond of Charles,
you can see that in her eyes. I myself will marry where I find
love. My father would never dream of pressing me into a
marriage I did not wish – and I would refuse it if he did! I mean,
if he had tried to get *me* to marry that lecher Barnard ..."

She clapped a hand over her mouth with impish
embarrassment, then took down another long swallow of mead.
Her voice was slightly less loud when she continued, "Oh, but I
forgot, his wife is here! She is so quiet, did she overhear me?"

Constance kept her eyes lowered, focused on the roast goose
before her. She heard the clink of a toast, and glanced up
enough to see Gabriel raising his glass to Gaynor.

"I salute your independence," he offered softly. "You stand
up for what you believe in."

"That I do!" called out Gaynor with pleasure, finishing off the rest of her mead in one long swallow. She called out to the musicians sitting to one side. "Let us have some song! A dance!"

In a moment the room was filled by a merry tune, and the two couples moved to do a set on the floor, joined by others as the music continued. Constance found she could not watch the swirl of people, not watch as Gabriel's long, lean form moved surely across the room, took Gaynor's hands in his own, touched her on the shoulder ... it was too much. She stood hastily and moved toward the stairs, heading to her room.

There was a voice at her shoulder. "My Lady, you are not ill?"

She did not turn. There was no need to. She paused for a moment, willing herself not to meet those eyes, not to see the pity or mockery or dismissal which waited there for her.

"I am merely tired, My Lord. Good night."

"Good night," came the quiet reply, and he was gone.

She reached her room in what seemed the flight of a swallow, but sleep did not come to her for many hours.

Chapter 7

Constance woke late the next morning and lay in bed for a long while, watching as the streaming sunshine moved slowly across the room. She could hear the keep hum with activity around her, but she felt no draw to join it. Finally, she forced herself to rise, to pull on a pale yellow tunic and make her way downstairs.

The rest of the household had apparently eaten already and was out and about their business. She scavenged a wedge of cheese and an apple from the panty, then made her way out the back door into the herb gardens. She spotted the children with their nanny by the duck pond, and with a smile moved over to join them.

Lucia cried out with a smile, "Look at the ducklings, Auntie!" Her dirty blonde curls bobbed in the sunlight. Constance dropped easily to a knee besides her niece, giving her a warm hug and looking where she was bidden. A white duck was nestled into one side of the pond, with four little yellow ducklings pressed up against her, remaining close.

"How darling!" agreed Constance with a smile. "There are four of them, just as there are four of you!"

"Which one am I?" asked Alond with keen interest. His gaze landed on a bright-eyed duckling with a white spot on its beak. "That one?"

"I should think so!" chuckled Constance, reaching out to brush a dab of dust onto the boy's nose. "For now you match perfectly!"

She sat on a nearby fallen log, and felt at the wood for a moment. "Here, this is a soft tree," she called out to the children. "Shall we make some boats, and sail on our ocean?"

A chorus of agreement echoed in her ears, and she smiled with pleasure. In a moment, the portly nurse had trundled inside to fetch a few scraps of fabric for sails, and the twins were busy seeking out sticks to serve as masts. Lucia helped pry off a few pieces of wood, and Constance pulled the dagger from her belt to begin whittling out the shapes.

It had been years since she had done this, but her fingers remembered the motions, her eyes recalled the shapes from when she and Gabriel had made their own boats during their trips to the ocean. Her movements faltered for a moment, but she pressed herself onward. That was long ago. The children would benefit from her knowledge; she would pass along the skills.

Still, it should have been her own children she taught this to … hers and Gabriel's …

"I see you have not forgotten," came a quiet voice beside her.

She started in surprise, her knife sliding down the length of the wood and nicking the side of her hand. The gash was shallow, but began bleeding at once.

Ava's cry was sharp. "A boo-boo!" Her blue eyes went bright with wonder.

Gabriel dropped to a knee at Constance's side, pressing his hand down on the injury. "I did not mean to startle you," he murmured, his voice contrite.

"It is nothing," assured Constance, looking up to see the nanny coming towards them at a trot. "Here, Joy has some fabric with her, for sails. One of those will do fine to bind me up."

Gabriel took one of the proffered squares from the nanny and folded it over several times before pressing it against the wound. He used a second square to seal the bandage to her hand. She felt the throbbing lessen, and the blood seemed to stop flowing.

Constance smiled at the children. "There, all better," she soothed them. "The boo-boo is all gone. Unfortunately, I am afraid I cannot finish the boats now ..."

Gabriel immediately spoke. "Let me." He sat down on the log next to Constance, picking up the hull she had been working on. He expertly finished off the boat in a few minutes, moving on to work on the next one.

Alain whistled, his eyes bright with surprise. "Wow, did Aunt Connie teach you that?"

Gabriel's eyes glinted with amusement. "No, I learned this skill when I was only a child," he responded to the tyke. It was only a few minutes later that four seaworthy little boats were lined up and ready for floating.

"There you are!" called out a high voice. Gaynor danced up along the pond walk to join the group, and smiled brightly when she saw what Gabriel had done. "You are so talented!" she enthused. "Look at how you have entertained the children! Come, I must tell my sister about this." She took his hands in hers, tugging at him to follow her.

He stood, looking down at Constance for a moment. "Fare well," he offered quietly, turning away. "Look after that cut."

Constance's throat was tight. "Thank you."

He nodded, and then he was gone, leaving her to the children and the flotilla. She knelt down in the mud, forcing herself to focus on the laughter around her, on the small boats wending their way across the waters of the pond.

By dinner time, Constance was soaking wet and covered with mud, but her heart had calmed. The children were a source of renewal for her, their simple laughter and joy a balm for her sorrows. She felt almost ready to face Gabriel and Gaynor's flirtations.

She was not prepared for the man who waited for her in the hall as she walked in with the children. He turned sharply as she entered, and his eyes were coldly dismissive as they ran down her bedraggled hair, her mud-stained dress.

Barnard's voice was icy disdain. "Good God, what *have* you been doing," he asked, sniffing haughtily.

Constance felt as if the entire room had stopped to watch the exchange. She walked to stand before him and drop a curtsy, her eyes lowered. "My Lord, I was spending time with my nieces and nephews," she offered quietly.

"Hmmm, well, yes," Barnard cut out, his tone dismissive. "It has been five days since your release, and I am surprised to still find you here."

Charles stepped forward, his voice smooth. "My sister is still not yet well enough to travel," he interjected calmly. "Our physicians insist it will be another week or two before she can make that trip. Rest assured that we are taking very good care of her."

Barnard's eyes roamed to the brood of children now peering nervously from around the nanny's wide skirts, and his eyes narrowed consideringly. "Maybe, indeed, a short stay here will help to undo the curse," he mused to himself. He glanced up again at Constance. "Well then, come along. It is time for dinner, and your place is at my side."

The couples arranged themselves down the length of the table, and soon the servants were ferrying in mugs of ale and servings of roast partridge. Constance's entire body shimmered with nervousness. Barnard had placed her at the end of the table, his own body between her and the rest of her family. She took in a deep breath, willing herself to relax, and reached out for a roll from one of the large baskets on the table.

Barnard's eyes shot to the bandage tied around her hand, and she flinched at the heat in his gaze. He grabbed her hand forcefully, twisting it in his grasp. Constance winced at the pain, biting down on a sharp cry.

She felt all eyes go to her immediately. She looked down so that she would not see the pity or amusement she was sure lurked there. Barnard's voice came in biting scorn.

"I was told you had been untouched. What is this then? Were you indeed abused? Were you tainted by them? Defiled?"

Constance blushed crimson, but she forced herself to speak in an even voice. "No, My Lord," she vowed softly. "I was hit, but they did not … touch me. I was very lucky. I was rescued barely in time. I thank God that the Angelus found me when they did."

She heard the sharp intake of breath from the two women, the rumbling growl from her brother. She found herself looking up despite her best intentions to seek Gabriel's eyes. His eyes were masked, as if he were holding back some emotion within. Confused, she turned away, shaken.

Barnard's voice was a bark. "What happened to your hand?"

"A minor injury from today, nothing more," she quickly explained. "It will heal soon."

"As well it better," pursued Barnard. "It would not do for you to be scarred. See that it does not mar you."

She bowed her head. "Of course, my Lord."

"So, Gabriel, do you hunt?" he asked, turning away and apparently putting Constance immediately out of his mind.

Gabriel shook himself, bringing himself back from a distant musing. "I do, sir, whenever I have the opportunity," he agreed with a nod.

"Well then, we shall all have to go hunting tomorrow," decided Barnard. "Charles has some of the best deer park in the region. With your permission, of course," he added, looking over to Charles.

Charles' voice was cordial. "I would not refuse an honored guest," he agreed. "We shall make a threesome of it, then."

Barnard drank down a long gulp of his ale, then leant toward the two men. "Did I ever tell you about the time I ..." He was soon immersed in regaling the men with stories of his many hunts, of slaying fierce wolves in Germany and fleet stags in France. Constance gladly cloaked herself in silence, finishing her meal as quickly as she could.

As soon as she was done she stood, nodding her apologies to the group. "I am afraid I am still a little weak, and will be heading to my room now."

Barnard rose at her side, downing the rest of his tankard in one long draw. "Well then, why not show me where *our* room is," he rasped, drawing his eyes in a long look down her body.

Constance's eyes flew wide in surprise. He had not shared her bed in five years. He was going to start now? Here? With Gabriel under the same roof?

She found herself gasping incredulously, "You wish to share my room?"

"It is my right," he responded, his voice gaining an edge, "to be in your bed any time I wish." His hand snaked out towards her arm to grab a hold of her, and panic flowed up her spine. She could refuse, admit the truth – but the consequences …

To her relief, Charles' voice cut in smoothly. "I think what my sister is saying is that the doctors have forbid any activity or travel until she heals up from her ordeal. They were very strict on this measure. Surely you respect their wishes."

Barnard's grip tightened on her arm for a moment, then he released her. "Of course," he cut out shortly. "I am sure you have another room available for me to sleep in, until I am back in her bed."

Constance heard a snap to his voice, and glanced up in surprise. She found he was looking not at her, but at Charles and Gabriel. Both men were staring at Barnard with directed focus, holding his gaze in an almost challenging manner. She wondered just what she had missed, but she did not want to prolong the situation any further.

"Thank you," she whispered, dropping a curtsy, then moving as quickly as she could up to her room. To her relief, Audrey was there to help her out of her clothes, to get her into bed. Despite her weariness, the events of the day swirled in her head long after she lay her head on the pillow.

Chapter 8

Constance woke early the following morning, feeling more like her old self than she had in weeks. She dressed quickly and headed down to the main hall. None of the men were in sight – only Alison and Gaynor sat together at the head table, laughing merrily together as they ate their sausages and eggs.

Gaynor waved. "You are awake! Come join us!" she called out with a smile. "It will be nice to have some time alone, just the three of us."

Constance's heart lifted at the welcome – it had been a long time since she had felt a part of any community. She moved over to sit alongside the two women, and in a moment a maid had brought a trencher and mug for her.

Gaynor spoke through a mouthful of fresh bread. "I was just telling my sister how different you were than I had expected," admitted Gaynor with carefree glee. "It is really quite amazing!"

"Oh? What do you mean?" asked Constance, intrigued.

Alison tried to hush her sister, but Gaynor pressed on, blissfully ignoring her.

"Well, Barnard has visited us several times over the years, and he always struck us as the last person on earth we would want to marry. He was cold, selfish, and ... well, inactive. I am surprised he wanted to go spend time with the other men today!"

She glanced at her sister, seeing the frown, but plowed ahead anyway. "When we heard that you had voluntarily agreed to become betrothed to him, we were jubilant that we were safe – and also convinced you must be just like him! Why else would you agree to such a match?"

Alison spoke up, apparently more willing to join in the discussion now that the ground had been broken. "Over these past few days, you have been so different than what I had thought. I am sorry I did not have you visit before now."

Gaynor nudged her sister in the ribs. "If she had visited, then she would have to bring *him*!"

Constance felt that she should defend Barnard from this ribbing, but she could not muster up the strength to do it. They were right, of course. He was all of those things, and much more. Still, she felt it her duty to say ... *something* ...

"I would be cautious speaking that way in his presence," she warned slowly, taking in a long drink of mead.

Alison nodded her head brightly, sending her blonde hair shimmering in waves. "Oh yes, I see the way he treats you! Charles would never behave in that manner to me. Even Gabriel was upset by it!"

Constance's breath caught. She tried to keep her voice even. "He was?"

Gaynor bobbed her head, her eyes shining. "Oh yes! Barnard left the table shortly after you did, and the rest of us were free to talk. You should have heard Gabriel questioning Charles, asking how long this behavior had been going on, and how your relations were with Barnard. Charles had to say he did not know; your paths have rarely crossed since you went off to be married."

Alison winked at her sister. "That Gabriel is quite the tender hearted one," she teased. "The way he cares for the children, how he dotes after you, you could do far worse, Gay."

Gaynor giggled with glee. "That I could!" She turned to Constance, her eyes bright. "Do you think he likes me? You knew him back when you were young, after all, right?"

Constance was at a loss for words. Back when she was young ... for she was old now, old and used up, and Gabriel would need someone to talk with, to go for walks with, to take by the hand...

The children bustled in as one noisy, excited mob, and she was spared the need to respond. She allowed herself to be led off into the far corner by the twins, waving her farewells to the two sisters. The children settled on a pair of stone benches at the far end of the hall, and Constance immersed herself in a world of blocks and stories. Anything to keep her mind off Gabriel.

It was after noon when the men came tromping into the room, dogs in tow. Constance looked up from the corner where she had been telling tales to the foursome of youngsters, and was surprised to see the men looked somber. She wondered just what kind of discussion they had shared while out in the woods.

Alison sprang merrily into the room, wrapping her husband in a warm hug. "So there you are!" she called out with mirth. "Ready for lunch, now, are you? Did you bring back any fresh meat?"

Charles pushed his wife off gently, shaking his head. "I am afraid our hunting was called off early, my dear," he apologized, his voice low. "There was trouble in the village."

Her eyes went round with surprise. "Trouble? What type of trouble?"

Barnard heaved himself into a chair, waving a hand for a drink. "Nothing for you to worry about, Alison. Just one of the local women, attacked by bandits. You are perfectly safe here."

Constance sprang to her feet, crossing the room in only a few steps, her heart in her throat. Her eyes sought out Gabriel's. "Who? Who was it?"

Gabriel held her gaze somberly. "It was Vera."

Constance's legs crumpled beneath her, and she sank onto a nearby bench. "No," she whispered hoarsely.

Gaynor came tripping into the room, drawing up at a stop upon seeing the expressions on everybody's faces. "What is going on?" she asked with curiosity.

Alison went to her younger sister quickly, putting on a bright smile, hooking her arm. "Just a little trouble in the village, nothing for you to worry about," she assured the younger girl, drawing her away. "I need your help in the garden, so off we go!"

Constance waited until the two had left earshot before turning to Charles. "Does Vera still attend church down at the village? Will she be well enough to attend tomorrow, do you think?"

Charles nodded, settling down beside Barnard at the table. "Yes, and yes. She married the baker, as you might remember, and they supply us with all of our special breads and cakes. She does quite well for herself, and has amassed a well-deserved reputation for her recipes."

Barnard looked between brother and sister, scowling. "Who is this Vera to you then? She is just one of the villagers."

Constance's throat was tight. "She was a friend when I was growing up," she explained, shaken to the core at the image of Vera's sweet face bruised by bandits. She looked over to Charles. "Do they know who the men responsible were?"

Barnard cut in, staring at his wife. "This is not appropriate for you to discuss, Constance. We are addressing the bandit issue in our own manner, on our own time. We cannot redeploy our forces every time a peasant woman is bothered."

A retort sprang to Constance's lips, and she bit it down with an effort. Deployed? He had not sent any troops in to rescue her when she had been captured. While he did patrol the Beadnell lands, the majority of his forces had been holed up in their keep, defending its walls, for as long as she could remember.

This was not a fight she could win. She turned on her heel and strode from the room, taking a long walk around the well-groomed grounds to help clear her head.

An hour passed, and then two. She slowly relaxed, the warmth of the summer sun seeping into her shoulders.

She came around the corner of the stables and pulled up short. Ahead of her were the flower gardens, and Gaynor and Alison were standing amidst the roses, laughing brightly together. Charles and Gabriel were with them, smiles on their lips.

Constance wrapped her arms around herself, a chill washing over her. How could the men laugh, knowing what had just happened? How could Gabriel be drawn to …

She turned away quickly, willing herself to be logical. Gabriel needed a wife. Gaynor was young, lovely, and fun to be with. What more did he need? She should be happy for him, that he was finding a way forward …

She needed something to do, something to focus her thoughts. Determined, she tracked down Ralph, and together they talked long into the night.

Chapter 9

Constance woke early Sunday morning, her mind newly resolved. She dressed quickly in her Sunday best, smoothing the embroidered, burgundy dress down and braiding her hair with care. She offered a quiet, heartfelt thanks to Barnard that, in his status-conscious world, he had felt it necessary to bring two trunks of her clothing for her to wear during her stay. It was nice to be back in her own dress again, to begin to feel like herself.

In a short while she and Ralph were walking down towards the village, heading to the grey stone church at its center. She smiled with pleasure as many friends from her childhood came up to greet her, to warmly hug her, to share stories of marriages, children, and the changes in their homes and lives.

She spotted Vera's thin form out of the corner of her eye, and started in shock. Vera's face bore several large bruises, and her movements were slow and cautious. Constance did not hesitate – she broke off from the group with a quick apology, then ran over to her friend. Vera's face lit up with a wreath of smiles, and the pair tenderly embraced.

Vera stepped back. "I had heard you were in the keep," she gushed with pleasure, "Still, I never thought I would see you so soon. You look beautiful, as always!"

"Oh, my friend," replied Constance, her heart in her throat. "Is there any serious injury that I can help with?" She looked over the bruises with careful scrutiny.

Vera blushed. "Nothing was broken, thank God," she vowed with gratitude. "Just some bumps and bruises. It was my strong box they wanted, not me."

Vera's husband came up behind her, nodding in greeting to Constance and Ralph. "I was out for the afternoon," he began by way of explanation. "They must have known she was all alone, defenseless." He put a hand gently on his wife's shoulder. "If they had done anything to my darling ..."

Vera nuzzled gently against his hand. "Luckily, they did not, Simon, and we will recover. It will take us some time, but we will be fine."

The church bells chimed, and the group headed in to the main building for the mass. The priest spoke about the protection of God, about relying on His strength, but Constance's mind whirled in other directions. As soon as the mass was over, she found Vera's side again. The two settled on a quiet stone bench in the shade alongside the church. Ralph lingered nearby, discreetly out of earshot.

Constance kept her voice low. "Vera, my friend, I have an idea. At my new home I have been helping the local women learn how to defend themselves. I am not teaching them to become soldiers, but simply to protect their homes and families. I was wondering -"

"Yes!" cried out Vera with delight, not even waiting for her friend to finish. Her thin face flushed with excitement, and she leant forward. "I know several of the women in the area would be interested. We could meet in the evening, after our daily chores are complete."

Constance was cheered to have her idea embraced so enthusiastically. "Where could we gather?"

Vera nodded her head at the sturdy stone structure behind them. "Right here! The priest has always wanted us to start a prayer circle, to strengthen our devotion. He has offered the use of the basement. We can bring in lamps and have complete privacy for our lessons."

"That sounds perfect!" agreed Constance with a smile. "When would you like to start?"

"Tonight," decided Vera without hesitation. "How about just after dusk?"

Constance nodded. "It is a plan, then."

* * *

Constance felt as if she was walking on air as she and Ralph strode up the long slope up to her childhood home. Vera had not been hurt badly, after all, and soon they would be spending time together. She would be helping Vera and others learn to keep themselves safe. Vera and Simon's bakery business was booming, and while the theft would set them back for a while, it would not bankrupt them.

The sun shown warmly down on the dirt path, and her cheeks were glowing by the time they reached the main gates of the keep. The stables were to the left in the cobblestone courtyard. These had always been one of her favorite places, and her feet headed there almost of their own accord. She stepped into the relative cool of the large, open building, standing in the doorway, smiling, allowing her eyes to adjust to the low light.

There was a movement to her left, and her eyes turned to follow it. It was Gabriel, removing his horse's tack and bridle. He stopped at her gaze, transfixed by her, his eyes unreadable in the dark. After a moment he finished removing the gear and hung it on a nearby hook before taking the few steps to close the space between them.

"My Lady," he greeted her in a low voice, his eyes still tracing her face with a look of almost surprised recognition in them. He paused for a long moment, and then began again, his voice soft, "Constance, you seem …"

Barnard's sharp voice boomed through the building. "God's teeth, woman, what are you doing in here?" A strong arm roughly pulled Constance out of the stable entryway and into the bright light of the courtyard. She blinked several times as her eyes adjusted, hurrying to match Barnard's pace as he pulled her toward the main building.

"It is almost lunchtime, and there you are lagging around the stables like some sort of servant," he scolded her imperiously. "Whatever were you doing in there?"

He glanced behind him again, and his gaze narrowed as Gabriel moved to stand in the stable's entryway, watching after them with serious eyes. Barnard gave an extra tug to the woman in his grasp, pulling her through the main doors and into a side entry chamber. He turned her hard, pressing her up against the wall in the small, empty room.

"Just who is this Gabriel to you," he asked with heat, his eyes boring into hers.

Constance's throat grew tight. "He was a guard when I was growing up," she responded quickly, feeling the guilt of the half-truth. She willed herself to keep her face calm, without any hint of emotion …

"When was the last time you saw him?" pressed Barnard, his voice gaining an edge.

Constance couldn't help herself. The memory was seared with blinding permanence on her mind.

* * *

It was the day of her handfasting. There was a blur of activity, a whirlwind of faces, the absolute certainty in her heart that this was the path she must take in life. She barely remembered the way her parents looked or the decorations of the church. However, she did remember …

It was the part of the ceremony she had dreaded the most. She had not seen Gabriel since that night at the tavern, not once in the long hours leading up to this rushed ceremony. Yet, as the priest intoned solemnly …

"If there are any present here who feel this joining should not go through, have them speak now or forever hold their peace."

Constance's eyes swept through the smiling congregation, past the bouquets of flowers, past the ribbons which trailed along the ends of the wooden pews. Out to the main doors …

He stood there, framed by the light, dressed in traveling clothes, ready for a long journey. He did not move or speak. His eyes moved slowly from her intricately braided hair to the richly embroidered burgundy dress her husband-to-be had bought for her. Then his gaze returned to her eyes, and for a moment she saw a glimmer of emotion – of loss, of passion, of heart wrenching longing.

Then he was gone.

"Let your partnership of one year flourish and blossom into a lifelong commitment" stated the priest with firm resolve, and Constance felt herself being turned by a pair of wiry hands, felt a pair of thin lips pressing possessively against her own.

"Well?" snapped Barnard, shaking her abruptly.

"I have not seen him since leaving home, since we were first joined," responded Constance quite truthfully, her voice low. "Not until I was rescued by the mercenaries and deposited at his home for safe keeping." Her resolve firmed as the memory of her kidnapping came to the fore. "Which reminds me," she added, her voice gaining in strength …

Barnard released her arms with a rough gesture, pushing her away. "It is time for lunch," he cut her off brusquely, turning on his heel. "It would not do to keep our hosts waiting." He strode out of the room without another word.

Constance took in a few deep breaths, composing herself. She had made her choices in the past, and she would live with her decisions. Resolved, she straightened out her dress and walked slowly after the man she had chosen to ally with.

* * *

Constance was thrilled with how easy it was to slip out of the keep grounds with Ralph as dusk approached. Constance knew all the back doors and quiet paths from her childhood years, and Ralph had been able to track down a tunic and pants from a page which fit her nicely. A thick scarf for her face and a heavy cloak finished off the disguise. They took a pair of horses, walking them through an unused gate with careful quiet, only mounting once they were well clear of the walls.

Constance was not sure what to expect when they reached the church. Vera had been enthusiastic in the bright light of day, but would she hold the same energy in the shadows of evening? To her delight, she found six women waiting for her in the torch-lit basement, the large, stone room lined with boxes and extra chairs. The central area had a solidly packed dirt floor, and seemed perfect for her purpose.

Constance recognized Colette, another friend from childhood, now married with three young children. She gave her friend a long hug, then made friendly introductions to the other women present. All had braided their hair tightly down their back, wore loose clothing, and were ready for action.

Constance and Ralph each took three of the women and began working them through simple blocks and defensive moves. The women were cautious at first, but once they realized that there were none here to see their actions, and great potential in their new skills, they threw themselves into the activities with passion. Constance was thrilled to see how quickly they picked up on the moves, on the benefit of each action and counter-action.

After an hour, Collete threw herself into an exhausted heap on one of the spare chairs. "You are amazing, Connie," she praised. "How did you ever learn all of these things?"

Constance brushed her tawny hair from her eyes, smiling in thanks. "Ralph here was a great help," she responded with warmth. "He makes time in his busy schedule to keep me in practice and well-tuned."

Ralph bowed. "It is my pleasure. You are an extremely apt student. You were quite good even when we first began."

"Well, that ..." Constance's face flushed and she looked away, hoping the shadows hid her discomfort. She remembered all too clearly the many long hours Gabriel spent with her, teaching her the basic moves, working with her with ever present patience, with unflagging concern, helping her master these skills. His eyes had held such pride and fondness ...

The women gathered up their cloaks, and Ralph escorted them up the stairs. Constance felt a touch on her shoulder, and looked up into Vera's bruised face.

Vera's voice was soft. "How is Gabriel?"

Constance turned away from that insightful gaze, willing the tears which welled in her eyes to dry unshed. She had shared everything with Vera; they had been inseparable as girls. There had been nobody else for Constance to talk with; her only sibling was her brother, six years her senior, off on the Crusades for several years. She had told Vera her deepest secrets, her desperate hopes.

"Oh, Vera," she sighed, and her friend's strong arms wrapped around her, holding her tightly.

Vera's voice came soft and somber against her ear. "I hope your family, and the people of this area, appreciate what you have sacrificed in their name," she offered quietly. "You are truly their guardian angel."

Ralph came back down the stairs, and Vera gave Constance one final hug before bidding them farewell.

A Sense of Duty

Chapter 10

Constance awoke late Monday morning, weary but content after her long evening out. She was happy to find the central hall deserted as she made her way down the main stairs. From discussions she overheard as she worked her way through to the pantry, the men were busy with the village leaders in discussions about the bandits. Barnard would be gone until late in the evening. The two sisters had taken the opportunity to go into town with them to do some shopping.

A sense of quiet contentment settled over Constance as she wandered comfortably through her family home. There had been changes, to be sure – Alison's red banners hung alongside the traditional white and yellow in the main room, furniture had been moved or added. Still, she ran a hand along the carved window bench with pleasure, thinking of the many long hours of happy time she had spent there as a child.

Her wanders took her outside, and she happened across Joy and the four children playing by the duck pond. The twin boys looked up with delight as Constance approached, running to grab onto her legs.

"We want to play tug of war!" they cried out. "Can you help?"

"Why of course," promised Constance with a smile. She walked over to the stables and grabbed a few spare pieces of leftover rope, and an assortment of gloves as well for good measure. She brought her stash back over to the duck pond and sat in the shade of a small oak while Joy told the children stories. Slowly, carefully, she created sturdy knots at the join points of the rope pieces. The finished length stretched a good ten feet. Once that was done, she began making small but protruding knots every foot. Against each one she created a small, flat loop. It would not catch the hand if your grip was sliding down along the rope freely, but if you wanted to you could slip your wrist within for better traction.

She gave each section a strong tug, satisfied that her work was well done, then stood and called over to the boys. They jumped up immediately, eyes round at what she had created.

Constance smiled widely. "Time to give it a try!" She helped the boys wriggle their hands into their gloves, then put on a pair herself for good measure. They found a long, flat area to one side of the pond, and Constance traced a center line on the bank with a stick. The two boys took up each end of the rope, their faces glowing with enthusiastic energy. Joy sat to one side with the two girls, clapping encouragement.

"Go!" cried out Constance, and the contest was on. She was impressed at how evenly matched the pair was. The center now wavered to the left, then to the right, but neither boy had a clear advantage. The spectators screamed with delight, egging them on, and both boys dug in their heels hard, pulling with all their might.

Then, suddenly, Alain's foot slipped as he moved closer to the pond. Alond took instant advantage of the traction loss, tugging hard on his rope. Alain flailed, lost his balance, and went back into the mud with a laugh. Everyone cheered and clapped as he ruefully picked himself up out of the mire.

Gabriel and Charles rounded the corner, their faces lighting up with interest at the sight. Charles squatted down, putting his arms out to his brood, giving an extra pat to Alain's muddy back.

"You will get him next time," he promised the twin with a chuckle.

Gabriel was examining the handiwork of the rope. "This is good," he commented off-handedly, "but we really should get you a solid length of rope. It would be safer without those joins."

Constance snorted, brushing hair from her face with one grimy hand. "Safer, my foot," she contested. "Those joins will not part before the rope itself does. Plus, this makes good use of unused end pieces. Waste not, want not."

Gabriel looked down doubtfully at the knots. "If you say so …"

Constance felt a feisty spirit run through her. She gave a tug on her gloves, seating them well against her fingers.

"Put on some gloves," she called out in challenge.

Gabriel's head came up at that. He glanced at Charles, then back at Constance again. "I do not think -"

Charles interrupted with a smile. "Oh, go ahead," he encouraged, his eyes twinkling. "It could be fun."

Constance's grin widened. "Let us see how well these knots hold," she added with a chuckle. "Unless you are afraid to get muddy …" she glanced suggestively at Alain's soaked clothing.

Gabriel pursed his lips, then reached down for a pair of gloves, sliding them on with practiced ease. "I will go easy on you," he commented as he moved to his end of the rope. He lifted it, examining the knots and loops. He gave an experimental tug at the end loop, his brows coming together. "*Very* nice," he murmured under his breath.

Constance glanced again at her brother, stifling a grin, then worked her way up to the third loop from the end of her side.

Gabriel raised an eyebrow. "You do know that brings you closer to the center line?" He shook his head in amusement. "You want this to be a quick test, I see."

Constance settled herself down low, bringing one hand into a loop before her, the other rested behind her back, keeping the line well seated along her waist. She gave each heel a twist, securely grounding herself. She took a long, careful look at where Gabriel stood, at the slick slope of the pond only a few feet away.

Charles watched her with a practiced eye, waiting for her nod. When he saw it, he gave one last look at Gabriel, then brought both hands up.

"Go!"

Constance leant back hard, ready for Gabriel's strength. She formed a wedge with her body; his pulling drove her more deeply into the soft earth. She only had to keep the angle correct to keep from skidding across the top of the surface. He was stronger, so much stronger, but so had Charles been all those years ago. It was not just about strength. It was about strategy, and traction, and ...

She heaved her body left, and Gabriel moved to counter, his feet steady on the ground, but inching closer to the slope. Constance knew this pond by heart, knew every dip, every curve. It was time for ...

She gave a soft cry, as if her hands were slipping, and she let the rope slide through her grasp to the next knot set. She grabbed securely at the next knot, jolting the rope. Gabriel stumbled back slightly, then caught himself. Again she leaned, again he followed with her, his eyes becoming more focused on the task.

She could see it in his face, that he was about to take the contest more seriously. If he dug himself in, she would have no chance. It was all about timing ... she watched his eyes, judging, waiting. The moment had to be just perfect ...

There, she saw the change, saw the moment he took in a deep breath. She let the final two knots fly through her fingers, catching solidly on the final loop, leaning herself with all her might to the left, digging in to the ground as if she were a tree putting down roots. Gabriel was just bearing down with a burst of strength to pull her in – and he flailed in surprise as the rope became loose in his hands, as the snap of its leftward angle pulled him toward the pond.

His foot slid, lost traction, and he tumbled sideways into the deep muddy puddle.

Constance threw both of her hands into the air in victory, crying out in delight. The children came running around her in glee, and she was swept up by her brother in a fond hug. She was still laughing when he put her down, as a soaked Gabriel climbed to his feet, shaking off his clothes.

She chuckled with mischief. "It seems the knots held after all."

Gabriel's eyes were bright with amusement. "You have done this before," he challenged.

"With an older brother? Of course I had," she retorted easily. "I certainly had to pick up some tricks along the way, too."

A pair of shrieks sounded from behind them, and they turned to find the two sisters standing, staring at the sight. Gaynor ran forward, her face pink with surprise.

"What have those children done to you now?" she called out half in horror. "We need to get you inside right away and get you out of those clothes!" Together she and Alison pulled at Gabriel, drawing him back into the keep.

Constance looked up at Charles for a long moment, and then they burst out in gales of fresh laughter, doubling over in mirth. Constance felt the merriness lift her, carry her through the afternoon, through the babble of dinner.

She almost wished she could stay for the dancing and music that began once dinner was finished, but she knew her other plans were far more important. It seemed second nature for her and Ralph to slip away, to change clothes and work their way outside the walls with their horses. In only a short while they had met up with their eager student group.

Constance lost herself completely in her training work, enormously impressed with how quickly the women picked up the skills, warmed with how dedicated they were to learning self-defense. The hours flew by in a contented blur.

But when the women had gone, and she was climbing on her horse to head home, it was the sight of Gabriel's smile that hung in her mind, the warmth in his voice that flowed through her blood and made her feel whole.

Chapter 11

Gaynor was, if anything, even more animated than usual when Constance made her way down to the sun-streaked main room the following morning.

"Oh, Connie, there you are!" she called out, tripping across the room with glee. "We are going to have a picnic!"

"Are you sure it is safe?" asked Constance with concern, her eyes glancing back to the main table where Alison sat nibbling complacently on an apple tart. The men were nowhere in sight, and Constance wondered absently if they were out talking with the village leaders about the bandit problem.

Gaynor wrinkled her forehead. "Of course it is, silly," she protested. "We have strong menfolk with us! We will be fine." She escorted Constance over to the table, talking non-stop about her plans.

As Constance ate, Gaynor envisioned every detail of the picnic from beginning to end. She enthusiastically began describing the foods they would bring, and the dances the musicians would play for them. Constance sat back and let Gaynor thrill in her dreams. Her own mind was distant, working out the next set of lesson plans for her evening group.

* * *

When lunch was done, Alison and Gaynor settled into the sun room for an animated discussion of exactly how the decorating and catering of the picnic would be accomplished. Constance left them to their work, walking slowly through her childhood home, heading out as she had so often in her youth to the freedom of the outdoors.

When she pushed her way through the thick outer door, she was immediately hit by a wall of heat and humidity. The heavy air seemed to dance in waves, and she pushed her damp hair back from her face before moving on.

She ambled through the fragrant herb garden, breathing in the rich aromas of tarragon and oregano. It was intoxicating, and she sat by a bushy sage plant, ripping one of the leaves from its base, pulling it into quarters to inhale its aroma. She closed her eyes, drawing in its rich scent. She had forgotten how wonderful the gardens were here.

She stood again slowly, glancing around at the quiet. The four youngsters were nowhere in sight – was it perhaps their nap time already? She began moving again, through the rose garden, among the lush, crimson blossoms. The fragrances were even more sensual here, and she found her footsteps slowed as she went.

Constance ran a hand idly along the back of her neck as she walked, wiping away the sweat there. She felt awakened by the sun, felt it soaking into her skin.

God, it was hot, though. She meandered over to the duck pond, drawn by its glistening blue. Holding up her skirts, she crouched at its side. Looking around to ensure the area was deserted, she cupped her hands and brought a shimmering fountain up over her head, the cool liquid raining down on her, bringing her instant relief. She ran her wet hands down her hair, drawing it away from her face.

She let out a deep sigh as the water soaked into her skin, washed over her. She felt a rivulet go down the center of her chest, where her medallion had been, and she pressed a hand against the spot, relishing the sensation. The sun warmed her face, the water brought an immediate and delicious coolness.

There was a noise from the right and she turned, staying low, looking through the dense hedges. Ralph was there, sword out, moving into a guard position. He took a step back, and Constance saw Gabriel was his sparring opponent. Gabriel was shining in the heat, and his light tunic was open halfway down the front, revealing the laced shirt beneath. He spun his blade through a rotation to loosen up his wrist, then moved in against Ralph with a laugh. The men danced up and down the meadow, crying out friendly challenges and encouragement to each other, raining down blows, raising blocks, turning and advancing and retreating.

Constance could not move. The sultry summer heat soaked into her bones; the cool water slowly trickled beneath her chemise. Gabriel's swordwork was a masterpiece of strength, of control, of careful strategy. He was not drawn in by Ralph's feint; he seemed to know instinctively to lean left rather than right to dodge the next strike. Constance had learned that trick after several years of daily practice with Ralph – how had Gabriel picked up on that so quickly?

She was transfixed by the way Gabriel moved, with a cat's grace, dodging low as a blow whistled past his ear. The muscles rippled in his arm as he swung his sword, driving Ralph back a step. She caught her breath, admiring the way his side did not give an inch when a full blow came down on his high guard. He was the consummate protector, the perfect guardian.

A shaft of desire pierced her through, filled her with a longing she thought long past. Here was a man she would be proud to have in her life, at her side.

If only -

She shook her head fiercely. She was in the public's eye a married woman; she could not be entertaining such thoughts. Even in dreams, such longings would do her no good. Still, watching him in motion, watching the way his sharp eyes read every move Ralph made, anticipating every nuance …

She was burning up; every part of her tingled with fiery heat. There had been a time when he would have gladly enfolded her into his arms. A time when she could have looked into his eyes and seen the smoldering desire there, always kept under a tight rein. She had felt those same cravings, had struggled to keep them tucked safely within her breast.

Now those long lost feelings billowed with fresh life, threatening to overwhelm her carefully built reserves of strength.

She threw herself back from the hedge, forced herself to rip her eyes from the man she loved. Turning, she saw the expanse of the clear blue pond before her. Without a second thought she stood, ran and dove in. The water was deliciously cool, washing over her at once, enveloping her. The passionate longings shimmered out of her, melted into the simple joy of streaming beneath the surface, lost to the world. She was safe, she was free.

She rolled easily, her tunic billowing in the pond's depths, drifting with her movement.

She swam underwater a few more strokes before surfacing far from shore, treading water with ease as she drew in a deep breath. She had loved to swim as a teenager, and had forgotten how delightful it was to be immersed. This pond in particular held so many happy memories for her …

There was the sound of heavy footsteps, and the two men came crashing through the hedge barrier, looking around in alarm. Their faces relaxed slightly when they spotted Constance holding her head above water in the pond.

Ralph called out in relieved exasperation. "What are you doing, lass? We thought you were one of the wee ones. Get yourself in to shore."

Constance stretched an arm to begin a gentle swim, and found to her surprise that her tunic had become incredibly heavy with the absorbed weight. She bit her lip to hide the effort from the men – it would do no good to turn this into a dramatic rescue attempt. Not in her own childhood pond! In a few moments she reached a depth where she could stand, then slowly waded her way through the mucky shallows, her clothing becoming heavier and heavier as she emerged from the water.

She stumbled as she came up on shore, her tunic feeling as if it was lined with lead weights. Gabriel's arm was there for her in an instant, and he felt rock solid beneath her. She thought again of the way he moved, of the power of his body, and the flush hit her again, the longing to be held by him, to be wrapped in his arms …

With an effort she pushed free of him, willed herself not to look up at him, not to allow him to see the turmoil she had fallen into. She stood wringing the water from her tunic with both hands, concentrating on the task with deliberate focus.

"I am fine now, thank you," she hoarsely managed when she was done. She lifted her still waterlogged hems with both hands, making her way steadily back to the keep.

She heard the men murmuring behind her, but she did not slow. If anything, she moved as quickly as she could, reaching her room and closing the door firmly behind her. Despite her drenched clothing, she could not bring herself to remove it; the fabric clung to her body as if she were in a damp embrace. She moved to the chair by the window, curling herself up in the corner, drawing her knees in to her chest. She sat there for several hours, willing the longing from her body, willing herself to focus on her training task for the night, on the path she had chosen for her life.

That evening, she threw herself into her training activities with a fervor the women had not seen before. Constance exhausted herself completely with blocks, with parries, with thrusts, driving the tortured demons out of her heart one lunge at a time.

A Sense of Duty

Chapter 12

As she lay in bed the following morning, Constance closed her eyes, taking in long, deep breaths, striving to find her center. She was grateful that the day's plan was for a picnic. It would do her good to get away from her childhood home, the familiar hallways and all the memories they brought up in her soul. A change of scenery would help her drive away old, long dormant feelings. Those longings would only bring her pain.

Resolved, she moved over to dress. She hesitated between the burgundy tunics which Barnard had brought and the yellows of her childhood from the dresser. She finally dug in the drawers for a more neutral, fawn colored tunic. Once she was ready, she headed down the stairs with a light step.

The group was all gathered, and the children were milling about in loud excitement at the adventure of it all. Constance helped to herd them into a large wagon waiting by the front door of the keep, then pulled Alison up after her. Joy climbed in with a handful of dolls, settling herself down besides Lucia.

Gaynor and Gabriel rode up on a pair of matching black horses, Gaynor laughing with delight. "What a glorious day for an outing!" the red-head called out to her sister. She glanced over at Constance. "I know my sister does not like horses, but surely you will travel astride with us! Gabriel tells me you used to adore riding."

Constance slid her eyes to meet Gabriel's. He had been talking to Gaynor about her? What else had he said? His eyes were shielded; she found it odd. Usually she could tell at a glance if he was angry … content …

A curt voice cut into the group. "My wife does not ride," insisted Barnard, drawing up to the throng on a steady, grey mare. "It would not be safe for her feminine disposition."

Gaynor spun her horse away, and Constance caught a glimpse of her rolling her eyes as she moved. Then the red-head and Gabriel were alight, charging ahead of the wagon, drawing out of sight. Constance sighed as her more staid conveyance jerked into motion to follow when Ralph gave a shake at the reins. Constance sat back, drawing Ava onto her lap.

The young voice rose in a piping lilt. "Will we see duckies?"

"Maybe we shall," replied Constance with a smile, willing herself not to look forward to where Gabriel and Gaynor cantered in the fresh sunshine. "We shall find out soon enough!"

She entertained the children with stories of ducks and fish for the short ride, and in no time the group had arrived at its destination besides the wide river. Blankets were laid out high on the hill, and soon the group was sprawled out in the warm afternoon sun. There was mead to drink, fresh bread and cheese to eat, and a babble of delighted conversation. A pair of musicians played a quiet tune on recorders.

Charles leant forward, eyeing his wife. "My dear, delight us with a song," he suggested.

Alison took him up on his offer immediately, launching into a lovely version of a local dance tune. Constance found herself clapping in time, and the four children got up on their feet, swirling and moving to the music in wild abandon.

Alison sung another quick tune after that, encouraging the little ones to even greater heights. They collapsed in a delighted heap by the time the song was done, the adults all clapping in pleasure.

Gaynor leant over with a smile. "Something slower," she requested, winking at her sister. Alison settled herself back, thinking for a moment, then began singing a languorous song of love.

Constance's heart caught. She remembered that song well. Gabriel had sung it to her, softly, as they sat together on the ocean beach, his arms warm around her. She turned her head away as Gaynor tugged Gabriel to his feet, pulled him into the grass clearing to dance around him …

Someone tugged at Constance's arm. "Duckies now?" asked Ava, her eyes bright with interest.

Constance swept her up in an instant. "Duckies now," she agreed brightly, drawing the other children along with her as they headed down to the river. Joy caught up with them in a few moments, taking Lucia by the hand with a warm smile.

The song faded away into the running burble of the water racing over rocks and reeds. To the children's delight, there was indeed a mallard family on the other bank, a green-headed father with his wife and five tiny children.

Lucia cried out in delight. "Look! They have five! Maybe we shall have five, too!"

Joy chuckled. "You never know!" she teased, her eyes shining.

Constance looked over at Joy in surprise. "Alison is with child again? Already?"

Joy shushed her and drew a little away from the children. "It is early yet to tell, but I believe she may be."

Constance frowned in concern. "I know Charles wants a large family, but surely it is not safe for her to have so many so quickly, without time to recover. Did she not just have a miscarriage a few months ago?"

Joy nodded. "I have been nanny to those girls since they were tiny. They always did exactly as they pleased, with none to gainsay them. I imagine that whatever Alison wants, Alison gets."

Constance looked back up the hill, at the figures dancing around in the clearing. Her brother was sweeping Alison around in a circle, her head thrown back in laughter. To the other side, Gabriel and Gaynor were close in conversation. Were they holding hands?

Constance looked away in a rush, moving along the bank with the twin boys. "Here, let us make some more boats," she urged them with a forced smile. "We can get a real race going here, I imagine!"

Time flowed by in a brilliant stream of blue and green, of racing boats and yellow ducklings. Ava napped for a while in a shady nook while Joy and Lucia built a stone castle. Constance worked with Alain and Alond to tune their boats, racing them further and further down the stream.

There was a shout from the hill, and Constance looked up to see Charles waving his hand in a sweeping motion, calling them back up. It looked as if the group was packing things away, preparing to head back home. Constance glanced at the sun, realizing how low it had slid in the sky. The day had sped past more quickly than she had imagined! Joy nudged Ava awake, then shook out both her and Lucia's dresses with easy routine, laughing as she did so. The three of them began moving in a loose group up the hill.

"That was my boat!" came the high shout from behind Constance.

"No, it was mine!" cried the second.

Constance turned with a chuckle. The twins were tugging and pulling at a single boat, faces set in determined passion.

"There were two boats a moment ago. Where did the second one go?" she asked with mock sternness.

Two pairs of pudgy fingers pointed downstream, to where the river raced and bubbled over rocks.

Constance shook her head. "How about this," she mused out loud. "When we get home, we will have an entire Olympics, and this boat will be the prize we set out for the winner. That way it goes to the best man."

The two sets of eyes lit up in delight. "Yes!" they cried out in unison, promptly placing the boat in her hands for safe keeping. She tucked the boat in her belt, then took one hand in each of her own and began moving up the long slope towards the crest.

They walked at a quick pace, laughing and talking about the events they would hold. They were halfway up the hill when they neared Joy, who was holding Lucia over her shoulder and tickling her gently. Constance looked around her as they neared.

"Joy, where is Ava?" She looked up ahead to see if Ava had run to be with her parents.

Lucia, hanging backwards over Joy's shoulder, pointed back down towards the river, her mouth wreathed in smiles. "She is on the boat!" she called out in childish delight.

Constance spun in horror, following Lucia's outstretched finger. The log she had been sitting on by the bank was beginning to drift out into the moving waters, and she could see a small figure astride it ...

In a heartbeat she was running, flying down the hill, her fingers stripping the belt off her in seconds as she moved. The water was deep ... fast ... the tunic would drown her in seconds. She pulled her arms in as she ran, sliding them down by her waist, and in another moment her tunic was tossed free over her head, leaving her light chemise. She streamed like quicksilver down the slope.

The log was caught by the current and began to move more quickly. Ava's cries of delight morphed into shrieks of panic. Constance's legs pounded the grass. She reached the bank and dove in as one fluid motion, slicing into the water without a sound.

She opened her eyes the moment she was beneath the water, swimming hard. Not far ahead she saw a bubble-rich splash, saw a pink shape plummet down through the waters. She kicked fiercely, moving toward Ava with sure strokes. She was nearly within reach ... Constance stretched out her right arm and grabbed the tiny fingers, pulling her roughly to her body. She kicked upwards, and breached the surface with a loud gasp, thrusting Ava up into the air. Ava gave a coughing heave, and then began screaming at the top of her lungs.

Constance turned in the current, going under for a moment as the child wriggled in her grasp. She sputtered again to the surface, desperately holding Ava up, her eyes stinging from the water. It was a struggle to stay afloat, between the twisting waves and the flailing child. It took her several moments to get her bearings in the roughening water. Once she oriented herself, she began to press hard towards land.

She leant herself sideways as she swam, angling her body so Ava's head stayed free of the waves while she made headway. Ava flailed with all her might, beyond panic. Constance was driven under by the motion, took in a breathful of water, and broke the surface again, coughing. She stretched out again with her left arm, moving desperately toward shore. Ava twisted again. Constance felt another lungful of water course down her throat ...

She was suddenly lifted high. A strong arm took a hold of her left hand, pulling her out of the water for a moment, giving her a chance to draw in a deep breath. She gasped for air, desperate to keep in motion.

"Grab a hold of my neck," called out Gabriel in a clipped rush, glancing ahead at the approaching rocks. "Hold on for dear life."

He pulled her left hand to him, rolling with it as he did so that her arm looped over his left shoulder and around to his chest. She pulled herself snugly against him, bringing her thighs in close against his hips, trying to position herself so as not to drown them both. With her right arm she kept a tight grip around Ava's waist, keeping the child as far out of the water as possible.

Beneath her, she could feel Gabriel set into strong motion, his arms and legs drawing hard against the river. She ventured a glance downstream, and saw with shock that the river was about to enter a section of rapids, The water jumbled and tossed against a bed of sharp rocks. A frisson of terror coursed through her.

"Do not let go," she heard Gabriel call up to her in a tense plea, every ounce of strength moving them closer to the bank.

"Never," promised Constance, pressing herself firmly against his body, feeling every sinew of his being, willing herself to be light, to be streamlined, to be a part of him.

She saw figures running, saw the bank draw near, and then suddenly there was wet mud beneath their feet, and Gabriel collapsed, exhausted, on the bank. Ava was pulled strongly from Constance's hands, and she let the child go, rolling weakly to her right, allowing herself to sprawl on her back in the mud. She sucked in heaving, deep breaths, feeling Gabriel doing the same at her side. He lay, still, on her left arm, and she made no motion to withdraw it.

She turned her head to the left, and found herself staring into his eyes, saw the relief and pride mixed in them.

His voice was hoarse. "You saved that little girl," he praised her, his breathing finally slowing. "She would have died were it not for you."

"You saved us both," murmured Constance, caught by his gaze, her heart pounding. "You came for me."

Gabriel raised a hand to gently brush the wet hair out of her face. He took in a deep breath.

Barnard's shrill voice bellowed out from above them. "Constance, what in God's name are you doing dressed like that?! Get yourself covered this instant!"

Constance stared up in shock at the apoplectic face, then looked down at herself. The thin fabric of her chemise, drenched to the core, clung transparently to her body, leaving nothing to the imagination. She pulled herself up to a sitting position, drawing her knees to her chest, then looked around.

Charles and Alison had Ava sandwiched between them, examining her over in minute detail for harm, their voices moving from shock to relief. Joy stood to one side of the couple, holding Lucia, who was crying in sheer panic. Gaynor knelt on the other side, her arms around the two boys, murmuring to them that their little sister would be all right.

Constance looked back at her husband in confusion, and saw he was staring down at Gabriel, his face hard. Gabriel rolled over and came up to his feet in one smooth motion, meeting his gaze with a challenging look.

Constance sprang to her feet in an instant, her body shaking with rage and exhaustion. "This is ridiculous!" she shouted at Barnard in exasperation. "His gaze did not leave my eyes! This man saved my life!"

Barnard rounded on her with fierce anger, his eyes looking up and down her body in a pointed glance. "I told you to cover up!"

Constance glanced around again. All eyes were now pointed at her, but what was she to do? There was no sign of anything to wear ...

Ralph came up to the group at a hard trot, carrying Gabriel's blue tunic and dagger in his hands. Gabriel swept up the tunic in a quick move, turning to stand before Constance. Suddenly she was a teenager again, Gabriel was standing before her, helping her don an old set of his leather armor before their training session. Obediently she put her arms up over her head, let him slide the tunic down over her wet body.

She was enveloped in the soft warmth, in the aromas of musk ... leather ... bergamot ... the rich scent of Gabriel, one she never forgot, one which came to her in her most secret longings. She closed her eyes, wrapped her arms around herself as the tunic settled down around her, held the sensation for a long, wonderful moment. Then she opened her eyes again, feeling fresh and new, her soul and emotion shining in her gaze.

She was almost surprised to see the real Gabriel there before her; it had been so long that he had existed only in her dreams. He seemed captivated, almost stunned, by what he saw in her eyes. He looked down at the blue tunic she wore, and his eyes softened ...

Barnard barged between them in an instant, grabbing Constance hard by the arm. "We need to get you back to the keep," he growled in command. "Get you into *proper* clothing."

He began dragging her up the hill, and she followed behind, half docile, half in shock. The rest of the party headed up the slope after them, the crying and soothing gradually subsiding to a low murmur.

Constance allowed Barnard to place her into the wagon, and soon three little bodies were tumbled up against her. Joy climbed in next, then Alison, holding little Ava tightly in her arms.

Alison's voice was a whisper "Thank you. I cannot thank you enough." She moved over to sit next to Constance. "You risked your life to save my child."

Joan moaned. "I thought she was behind me," she apologized, her eyes locked on the tiny body. "I never dreamed that she had gone back down to the water."

Constance closed her eyes, leaning back against the wagon frame as it bumped into motion. She pulled her arms tightly around herself, her hand dropping to press against her chest, to where the medallion had hung. She could smell the aroma of Gabriel all around her, feel his warmth in his tunic. She knew it was wrong to encourage her memories of him, to allow herself such pleasure at being wrapped in the embrace of his clothes.

Even worse, she was putting Gabriel's heart at risk. She had been unguarded, allowing him to see into her soul like that. She must do better in the future, for his sake, and for her own. If at all possible, she had to undo the damage that had been done.

Still, just for now, she would relish the feeling of his tunic enveloping her, of being held close by his scent. The miles rolled on in a dream of long lost hopes.

Constance shook off her reverie as the wagon bumped its way into the cobblestone-clad courtyard. The wagon had barely stopped moving when she leapt from its back, sprinting into the main building. She swept up Audrey as she went, drawing the young maid with her up into her room.

She gave a sigh of relief as the door closed behind them, then turned to smile reassuringly at the confused girl before her.

"We had some excitement while on the picnic," she let Audrey know in a weary voice, the exertions of the day catching up with her at last. "I am sure you will hear all about it in a short while. However, it has left me exhausted. Please let the others know I will take a long nap, and do not wish to be disturbed for any reason."

"Of course, My Lady," agreed Audrey, her young eyes wide with interest. She did not ask any further questions, although her eyes looked over Constance's tunic with sharp curiosity. She helped Constance climb out of the oversized outfit, then gently tucked Constance into bed before retreating from the room.

Once alone, Constance found that her ruse was only half invention. She was, indeed, quite worn down, and welcomed the long nap that beckoned.

She awoke in the early evening, the sun's light a soft glow at the horizon. She found herself refreshed and ready for activity. Audrey had left a serving of bread and cheese by her bed, which she gratefully ate, sipping the mead that sat alongside it. Once darkness had truly settled across the landscape, she got up quietly, slipping on her excursion clothes in the gentle light of the fire.

By the time Ralph's soft knock sounded on her door, she was ready. Together they slipped down the hall, heading out to the stables. In a short while they had reached the growing group of women who listened and learned in the church basement.

But when the evening was done, and Constance had mounted to head towards home, nervousness skittered through her heart. Gabriel had glimpsed what lay behind her mask, what lay nestled in the depths of her soul. The years she had sacrificed, all the innocent lives at stake, now depended on her ability to craft an explanation he might believe.

She only hoped she had the strength to see it through.

Chapter 13

Wednesday morning dawned with bright sunshine. Constance stood and stretched. Her shoulder ached, her left calf throbbed as if it had been kicked by a mule, but a freshness filled her with each breath.

She looked over at the blue tunic which still lay neatly folded in a corner, then turned away with a sigh. She reminded herself with harsh discipline that she had to keep Gabriel at bay. Every time she was near him, every time she looked in his eyes, she was tangibly drawn to him. She did not have that luxury, and it was cruel for her to encourage him in any manner.

Her own burgundy dress had been cleaned and laid out at the end of the bed. She slipped it on, holding back a dejected sigh as it slid over her shoulders. It had been so wonderful to wear Gabriel's tunic … she pushed the thought out of her mind. She would not go down that road.

She walked down the stairs and into the main hall, and instantly she was surrounded by cheers and cries of welcome. Alison came running over to give her a warm hug, and Charles was close behind her with an embrace of his own.

"Anything you want, it is yours," he offered heartily as he held her back to look at her. "That is quite a thing you did out there."

She saw a movement behind him, and her gaze was met by Gabriel's. She realized in a heartbeat that he had understood the full import of her look yesterday, that he knew her heart had never truly left him. His gaze shone as it had when they were younger, glowed with tender care and fierce protection.

She spun away from him, her heart in turmoil. She had to try to undo the damage she had done, and quickly. She had made her choice, and she could not abandon the villagers of Beadnell now, not when the bandits had become so dangerous.

She heard Gabriel's voice murmur something to Charles, and the sound of it was like a dagger in her heart. She was overwhelmed by the sense of his nearness, the knowledge that he still cared for her. All she had to do was turn and tell him the truth, and he would be at her side. She knew he would be. He was so close, so incredibly close …

She closed her eyes, taking in a deep breath. She could not do it. The villages would be burned, the innocents slaughtered. Only her resolve kept that fragile hold on the Beadnell's safety.

She forced herself to move around to her seat at the head table. Barnard was at her side in an instant, putting himself between her and the others. Despite her angst, Constance almost chuckled at his active involvement in her life. For so many years he had avoided her, neglected her. Now, suddenly, he was energetically seeking her out?

As if sensing her thoughts, he turned to her, taking a hold of her arm and gazing at her with a sharp look. "I do not like how you have been behaving while back at your old home," he clipped under his breath. "The presence of those sisters is affecting you. You have lost the docile obedience which is proper. I am most displeased."

The last thing Constance wanted was a fight, not here, not with Gabriel a few seats down. She dropped her eyes submissively. "I do not understand," she answered truthfully. "I have spent most of the time with the children, attempting to heal."

"You have spent far too much time with Gabriel," shot out Barnard with heat. "You will have no further contact with him."

Constance's face flushed, but she did not raise her eyes. Had she been spending time with Gabriel? She would have said she was avoiding him, trying to keep herself clear of temptation. And yet, she could remember clearly every moment they had been together, every phrase from his lips, every look in his eye.

Her hand went absently to where the medallion had hung, feeling the hollow spot at her chest. She let out a long sigh. She had to convince Barnard that Gabriel was no threat, to ease the remainder of their stay here. The people of Beadnell depended on it.

Her mind skipped back to that evening, long ago, where she sat with Gabriel. The words she had said then remained burned in her memory, etched as if in stone. She pitched her voice to hold the same dismissive coldness.

"Gabriel was my guard, nothing more. Yes, we had an amusing few years. However, now you and I are together. You are a real noble; we will have a title for our children. We have a fine house to raise them in." She raised her eyes to meet Barnard's squarely. "Surely you know this."

Barnard appeared mollified. "Of course, you are right," he agreed after a moment. "I am perhaps overly possessive of your charms, and I rarely see you with other people. After all, just because I like fine bread, I would certainly not marry a lowly baker!" He laughed in amusement at his own joke.

"You are very right," agreed Constance, keeping her tone light, soothing him. "Only a fool would do such a thing."

Barnard finished the last of his drink, his face relaxing slightly. "Certainly you are far better behaved than the other two women in our company." He leaned back, eyes searching for a maid. "In any case, we will be home soon, and things will be back to normal."

He spotted one of the servants behind him and called for another mead. Constance glanced down the table, hopeful that none of their soft conversation had been overheard. Alison and Gaynor were turned in their chairs, answering a question from Lucia. Charles was taking a long drink from his mead. Gabriel

...

Gabriel was staring at her, a stricken look on his face, of surprise and dawning understanding. She looked away quickly. She could not tell if he believed her indifferent now, and was upset by that – or if he realized how she had deceived him so many years ago. She did not want to know. Either one would undoubtedly cause trouble.

As soon as breakfast was finished, she walked quickly out into the front yard, looking for Ralph. If she could focus on her evening activities, she might keep herself occupied for the day. She found him in the stables, and pulled him aside.

"Ralph, do you think you could get your hands on one of those straw training dummies for tonight?"

His seamed face split into a smile. "That is a wonderful idea, My Lady," he agreed. "I think the women are quite ready for that step, and it will help with their training."

"So you can do it?" asked Constance, her face brightening.

"Consider it done," he agreed readily.

He glanced up over her shoulder, frowning, and Constance turned at once. Gabriel was bearing down on them, his face set.

The moment he had reached them, he fixed Constance with his gaze, his voice low and firm.

"I need to talk with you. Alone."

Constance shook her head at once. "You know that would be highly improper." Visions of Barnard catching them together – of his explosive rage – spun through her head. She glanced sideways at Ralph. "Say what you have to say now, or hold your peace."

Gabriel hesitated for a long moment, and Constance moved to turn away. Then, to her surprise, his voice burst from him, low but forceful.

"You would never believe what you told Barnard earlier. You were proud of Vera marrying her baker, the man she loved."

Constance flushed, her loyalty to Vera overwhelming her. "I am proud, very proud of Vera for many reasons," she retorted hotly. "She is an amazing woman. I wish I had one tenth of her strength."

"What about the rest?" pressed Gabriel immediately, his voice hoarse. "The remainder of what you said? Your need for a title? Noble blood?"

Constance knew she had to maintain her story, to keep a shield between her and Gabriel. She opened her mouth ... and could not do it. She could not force herself to say the words to him. Once had been difficult enough, all those years ago. She could not bring herself to do it a second time. Slowly, she closed her mouth again, letting out a deep breath. She lowered her eyes, looking away in shame.

Gabriel's eyes widened in shock, and he took a step back. "Good God, Connie ..." he gasped, awareness flooding his face. He looked at her for a long moment, then his eyes sharpened with anger.

"You had *no* right to lie to me!" he growled, a wealth of emotion resonating in those few words. "I was ever truthful with you, completely open and honest! I put your life before mine, I pledged my honor to you. I thought you would give me that same respect. You betrayed my honor, betrayed my trust!"

Constance whirled, her mouth open in shock. "I betrayed you?" she repeated in shocked confusion. "You threatened that you would love no other! That you would spend your life alone. I could not let that happen! I sacrificed myself for you!"

Gabriel shook his head, his eyes fierce. "You sacrificed yourself for your brother, for these villages around you. They, at least, you treated with respect. How did you treat me? You drove me to believe in lies, to believe all we had was a sham. How could you do that?"

Constance gestured at the keep. "You had healed as a result! You were courting Gaynor, were finding joy -"

Gabriel's face twisted in anguish. "I tried, believe me I tried. No matter what I did, at night it was only your face which I saw, in my dreams it was only you at my side. I thought you had turned from me, that none of it had been real. If at least we had loved and lost, I would have had those memories to keep me warm. You stole even those from me."

Constance turned away, haunted by the look in his eyes. She took in several deep breaths, fighting to control her racing heart. "This will not do either of us any good," she finally whispered softly. She did not mean to say any more, but the words slipped out of their own accord. "The loss of your presence has already hurt me more than I can bear. Please, I cannot shoulder much more." Her hand moved to press against her chest, against the absent medallion.

Gabriel saw her movement and his eyes narrowed. "You abandoned the amulet rather quickly, I noticed," he bit out in anger. "Perhaps women do not feel the loss of a soulmate as strongly as men do."

Constance spun at this, stung by the injustice. "I never let that pendant leave my body – not for one day – since you placed it around my neck," she swore with fierce heat. "That pendant was my life's blood!"

Gabriel ran his eyes down to her chest, then back up again, his eyes burning. "Another lie. I saw you by the river, when your chemise outlined your form. There was no pendant at your neck."

Constance took a step to stand right in front of him. She ran her hand around behind her neck, sweeping her hair up and on top of her head in a swirl, revealing her marked neck. "That is because the kidnappers *ripped it from my body*," she hissed out in a furious snarl. "They stole it from me, and threw me into a windowless cell, and I was lost … I was lost …"

Sobs racked her body, the overwhelming sense of loss hitting her as a physical blow. Staggering, she closed her eyes, shutting out the world, swept up by her torment. A gentle hand touched her neck, tracing the outline of the scars, and then she was being folded in against his chest, wrapped in his arms, rocked against his body with a soothing murmur.

Constance could not help it; she collapsed against him, crying, letting him take on her weight, letting him support her as he always had. She brought her arms up around Gabriel's back, holding him close. She neither knew nor cared where Barnard was. Let him find them.

Time stopped …

After a long while, Constance's sobs diminished, then ceased. Complete exhaustion overtook her. She knew she needed to get back to her room before she said or did something she would regret later.

She pulled herself back, eased her hair forward over her shoulders again to hide the scars. She turned away from Gabriel, unwilling to meet his eyes, and walked back toward the keep.

Gabriel did not say a word, nor did he follow her in.

Constance returned to her room, again leaving word with Audrey to turn away any visitors. She lay on her bed, willing herself to fall asleep. No matter how hard she tried, all she could see was Gabriel's eyes, all she could feel was Gabriel's arms wrapped around her. She knew she had been weak – she should have denied her feelings, should have kept up the charade.

She could not. Gabriel's charge about her honor had driven deep into her heart. They had sworn to always be truthful to each other, and she had betrayed that trust. She had thought it justified, but she realized now that she had no right to make that decision for him. It was not her place to tell him how to feel. It was wrong for her to try.

Where did this leave her now? She could not abandon the Beadnell lands. Without Barnard acting as her husband, those villages would become lost to the bandits. The women would be raped, the children slain. She could not live with that on her conscience.

If she must stay with Barnard, was knowing that Gabriel was out there, loving her, caring for her, a good thing?

A sense of peace washed over her.

Yes. It would be enough.

A Sense of Duty

Chapter 14

Constance was alert and ready to go long before dusk, but she bided her time, allowing the others to believe she had gone to bed. She waited until the appointed hour before dressing and slipping out the door to join Ralph. True to his word, he had a straw dummy tied to the back of his horse. They made the trip to the church in record time, the brightness of a full moon lighting their way.

Vera's face lit up with delight when she saw the new toy Constance had brought for her to play with. There were twenty women in the group tonight, so Ralph and Constance each took five women, while Vera and Colette felt comfortable enough with the basic moves to take four women each under their wing. They worked through the thrusts and parries, then began practicing with the dummy. Constance was delighted with how quickly the women became used to the moves, how much they improved each session.

She sat back once the lesson was in full swing, taking a moment to watch Vera and Colette lead their groups through the exercises. The two women were good, and the students followed their example with focused attention. Vera's bruise was all but gone now, and her face was bright with energy.

Constance realized with surprise that the women would be able to continue their practices even after she had to return home; they would be far better able to defend themselves as a result of the one seed she had planted. The thought made her proud, and humble at the same time. If only someone else had made this effort, years ago, who knows how many lives might have been saved …

It was much later than usual when Constance and Ralph finally bid farewell to the last students and began packing up their gear. The women were long gone by the time they put on their heavy cloaks. Ralph slung the straw dummy over his shoulder and they headed out toward their horses.

Ralph had just tossed the target over the back of his steed when a trio of shapes separated themselves from the nearby woods. Ralph and Constance drew their swords as one, moving in close to one another. They watched the figures with a careful eye, not saying a word.

Constance pulled her scarf more closely around her face and ears with her left hand, hiding her identity more carefully. If they realized who she was ...

The three intruders came to a halt about ten paces away, still hidden in the shadows. The taller one in the center – apparently the leader - took another step forward. He glanced over his shoulder at the stocky man to his right. The subordinate nodded, then called out in a low, decisive voice. His voice seemed muffled and odd through her swaddling, but she could not risk pulling it loose.

"Turn her over to us, and we can resolve this peacefully," the junior man ordered.

A sense of dream-like unreality settled over Constance. The bandits were nothing like the men who abducted her from the tavern; something buzzed in her head about the way they moved. They had not charged in and attacked; they were being almost cautious. What was going on?

Ralph protectively took a step in front of Constance, holding his sword out at an angle to further shield her.

"No," he called out in challenge, his voice firm and unyielding.

The trio facing them drew swords in unison, and began walking forward. "Well then, we will do this the hard way," offered the heavy man.

The leader put his sword through a rotation, shrugging his shoulders loose, and Constance's world tilted even further. It was as if her dreams were melding with her realities ... but she had no time to think. Without another word the three charged, and the fight was on.

Ralph strove to keep Constance behind him, but Constance refused to allow him to attempt a three-way battle. She rushed in at his side, keeping his flank clear of trouble as he blocked with both sword and dagger. Constance used her smaller size against her opponent, tucking and weaving with expert skill against the blade which came down at her.

It only took a few blows for her to realize that the man she faced was attempting to disarm her, not to harm her. The knowledge made her bolder, but at the same time more cautious about attempting lethal blows on her enemy. She tried one disarming move, then a second. Her opponent seemed surprised at her attempts to disarm rather than wound, but slipped the actions deftly. He was good ... very good.

Constance spared a glance to her side, and saw that Ralph did not have the luxury she did. He was being pushed back by the two men, their combined attack proving more than he could hold off at once. As she watched, his dagger flew from his hand, and without its protective action, his sword was out of his grasp only moments later. Constance dove before him, but she knew it was hopeless. A sharp rap on the side of her arm forced her to drop the sword, her forearm ringing with pain.

The men brought their swords up to point at her neck, and at Ralph's. There was a long pause.

The taller man nodded with his head. "Get her," he ordered his partners in a low, gutteral voice.

Ralph's voice rang with desperation. "No!" He swept the attackers with his eyes, and then without further hesitation dove towards the blades, seeking to muscle his way through by force, to take them down in hand to hand combat.

The leader pulled his sword to the side to keep Ralph free of the blade, then brought the hilt sharply across to smash into Ralph's head.

Ralph went down like a stone. His body sprawled against the dirt, and lay there, still.

Constance's heart stopped. "Ralph!" She flung herself to the ground at his side, running her fingers to his neck to seek out a pulse. "Ralph, please speak to me!"

Ralph fluttered his eyes open at her voice, looking up groggily. "My Lady," he rasped out hoarsely. "I have failed you."

Constance exhaled in relief, sitting back on her heels. "You did not fail me," she promised softly, her eyes shining in gratitude. "That was the most valiant -"

"God's Blood!" swore the tall man above her, looking in startled surprise between the two. She winced at the strength of his shout, instantly throwing herself across Ralph, shielding him with her body.

To her surprise, he did not make a move towards them. Instead he crossed the distance to the horses in three long strides. He examined the bundle on the back of Ralph's horse, then turned in shock, holding it high so his comrades could see the shape.

The stocky man standing above Constance looked down at her in bafflement. "Straw? It was a straw woman?"

Constance shook her head in confusion. "Not a woman, a dummy," she retorted, standing up protectively over Ralph. "For our training."

The man standing by the horse took a step forward into the moonlight, and Constance finally got a better look at him. He wore dark leggings and a matching tunic. His head was hidden, as were all the bandits', by a full helmet, although with his the faceplate seemed to shimmer more than the others. On his chest ...

She gasped in surprise, recognizing the emblem in an instant. "You are with the Angelus?" she called out in confusion. "We thought you were bandits!"

The man shook his head, and all three slowly lowered their swords. His voice was pitched low when he spoke. "We took you for kidnappers, stealing off with one of the women from the prayer circle."

"Prayer circle?" echoed Constance, her voice faint.

The man waved a hand in the direction of the church. "Why else would women be congregating at a church at night?"

"Perhaps learning to defend themselves from the likes of you!" shot back Constance in heated retort, leaning down to help Ralph struggle to his feet. "Do you never ask questions first, and attack later?"

She thought she heard a hint of amusement in the man's quiet response. "We thought a woman's life was in danger," he pointed out calmly.

"Well there was. Mine," bit out Constance shortly.

That seemed to silence the mercenary for a moment. When he spoke again, his voice was somber. "We never would have hurt you. We were hoping to take you in unharmed, to learn more about who you were working for."

"Well go then and seek some real bandits," retorted Constance, helping her injured friend over to his horse. "I have a wounded man to tend to, and we have to get home."

The tall man made a move with his hand, and one of his fellows ran into the woods, returning in a moment with three horses. "Let us escort you, then. It is the least we can do to atone for our mistake."

Constance waited until Ralph was fully mounted, then climbed easily onto her own horse, wheeling it around. "We do not need your help."

The mercenary climbed onto his steed and pulled in alongside Ralph. "Yet we will offer it, just the same. I believe you are going to the keep at North Sunderland?"

Constance blushed and looked away. She knew her gender had been given away immediately when she called out for Ralph, but she had hoped to keep her full identity a secret. Once the others found out …

The mercenary's voice came again, low and rough. "Your secret is safe with us, My Lady," he offered quietly. "Do not fear for that."

Constance glanced up at him in gratitude. She had not expected this gift, and nodded in appreciation.

The mercenary turned his gaze immediately, and rode the rest of the trip with them in silence. The men drew off to one side as Constance and Ralph approached the main keep. Constance glanced back after a few steps, and the trio was gone, melted into the trees.

She knew she should be angry with them for harming Ralph, and for interfering with her evening. But somehow she felt reassured that they were on the guard, helping to keep a watchful eye over her friends. There was something else, another feeling ... something elusive. She could not put her finger on it, no matter how hard she tried.

Chapter 15

Constance dressed quickly as soon as she awoke, heading downstairs, waving absently at her relatives as she passed through the main hall. In only a few moments she had moved into the quiet of the guard barracks. Long bunks stretched out on either wall, with a chest at the side of each bed. There was little adornment in the room; everything was tidy and neat. Most of the guards were out at work or breakfast; only a few men lay curled up under their blankets, sound asleep.

Constance moved toward the back of the room where a pair of men sat comfortably on one of the beds, talking quietly. They looked up at her approach, and she realized in surprise that Gabriel had come to speak with Ralph.

Gabriel was staring at her with a new look in his eyes. She found herself caught in his gaze as she walked up to join them. What was going on in his head? There was curiosity there, but also … the feeling clicked in her mind. It was pride, admiration. She had seen him look this way once when one of the keep's young squires had defeated him in mock combat. A shiver of delight moved through her, and she found she could not look away.

The question burst from her before she gave it thought. "What are you doing here?" She realized at once that she sounded brash, almost rude. She quickly amended more gently, "You seem quite comfortable with Ralph; had you met before this week?"

Gabriel's smile was warm. "Ralph and I have a long history," he responded easily. "We served together for many years in the Crusades, when I was young." He looked fondly at his friend. "Ralph saved my life once or twice, and taught me a great deal about life."

Constance turned to look at Ralph with curiosity. "You never told me you knew anyone from the area during your time in Jerusalem," she stated, intrigued.

Ralph looked uncomfortable, and Constance flushed. It occurred to her suddenly that Ralph probably kept this knowledge from her in order not to upset her with reminders of her past; this was hardly a topic she wanted to get into in front of Gabriel. At a loss for words, she sat down on Ralph's other side, inspecting the injury on his head.

"How is the lump doing?" she asked, probing at his skull gently with her fingers, anything to change the subject. "Tender, I assume?"

Ralph winced as she touched him, but his voice was even. "No worse than an average day on the practice field," he responded. "I will heal."

Constance waited for Gabriel to ask how the wound had been acquired, but to her surprise he did not speak. Perhaps he was used to the daily bumps and bruises of guard life from his years as a soldier.

She thought back to the previous night's activities, to the encounter with the Angelus. She wanted to ask Ralph more about the organization, to find out what he knew of them, but she would not broach that topic with others nearby. It would have to wait until later.

Satisfied that the wound was not serious, she stood again. She looked down fondly at the man who had so valiantly defended her from harm. "I am sure you will be as good as new in a few days," she affirmed. "Please let me know if you feel faint or dizzy in the next few days. You can never tell with head wounds."

"I know the drill," he agreed readily. "I will be sure to turn myself in if things seem to be getting worse."

Constance turned back towards Gabriel, and once again she was caught by his eyes. She felt as if he was looking into her soul, was approving all he saw with heartfelt admiration. It was an intimate look, one which warmed her from head to toe. She felt the power in the connection, and the danger. With an effort she wrenched herself from his gaze.

"Until later," she called, turning quickly and heading back into the main hall.

Constance played a dance with Gabriel for the next few hours. If he came into a room, she found a reason to leave it. If he joined them for lunch, she took a snack off to eat with the children, offering to entertain them with stories. Barnard kept a close eye on her, but she deliberately gave him no reason to become upset, not by a movement, glance, or word.

Her efforts began to pay off. Slowly Barnard lost his jealous glare and settled into a surly calm. As she gathered up the youngsters for some time outside, she left him sitting back in the main hall, talking politics at length with Charles.

The late afternoon sun was drifting into the shadows of evening as Constance sat out in the herb garden playing with the four children. They were weaving together chains of daisies, draping each other with garlands of flowers. Constance relaxed in the warm sun, listening to the gentle drone of a nearby bumblebee.

Looking up, she was captivated by the tracery of clouds floating languidly across the sky. They were like wisps of smoke, curls and swirls in the deep blue canopy. The thin loops glimmered in the sunshine ...

She sat up suddenly, awareness washing over her. The tracery on the helmet of the leader, that night at the church. It was the same as the man who had rescued her from the prison cell. It was undoubtedly why he had seemed so familiar, in his movements, his actions.

Was he the leader of the Angelus? Her memories of the rescue were so fragmented that she struggled to remember. The other men had not spoken, there had been no commands given. But the way they moved, the way they acted, seemed to indicate deference.

Even the night at the church, there had been nothing stated, but it had been clear to her from the start who was in charge.

Her mind was brought again to the idea that the Angelus were actively protecting the poor, not simply the interests of the wealthy guild. If so, who was funding their efforts? Surely not the wool merchants.

Voices bubbled over a nearby hedge, shaking her from her thoughts. Constance looked up to find Gabriel and Gaynor walking slowly together through the sunshine, Gaynor's reddish curls bouncing gently with each step. Constance looked away quickly, hoping they would pass her by, but to her consternation they turned in her direction, Gaynor's laughter chiming out across the greenery.

"See, look, I knew I could find her for you." Her eyes swept the children and their petaled crafts. "Why, how lovely your flowers are! You are quite a talented teacher, Constance!" she called out in delight. "May I have one?"

Lucia stood primly, her eyes shining with pleasure. "Here, you may have mine, Aunt Gaynor!" she announced, removing her own long garland. Gaynor knelt down at the child's feet, and Lucia carefully placed the strand over the woman's shoulders, as if bestowing a medal.

Gaynor stood again, fluffing her hair out over the flowers. "How does my necklace look, sir knight?" she asked Gabriel playfully.

"It is quite fitting," he responded with a smile. "Flowers suit you nicely."

She dropped a curtsy to him, "Why thank you, My Lord," she flirtatiously responded with a grin. "I shall have to wear fresh flowers for you every day, if it pleases you."

Constance turned away, her heart tight at the exchange between the two. She had chosen to remain with Barnard - could she expect Gabriel to vow chastity and spend his life pining for her? Gaynor was beautiful and vivacious. Could Constance jealously doom Gabriel to a life of unrequited longing, never to look at another woman again?

But could her heart shoulder the burden of seeing the man she loved wooing and marrying another?

Her heart raggedly ripped down its seams, and she turned away, drawing in a long, deep breath. Getting up from where she sat with the girls, she walked to where the twins were playing, seeking a distraction.

"Would you two like to start another garland?" she asked the twins, her voice deliberately light.

Alond's answer was immediate. "No, we want to ride horsie!" he called out with delight.

Alain leapt to his feet, his eyes sparkling. "Yes, please!"

Constance flushed with embarrassment. She did not mind rolling around with the boys when none were watching, but to have Gaynor looking the part of a flower-strewn princess while Gabriel watched her wallow in the mud was more than she could bear right now.

"Not this afternoon," she tried to dissuade the pair, hoping against hope that they would not make a fuss. "Maybe later."

She heard a low voice over her shoulder. "Let me," Gabriel offered with a smile in his voice. "I am more dressed for horseplay."

She glanced up at him in surprise. "You do not need to -"

Gabriel had swept up both boys in his arms before she could finish, and somehow managed to get both on his back, trotting around the area to their delighted calls and screams. He lifted one in his arms, somersaulting the boy over his head to land gently in a hay bale. The other soon followed, and in moments the trio was turning and rolling in the hay, the boys attacking Gabriel with glee, Gabriel gently turning and spinning the boys off of him.

Constance's mouth fell open in surprise. She had known Gabriel was gentle, and he had always treated children with kindness. Still, to watch them, they were like a pile of puppies tumbling in the sunshine. Her heart glowed with adoration. She could never imagine Barnard playing with their children, connecting so closely with them.

Alond's voice rose high. "Ow!" he called out, pressing a hand to his forehead. Constance skipped forward in a moment to where the boy sat holding his hay-strewn head, his face creased with surprise rather than pain. She ran her fingers gently along his scalp, finding a small bump near the back.

"Just a little boo-boo," she smiled at him. "Nothing to worry about. What did you hit?"

She looked around at the other two, equally covered with hay and askew. Alain looked at her with an open grin, shrugging. Gabriel ...

Time froze. His shirt's laces had loosened, and a silvery pendant had fallen out from within its folds. She knew that pendant, knew every curve of its shape, knew the feel of it beneath her hand, knew the weight of it around her neck. Her hand flew to the spot on her chest where it should have hung, and her mouth dropped open in horror.

Gabriel was associated with the bandits.

There was no other reason, no other excuse for him to have that medallion. He knew it was hers. If he had seen it in a shop, or come across it in another way, he would have given it back to her. It was only if he had acquired it surreptitiously ... through an association he was not proud of ...

Gabriel looked baffled at her stunned silence, then followed the steady focus of her gaze down to his own chest. His face wrenched in a twisting blend of emotions, then he rolled and sprang to his feet, coming towards her.

Constance did not wait one more moment. She turned and fled, racing at top speed toward the keep. Her heart pounded as her feet flew along the path and through the door.

She was sprinting across the main hall when a strong hand grabbed at her wrist, a steadfast arm spun her in a turn to look at him. Gabriel was breathing hard from his chase, his voice coming out in gasps.

"Con ... wait ..."

She jerked her arm away from his grasp as if his touch burned her, her face livid with fury. "You dare! You dare to look me in the face, after what you have done!" Her mind flared back to that day she was dragged into the ruined basement, to the bandit who had fondled the medallion in his grimy hands, who had ripped it painfully from her neck. Her hand went by instinct up to the scar there, running her fingers along its rough edge. Her eyes became cold and steely.

"Tell me you were never in that bastion of hell," she hissed, her voice grating. "Tell me you never set foot in that prison."

There was a long pause; the hammering of her heart shook her body. Gabriel did not look away, his eyes held the somber truth in them, his breath coming under control. He was clearly searching for words.

"Connie ... I would never lie to you ... let me explain ..." He reached a hand out to her.

Constance took a step backwards, shaking. He could not deny the charge. His admission was the knell of doom. All her hopes, all her dreams of Gabriel as her shining hero came shattering down around her in one crystalline moment, in the tortured look in his eyes.

Tears welled in her eyes. She would not break down, not here in front of him, not after everything that had happened. She turned on her heel, preparing to run up the stairs to her room.

She nearly slammed into Barnard's chest, and looked up, startled. His face moved from annoyance to jealous anger in the blink of an eye as he moved his gaze between her face and Gabriel's.

"What in God's teeth is going on here?" he demanded fiercely.

His gaze swept down to Gabriel's chest, and his look darkened. He grabbed Constance's arm hard with his left hand, shaking with rage.

"That cursed medallion! I ordered you to melt that pendant down years ago! Now I see it on another man's chest?"

Gabriel's eyes went wide with shock as he looked between Barnard and Constance. He looked automatically at Constance's chest, at where she had secretly worn the pendant until recently.

Barnard was not finished. His voice rose in pitch, reaching every person who stood in the hall. "You have betrayed me, publicly humiliated me! You cheating slut!" His right hand raised high, aiming at her head. Constance instinctively tried to pull free, to shield herself, but his grip was far too tight. His arm swung …

It never connected. Gabriel moved with lightning speed into the space between the two, grabbed Barnard's arm with his own, held it motionless in the air as the two men struggled. Finally Barnard pulled his arm back, his look fierce.

"You would dare to interfere?" he asked coldly, his breath still coming heavily from the struggle.

"I would rectify a mistaken impression," responded Gabriel shortly, his look heated. "The pendant I wear around my neck is my own, given to me by my father on his deathbed, when I was ten. It has not left my neck since that day."

Constance swiveled her head in shock to stare at Gabriel. Surely he did not think such a blatant lie -

Barnard obviously was of the same impression. "You hold your honor lightly, if you would sell it so cheaply," he challenged in a flat tone.

Gabriel's eyes flashed, and his hand dropped to his sword. He took in several deep, steadying breaths, visibly steeling himself to be still. Then he turned and looked straight into Constance's eyes. His voice was quiet, and yet it held a vast reservoir of emotion.

"My dragon gazes to the left."

Constance lost herself in his gaze, wrapped herself in the comfort of his words, and the tension in her body melted away as dew on a golden spring morning.

It was true. She had seen her pendant's image in her mirror so many times, it looked natural on him. She had never taken off her medallion and gazed at it directly. It was suddenly as clear as day. What she saw was what a mirror would show her – but if she were to hold it in her hands, it was a reverse image. Her dragon had gazed to the right, always to the right, where Gabriel stood ready by her side. And his …

Barnard was not calmed by this news – if anything, his fury seemed to grow to even greater heights. He rounded on Constance, the veins in his neck standing out in throbbing lines.

"You told me you got your medallion at a fair!" he snarled furiously, every muscle in his body shaking with anger.

"Yes, yes," she agreed quickly, desperate to defuse the situation, wincing as Barnard's grip grew even tighter on her arm. "That was long ago; I was barely sixteen! I liked the design, that is all."

Her eyes pleaded with him to believe her; her mind flailed for something innocent to prove her case. "The vendor said it was a guardian symbol ..."

Barnard's face relaxed as he saw the truth in Constance's eyes. He drew strength from her meek attitude, and gave her a small shake. She watched as his cock-sure attitude boiled back up to the surface. He rounded on Gabriel with a sneer, his anger sliding into arrogance. "So these are guardian dragons? Yours did not seem to have helped your father, did it?"

Gabriel's eyes flashed with shock and pain. Constance's heart dropped at the sight, and her temper roiled. Her emotions were see-sawing wildly, and she could not rein in her words. They rose in a heated shout.

"At least his parents died making an effort to save their lands. They sacrificed everything for their people. You will not let even one of our best soldiers outside our walls, for fear you might lose power – and our people suffer for it!"

She shook off Barnard's grasp, her eyes blazing with fury. "You hired local drunks to accompany me to the nunnery – and when they were slain, you made no effort to rescue me! No attempt at all! While I lay imprisoned in that hell hole! It is only thanks to the Angelus mercenaries that I am even alive!"

Her voice rang out, challenging him. "I was given over to a coward, and if there were any way for me to undo this bond while keeping the Beadnell lands safe, I would take it!"

The room went dead silent, and Barnard's eyes burned into her with the heat of a thousand suns. Constance found she was shaking with passion, fear, and exhaustion. She could not un-say what she had just shouted. God only knew what Barnard would do to her now.

Barnard's eyes slowly swept the room, and Constance could see what he found there – dislike, disdain, and disapproval. Charles had come to join the group, with Alison and Gaynor right behind him. All three stared coldly at Barnard.

Barnard brought his gaze back to stare down at Constance. "I see now that your stay here has tainted you; your disposition is normally tolerable at best, and now it more closely resembles the ill-mannered family your brother has married into."

Alison and Gaynor both drew breath, aghast, and Charles' eyes became steely. Barnard did not hesitate; his orders came swiftly and without equivocation.

"It is time you were back home fully under my control where you belong. If your coach were here we would leave immediately. As it is, you and I will return home at first light tomorrow morning, doctors' orders be damned." He looked up, his eyes searching out one of his guards. "You there, go back and ensure the coach is ready at dawn." The man bowed and fled from the room.

Barnard's eyes rose to hold Gabriel's with an open challenge as he continued to bark orders at Constance. "If you are healthy enough to fight with me, you are healthy enough for your other intimate duties as well. You will join me in our bed … now."

Gabriel went very still. Constance could see the tension in every muscle. She had seen this look before, knew the myriad signals broadcasting that he was preparing to launch his attack. His hand slid slowly down the hilt of his blade.

Constance could not let it happen. If Gabriel attacked Barnard, no court would justify the action. He would be hung … put to death …

Anything was better than that consequence.

She tossed back her head in challenge, knowing she would have to goad Barnard to distract him from the rising threat in Gabriel's stance. She forced her voice to be calm, almost disdainful.

"You have shown no interest in me these past five years, My Lord. I thought you were becoming interested in a position with a monastery. Fine, then, let us see if you still have the energy to be a man." She gazed dismissively at him, then turned and began striding purposefully up the stairs.

She sighed in both relief and nervousness as she heard him turn, heard the fast footsteps come up behind her to join her. Whatever came next, she had lured him away from Gabriel, had bought them some time.

She steeled her inner strength as Barnard stalked into her room after her, as he turned to drop the heavy bar across the door with a solid thud.

He strode over towards her, ripping loose the laces of her tunic with one hand, yanking the material down with a savage fierceness she had not seen before. She did not resist as he pulled the tunic down to her waist, then slammed one hand against the chemise at her chest, searching.

His voice was terse. "You do not have your medallion," he snapped, his eyes sharp on her.

She dropped her eyes. "You ordered me to destroy it," she responded simply. He had her at his mercy, here in this room. She did not want to goad him into a rage. She knew it was a lie of omission to hedge like this, and mentally promised to pray out her sins as soon as possible.

He held his hand there, against her body, and she felt his eyes searing into her.

"At this fair ... was Gabriel there?"

She turned away, flushing crimson at the thought. Yes, Gabriel had been there. Hhe had become still with shock when he saw the medallion in her hand. He had bought it instantly for her, no haggling, no questions. He had been like a man driven ...

"Yes," she whispered, her voice low.

Barnard stripped the tunic off of her in one fierce move. He pressed her down onto her bed, climbing on top of her and staring down at her with fierce possessiveness.

"Did he buy the medallion for you?" he snapped, his eyes bright with dawning realization.

Constance could not lie. Not about something as important as this – not about the pendant which had kept her strong, had kept her sane.

"Yes," she replied, her voice more steady.

Barnard's face mottled with rage. "You knew he had the matching pendant!" he screamed with fury. "You knew he was pledging himself to you!"

"No!" shot out Constance immediately.

She barely saw Barnard's fist flying toward her face, barely had time to turn before it slammed into the side of her head. Her world burst into brilliant flares of pain. She screamed in agony; the waves of torment which followed left her gasping for breath.

"Do not lie to me, whore!" cried Barnard, his hand raised again. She could see blood on his knuckles, could taste its metallic tang in her mouth. Her vision unfocused, then came back into alignment. She struggled to see through the shimmering waves, to focus on survival.

"I swear I speak the truth," she gasped, and the knowledge flooded through her, filling her with anguish. She drew in long, deep breaths. "Gabriel never told me he had a medallion," she added in a whisper, her heart torn. The pain became visceral, became a swamp which enveloped her entire being.

Why had he not told her of her medallion's true origin? Undoubtedly it had belonged to his mother, and had been stolen or lost long ago. Why had he not told her of the one he carried? That she had worn hers all those years, not realizing …

There was no further blow, no motion from the man above her. She warily looked up again, and saw an expression of understanding dawn on Barnard's face. "It seems you were in fact deceived," he murmured slowly, a cynical smile spreading. "It serves you right. Your little boy toy is not so noble after all, is he?" He chuckled for a moment. "I wonder what he is doing this very moment, knowing that you are mine, that you are in my bed, feeling my hands upon you …"

Constance blanched, her stomach roiling, her head throbbing. Barnard slid her chemise up in one quick movement, exposing her lower half, and then began fumbling at his pants.

Constance did not resist or turn. Once, years ago, she had gone through this process almost willingly, hoping to grow a bond between herself and her new ally. She had dreams of children to love, a family to nurture. Now she fought off a shiver as his cold and clumsy fingers grasped at her, as he slid himself up against her with insistent focus. Fighting him off would only bring more pain. Best to endure as best she could, and get this over with as quickly as possible.

But ... nothing was happening. Confused, she looked up at Barnard. The look on his face was ... frustration? Anger? She realized suddenly that he had not entered her because he *could* not. Despite his best efforts, he was completely limp.

Constance bit her lip and turned her face away, willing herself to portray no emotion. She lay absolutely still. If she sent Barnard into a rage with a look, a sign ...

Barnard rolled off her with an angry growl. "That medallion is cursed," he ground out between clenched teeth. "I will have no peace while I am under the same roof with it." Constance laid stock still as he climbed out of bed and reassembled his clothing. He ran his eyes over her with dismissive contempt.

"I will not stay one second longer in this damned house," he shot out hotly. "I ride at once. I expect you to follow in the coach at first light tomorrow morning." His voice took on a more sinister tone. "I will send an armed guard with it to ensure you follow my orders."

Constance fought to hold her face motionless. A steely resolve coalesced in her core. She would never return to Barnard's keep, never put herself under his control again. She would find some solution – any solution – to ensure the Beadnell villagers' safety. One that did not require her to maintain this charade of a marriage any further.

Barnard's eyes narrowed, and a cold grin spread across his face. "Thinking of following through on that little threat of yours earlier, are you? The whole land thinks we are married. That gives me legal rights over you. You are my property. Just as the Beadnell lands are my property."

Constance could not help herself, the wound was too raw. Against every instinct screaming in her body, she found herself whispering, "you are *not* my husband."

Barnard's grin grew wider. "I am afraid, my dear, that I have legal documentation that proves I am indeed your lord and master."

Constance's blood ran cold. She opened her mouth to speak, but no sound came out.

Barnard straightened out his tunic with a look of keen satisfaction. "A forgery, of course, but completely legitimate looking. You would never convince anyone, after all this time, that it was anything but authentic." His eyes narrowed. "You will be on that coach in the morning, or I will bring the full power of my estate against your brother's keep – and the backing of every lawman in the region will be on my side."

Constance turned away, her world crashing in on her, feeling as if she were sliding into a black pit with no bottom. She was lost. She was hopelessly lost.

There was a long moment of silence. She heard the bolt slide free, and the door open and then close again as he left the room. Constance pulled herself away from the abyss and moved into desperate action. The moment the door was closed again, she flew from the bed to slide the bolt quietly, carefully, into the sealed position again. She stood by the door shaking, waiting – but he did not return. She heard the sound of raised voices from the main hall, but could not make out any words. Then nothing.

She waited … waited … there was the sound of footsteps coming down the hallway to her door. Audrey's quiet voice came hesitantly through the solid wood.

"Constance, are you all right?"

Constance leant back against the door, closing her eyes, fighting away the dizziness. She did not want to deal with questions, did not want to think about what tomorrow held for her. She wanted time to stop …

Audrey's voice cracked with concern. "Constance?!"

Constance suddenly realized that Charles and Gabriel were likely to break down the door if she did not at least give an answer.

"I ... I am fine," she called through the door, trying to keep her voice even.

There was a moment of low murmuring, then silence. Audrey's voice was gentle. "Please let me in."

Constance shook her head, and immediately her world grew fuzzy. A warm rivulet of blood trickled down her cheek. The thought concerned her. If she was going to be able to plan any sort of action, she needed all of her wits about her – and her senses. Still, not Audrey ...

"Send Ralph in, please – and *only* Ralph," she requested in resignation. She slid the bar back from the door, and stayed behind it as Ralph pushed it open and walked into the room. He looked around in surprise, then turned as she pushed the door shut behind him.

"Oh, Constance," he groaned as he looked at her face, stepping closer.

"You have seen worse, I am sure," she pointed out pragmatically, standing stoically beneath his scrutiny. "The pain is intense, but I am hoping the injury is superficial."

He stepped forward, using his sleeve to carefully mop away the blood from her forehead. "Head wounds always bleed a lot," he murmured to himself, "even if they are minor." He probed gently for a few minutes, then looked down at her.

"It will leave a nasty bruise, but if we can stop the bleeding, you should recover soon enough."

"A steak, then," she requested, relieved at the diagnosis. "Could you bring one, please? With a mug of mead?"

Ralph nodded and left the room quickly. Constance leant back against the door, closing her eyes with exhaustion. Barnard swore he would attack her brother if she did not return to his home. The war would tear the lands apart – and the bandits would have easy pickings from the survivors. But to willingly go back into Barnard's power ...

There was a knocking at the door, and she slid it open again, reaching out to take the mead from Ralph's hand.

It was not Ralph. Gabriel stood there, mug of mead in one hand, steak in the other, a shocked look on his face.

His voice was rough. "God's blood, I will *kill him*."

Ralph stumbled into the room, his tunic askew. "I am sorry, My Lady. He saw the blood -"

Constance shook her head. "It is all right, Ralph. Leave us, please."

Ralph retreated, pulling the door shut behind him. Gabriel stood still for a moment, then set the items on a side table. He stepped forward to wrap an arm around Constance's waist, carefully helping her to sit on the bed.

"Connie, what have you gotten yourself into," he murmured softly, his voice almost breaking. He reached over to take the steak, sitting beside her and pressing it carefully to the side of her head.

It was so familiar to Constance. The gentle way he had tended to her after their training rounds, caring for the numerous scrapes and bruises she collected so easily. She found herself leaning against him, and his arm came up around her shoulder as it always had.

"Oh, Gabe," she sighed, resting her head against his shoulder.

He ran his fingers through her hair, pressing a gentle kiss down on the top of her head. "Please tell me this is the first time he has hit you," he asked, almost hesitantly.

She nodded against his chest. "The first ... and the last," she vowed.

"Tell me how I can help," he insisted, his voice full of steel.

Constance thought for a long moment of telling Gabriel the full truth, that she was not married to Barnard, that she was a free woman. She knew how that discussion would end. Gabriel would insist she go with him, to hole up at his ocean-side keep. Barnard would then produce his illegitimate marriage documents and level kidnapping charges against Gabriel. The full might of the justice system would slam down on Gabriel's neck. There was no way he would survive that full-on onslaught.

She would not take that path. There had to be another solution.

Constance took in a deep breath, then let it out again. She reached over for the mead, taking in a long swallow.

"If I could do this on my own, I would," she stated quietly. "I hate to involve you in this; crossing Barnard could cause you no end of trouble."

"Do not even think of keeping me out of this," bit out Gabriel tersely. "If you try, I will just follow you on my own."

"I know," Constance soothed, patting his hand. "He insists I return to his home – but he gave me leave to go to the nunnery for two weeks. I never had that time there."

"The ... nunnery?" asked Gabriel, his expression torn between hope and concern. "You are not thinking -"

Constance shook her head, wincing at the pain that came with the motion. "I just need time to think. I cannot stay here – and I cannot go home. I need a safe haven where I can gain some breathing room." She turned to look out the window at the stars in the night sky. "If I can get to the nunnery, that should give me at least two weeks, if not more. Maybe something will come to me during that time."

"It is a start at least," agreed Gabriel resolutely. "However, it will be a race. If we leave at first light, the coach team will send the alert back to Barnard. He will then send an intercept group to block your flight."

Constance nodded in agreement, her mind clicking through the possible moves. "I imagine the ambush would be laid at the bridge at the old ford. His team could try to make it there just before we did. That would give him a choke point to stop us. If we took the ride at a fast canter, we could clear that an hour earlier than he could, easily. Maybe even two."

Gabriel looked into her eyes with concern. "Are you sure you are up to that?" He lifted the steak away for a moment, checking her wound. A black anger moved into his eyes, then dissipated again as he forced it away. "You should rest for a day ... maybe two ..."

"I do not have the luxury," pointed out Constance. "If I get a solid night's rest, then yes – I will make the ride. I need to."

"Ralph will come with us, and perhaps some of your brother's men -"

Constance shook her head. "I cannot bring a war down on Charles' head. Also, Ralph is Barnard's man and -"

"Ralph is *your* man," corrected Gabriel. "You can ask him yourself, of course, but I know his answer. He will go with you, rather than return to Barnard."

"Will the three of us be enough?" asked Constance with concern.

"For the likes of the soldiers Barnard will 'spare' to bring you in?" snorted Gabriel with the hint of a smile. "We will be more than enough."

Constance allowed herself a wry grin. "Then I will leave my fate in your hands," she agreed softly, looking up at him.

She melted as she saw the tender look in his eyes, a gaze full of longing and protectiveness. He lingered for a long moment, then leant forward to press his lips gently to her forehead.

"I must go make plans, if we are to succeed. In the meantime, you need every moment of rest you can manage." He paused for a minute, looking down at her. "Sleep well," he rasped gently, then stood and walked slowly to the door. She saw several people gathered around the door as he left, and in a moment Audrey came in to help her into bed. Constance allowed herself to be guided under the covers, and in a moment she was falling fast asleep.

Chapter 16

Constance woke to a throbbing headache, a feeble thread of early morning sunlight entering the room. She rolled over and buried her head back into her pillow.

The knocking came again, more insistently. She sprung awake suddenly, the events of the previous day flooding back to her. She sat awake in the bed, pulling the blanket up around her. The room swayed dangerously, then settled back down again.

"Come in," she called out in concern.

Audrey entered the room at once, bustling around her. "The coach is here, and they are becoming agitated. M'Lord and Ralph are both ready to ride, and your horse is prepared as well. The moment you leave, Lord Barnard's men will head back to alert him, so it is important you get out as soon as you can so you can make it to your aunt's by nightfall."

Constance chuckled even through her headache. Apparently Gabriel had been busy last night! She wondered if there was a person in the building who did not know of their plan.

Audrey helped Constance to her feet, and assisted her in preparing as quickly as possible. Soon Constance was heading down the main stairs towards the great hall.

Gabriel and Ralph were there, talking in serious tones with Charles while Alison and Gaynor hovered nearby, their chatter nervous and high. Constance did not see the children around. Three of Barnard's men were grouped to one side, conspicuously apart from the rest. When they saw her descend the stairs, they sprung to alertness and headed towards her.

Gabriel and Ralph drew swords in unison and moved in between Constance and the approaching men without saying a word. Several guards from nearby tables rose at the same moment, their hands hovering at their hips.

The trio stopped at the motion, gazing around them with wary concern. The lead man took another step forward, his gaze challenging.

"Lady Constance, your husband insists you return to his home, where you belong. He has sent us to ensure you obey his order."

Constance moved to stand between Ralph and Gabriel, her eyes steady. "Barnard gave me permission to visit with my aunt for two weeks. I was delayed in my trip, but now I am healthy enough to proceed. I will be heading there, as planned, and as agreed."

The man's face creased in confusion for a moment, then a crafty look came over his face. "We can certainly take you there in the coach, if you will come with us. You know you do not like to ride horseback."

Constance's mouth quirked into a smile. "Actually, I adore horseback riding," she countered. "I find it quite refreshing, and will enjoy the trip. Please return the coach to Barnard, with my apologies."

There was a long pause as the man ran his eyes along the guards in the room, settling on Gabriel and Ralph. He appeared to come to a decision, and nodded. "Yes, we will return to Barnard, and let him know of your choice."

He turned on his heel, and the trio was gone in a flash.

Gabriel resheathed his sword in one quick move. "That is our cue," he commented, moving to shake hands with Charles. "Thank you again, and I will be in touch," he vowed quietly.

Constance moved to give her brother a warm hug. "I am sorry that I have caused trouble for you," she sighed as she pulled back.

Charles laid a hand gently against her bruised face for a moment, his brow darkening. "It is I who should apologize for letting your life get so out of hand," he responded in a low voice. "I am the only family you have left, and I have been lax in my responsibilities. Believe me, I will make up for it."

Alison came forward to give her a hug, then Gaynor did the same. "Good luck," whispered the younger girl. "I think I am suddenly less eager to get married. It might be worth it to take my time, and consider my options more carefully."

Constance smiled. "It is good to thoughtfully consider anything you attempt in life," she advised gently.

Joy poked her head into the room, scanning it for danger, and in a moment four young bundles of energy poured in, gathering around Constance to give her hugs. She picked each child up in turn, providing a fond farewell.

Ava's voice was high with concern. "Boo-boo!" she cried out, pointing a finger at Constance's large bruise.

Constance smiled, reassuring the child. "It is fine," she promised. "It will heal, and it will not happen again."

"That is good!" agreed Ava, allowing one more hug before running back to Alison's leg.

Gabriel's voice was steady. "We really should get going."

Constance nodded and stood. She followed the two men out the main doors, and in a moment they were mounted and cantering out the central gate.

Constance knew she should be concerned, should be looking over her shoulder as she rode along the path, flanked by Gabriel on her right and Ralph on her left. She found she could not regret the events of the previous day. She felt free ... she felt free. Her hair streamed behind her in a long ribbon, the sun shining brightly on her face as they flew down the path.

She glanced to her side, saw Gabriel return her look with a face half tense, half released. She knew the feeling, echoed it back to him. There had been so many days like this in the past, so many times where they rode on together for hours, racing the wind. He was older now; there were lines on his brow, a new strength and breadth to his shoulders.

The hours rolled along in a joyous stream of singing birds and roadside wildflowers. Finally Gabriel indicated they should pull in at the next tavern, a squat building sitting next to a slow running river. A lad of ten ran forward as they approached, taking the reins of the horses and leading them off to a nearby stable. Gabriel strode forward to press open the door of the tavern, scanning the interior before waving Constance and Ralph over to join him.

"Gabe! Welcome!" cried the innkeeper, waving a beefy hand. "Sit anywhere. Ale?"

"Three, yes," agreed Gabriel with a smiling nod, as the trio moved towards a round table in the back. In a moment their ale had arrived, and the man wiped his hands on his apron before heading out back to prepare three bowls of stew.

Constance shook her head, a grin on her lips. "How is it that you still know every tavern keeper we come across?" she asked jokingly.

Gabriel shrugged, taking a long draught of his ale. "One of my many talents," he responded, winking conspiratorially.

Constance suddenly was brought back to another tavern, another innkeeper, with a dagger at her back and a last chance caught in her throat. She thought of her vain, foolish hope in passing a message along to Gabriel. Her childish dreams …

She looked down, her cheeks flushing, ashamed that she had even thought to ask for him in her moment of weakness, after how she had lied to him. She took a long pull on her drink, looking away. When she finally looked back at the table, she found Gabriel watching her, concern in his eyes.

The sound of footsteps brought her back to her current situation. The tavern keeper came over to the table with a large tray, balancing three bowls on it. He handed them around the table, and Constance focused on eating the warm mixture. It was simple but good, and she ate through her portion in haste, washing it down with the fresh ale.

They were done in record time, and Gabriel walked over to the innkeeper to pay. Constance could hear them talking; heard the innkeeper turn down Gabriel's money. "Not after what you did for us," he insisted calmly. "Go, take the lady on her way, and good luck to you. God bless." Constance watched him with curious eyes, but said nothing as he returned to the group, heading back out into the bright sunshine.

In a moment they were mounted on their horses and riding along the pathway. Constance knew they were making excellent time. At this rate they should be at the bridge in another hour, and to the nunnery before nightfall. Her shoulders relaxed and she stretched out her mount into a long, easy canter, falling into the rhythm of the steed's movements. Beside her Ralph and Gabriel matched her pace, their eyes alert. No hoofbeats sounded from behind them; the few travelers they passed waved a friendly hand as they went by.

Constance almost felt a sense of sadness as they approached the bridge. It marked the beginning of the end for her and Gabriel. On previous trips to the nunnery it had always been a point of excitement, an indication that the destination was almost upon them. Now it was a sign that she would be soon parted from Gabriel, that the nunnery's walls would separate them, leaving her isolated within. Would she ever see Gabriel again after that? Just how would she resolve the mess she was embroiled in?

Beside her, Gabriel tensed suddenly, sitting up higher in his saddle. Constance reacted to his change viscerally, pulling in more closely alongside him before looking around to see what had triggered it. The bridge lay in the far distance up ahead, arching over the ribbon of blue ...

She let out a long breath. She could just make out the figures behind it, the horses grazing in the meadow, the men slowly standing up from the side of the road. Two ... three ... four ...

Gabriel put a hand out to her and she instinctively slowed her horse, keeping it alongside his, bringing it down to a trot, then a walk. Ralph was near on her left side, his hand resting on his hilt. Constance felt as if a steel band was wrapped around her chest, constricting it in tight ratchets. She could not breathe ... she had to relax. If they were to get out of this at all, she had to calm herself, to think.

They walked their horses to the near end of the bridge, watching as ten men in leather armor formed a line across the far side. A pile of packs were heaped to one side of the path, and the horses were tethered against the trees. Apparently the men had been eating a casual meal when they rode up. The remnants of bread and cheese were laid out on a large cloth. Constance shook her head in confusion. How could the men possibly have gotten here so far ahead of them?

Gabriel reined his horse to a stop at their end of the bridge, and Constance and Ralph mirrored his actions. All three now had their hands on the hilts of their swords. Constance's heart pounded in her chest. She very much respected Gabriel's talents, and Ralph's as well – but there were simply too many opponents for them to prevail. The moment that one of the soldiers got a grasp on Constance, her two protectors would be forced to drop their weapons, and she did not trust Barnard one whit. He could easily have left orders for the two men to be slain.

Gabriel's voice came out smooth and even. "You have been here all morning, it appears. Barnard must have known that Constance would never return to him."

One of the men stepped forward, his dark curly hair shining in the sun. Constance nodded in growing understanding. "Frank – I wondered why you were not there to accompany the coach, if Barnard felt it so critical that I come home. Now I see that he never expected me to set foot in it."

Frank bowed slightly. "Your *husband* understands your moods very well," he commented snidely, his eyes flickering to meet Gabriel's for a moment. "It is time for you to send these playthings of yours away and return to your proper place."

Gabriel bristled visibly, but said nothing. Constance looked again at the array of men, then spoke softly to Gabriel. "I am afraid we have no choice," she admitted under her breath. "With these odds ... I cannot see you hurt."

Gabriel's voice was tight. "There is no way I will allow you back into the grasp of that bastard without a fight."

Constance sighed, looking down at her hands. "We had a chance, but it is gone," she ground out. "The next ford is too far away. If we make a run for it, they will catch us before we make it. Our horses have been on the road all day, while theirs are fresh."

Gabriel turned and looked at her full on. "The Constance I knew would not have given up so easily," he insisted steadily.

"It is one thing to risk my own safety," she returned with emotion. "I will not risk yours. I cannot … the only thing which has kept me sane is knowing you are out there, that you are free …" She turned away, feeling as if her heart would break. She could not jeopardize his life. It did not matter what she suffered. All that mattered was him.

"Connie," came the soft call, and she turned back to look at him. His eyes were steady and blue, the deep depths of the ocean, and she was lost in them.

"Trust me," he whispered.

God help her, she did. She took in a deep breath, then nodded.

In a moment, he had spun his mount and was driving at a hard gallop due north. Constance and Ralph moved in with him, staying in a tight formation. She heard the shouts of anger behind her, the scurrying as the men leapt onto their horses and charged in chase. Constance wondered how long they could keep up their lead. Their horses had been ridden hard all day, where the pursuers' steeds were fresh and rested. Still, for the moment at least, she was free, and she would treasure every hoofbeat, every breath. Her heart pounded as they rode full tilt, flying across the landscape.

The miles rolled by, and their pursuers began to close the gap. Constance leant lower over the mane of her horse, willing him to go faster, willing the bridge to draw nearer. Perhaps if they crossed it, they could lose themselves in the forest beyond, hide out until nightfall …

The bridge came into sight, and her heart leapt – then sank like a stone. A company of a full dozen mounted men waited on the span, facing her party. Even as she watched they spread out, forming a long line. Gabriel did not slow up at all – simply rode straight for the line, and Constance plowed steadfastly at his side. If this was to be his choice, she would not falter.

Then, to her surprise, the line began to separate, began to open up to form a hole – and behind her, she saw those chasing her begin to draw off, to rein in. Confused, she scanned the men before her more closely. They wore leather armor, with full helmets, but they were not in Barnard's colors. Instead, they were ...

She gasped in surprise as the trio flew through the center of the line, reining in and turning as the line reformed in a solid band behind them, separating her from the pursuers who were circling in a confused group some twenty yards away.

The Angelus. She had just been saved by the mercenaries. Questions buzzed around in her head, but she pushed them aside, staying close to Gabriel, taking full measure of what lay before her.

Gabriel rode up to talk quietly with one of the men in the line, then waved Constance to come forward with him. Ralph stayed close in on her other side, and together they joined the full line of men. Constance swept her eyes down the group. First they had come to her rescue in the dungeons, and then they had tussled in a case of mistaken identity. Both times had been dark, and she had barely gotten a glimpse of them. Just who were these soldiers for hire?

She had thought of them as the meanest of cast-offs, but in the full light of day she saw now that she had been mistaken. They were extremely well outfitted, with high quality armor and well-made swords, which each man had drawn and held at the ready. The crew all wore full helmets, hiding their features, but their jaws were set and they were clearly prepared for any action. Their shoulders and arms were well toned and in fine shape.

They were a far stronger military fighting force than any of the men in Barnard's guard, or her brother's. She wondered just where this mercenary group had found such men.

Hoofbeats sounded from downstream, and she looked up to see Frank riding towards the line, his face surly. He scanned down the ranks of mercenaries, seeking out a leader. He settled on speaking to the group as a whole.

"You, Angelus, this is not your fight," he barked in anger. "This woman is the rightful property of my lord and master, Lord Barnard. You would do well not to meddle."

There was a long silence which none of the Angelus sought to break. Finally Gabriel spoke out. "You see that your case has little merit here. Your troops would not last five minutes against these men. Head home and tell your master that Constance will be taking her prayer time with her aunt, as agreed. If he wishes to discuss her return, he will find her well protected at the nunnery."

Frank's eyes narrowed in anger, but looking again at the line of fighting men facing him, he shook his head.

"This is not the end of it," he promised Gabriel with a snarl before whirling his horse and heading south at a hard gallop. The rest of the Barnard's force joined in the retreat. In a few minutes they had crossed the horizon and were gone from sight.

Constance let out a long, shuddering breath. She had not realized she was holding it until then. They had won. If only for the moment, they were safe. She turned to look up at Gabriel, opening her mouth to ask him what was going on.

He spoke before she could form any words. "We need to get you into that nunnery," he stated quickly. "There are still many dangers out there." He spun his mount, and in a moment he was in motion. Constance did not hesitate; she urged her horse until she was alongside him. To her surprise, the mercenaries formed up around them with ease, folding into a long diamond pattern around her without any words or signals. They reminded her of a flock of birds in flight, turning and wheeling as if part of one large entity. The remaining miles of her trip slid by in a rolling echo of hooves and a motion of men. She felt as safely ensconced as if she were being carried in an armored bronze boat. None could breach the wall of skilled soldiers surrounding her.

It seemed only a short while before the large stone walls of the nunnery rose before her. She could see the tavern and main street shops off to the south, but she barely spared a second glance, focusing all of her attention on the nunnery and its large wooden doors, which stood open. As they drew close, she saw that the entire nunnery's occupants had apparently turned out for her arrival, standing around the entry gate and interior courtyard. The men around her began to slow, and she reined in with them, coming down to a trot, and finally a walk. As they approached the main gates, the mercenaries formed a half circle, reining in to stop in a protective arc. Only Gabriel and Ralph moved forward with her towards the main doors.

Constance's aunt Silvia stood in a brown habit and wimple next to the abbess. Both smiled fondly at her as she dismounted. Gabriel and Ralph joined her on the ground, walking alongside her to the gates.

Silvia stepped forward to warmly embrace her niece. "My dear, I cannot express how glad I am that you made it here safely," she welcomed with relief. "We had feared the worst."

"It is all thanks to these two men, and to the Angelus," praised Constance with a smile. "I never could have made it this far if not for their concerted efforts."

The abbess stepped forward at this, her wrinkled face creased into a smile. "We will say prayers for each of you tonight at mass," she called out to the group of men. "You have done a good deed here today, one which will not be forgotten."

The row of men crossed themselves reverently, saluting the woman with a bow.

Constance turned to Ralph. "What will you do now? Surely you cannot return to Barnard. You have risked so much on my behalf …"

Ralph glanced at Gabriel, then smiled fondly at Constance. "As long as you are free of Barnard, I will stay with Gabriel. He has offered me a position with him."

Constance put the alternative – her returning to Barnard's control - out of her mind with a fierce effort. She stepped forward to embrace Ralph tenderly. "Thank you," she whispered in his ear. She then turned to Gabriel.

Her heart caught as she gazed into his eyes. He had stayed with her every step of the way, never faltering, her steady rock. His eyes shone with resolution and concern. She raised a hand to rest against his cheek, and she felt the strength, the power that shone within him.

"How did it get to this, Gabe?" she asked softly, her voice breaking.

He put a hand tenderly over hers, bringing it down to hold to his lips for a gentle kiss.

"I will be at the gate each morning, from eight to nine in case you need me. I will be here, to spend time with you, to sit with you, to ferry a message to your family if need be. Together we will figure something out."

Constance wanted to think there was a solution to all of this, and she allowed herself to believe an answer was within reach, if only for now. She nodded, forcing herself to smile. Then she raised her gaze to look out at the Angelus who ringed her.

"If there is any way I can repay your help, I stand ready to do everything within my power," she vowed to the men. "Truly, you have saved my life. I offer you my heartfelt thanks, and I will add my prayers to those of the abbey nuns for your safety and success in whatever your missions may be."

The men bowed to her solemnly.

Constance allowed herself one final look at Gabriel, then she turned. The Abbess and her aunt fell in on either side of her, and together they entered the nunnery. Behind her, she heard the large, heavy oak doors of the main gate draw shut, and the heavy bar was pushed across them to seal the way.

"First we will get some food into you," stated the abbess, her voice creaking with age but replete with inner strength. "Then you will tell us everything, from the beginning up to this very moment."

Chapter 17

Constance stretched on her bed, a sense of peace and safety beginning to drift into her aching world. Her room at the nunnery was neat and clean. The blanket was embroidered with delicate white primroses, and the trunk at the foot of her bed was simple, yet glowed from tender daily polishing. The morning sunlight streamed in through the open window, sending shafts of gold across the swept wooden floor.

She knew the rhythms of the nunnery by heart, having come here every year for most of her life. She would have missed the dawn service of Matins already. Prime, starting at 7am, would be going on now. Then at 9am was Terce, noon was Sext, 3pm was None, sunset brought Vespers, bedtime was Compline and then the midnight office. Each meeting had its own focus, its own rituals.

A simple robe lay in the trunk and she put it on, washing quickly before heading down to the sanctuary. She slipped quietly into the rear of the nave, moving silently so as not to disturb the roomful of women in their prayers. She appreciated the quiet meditation of the office, and gave herself a few minutes before focusing her attention on the sermon.

The abbess was talking to the group about the banishment of Adam and Eve from the Garden of Eden; how their desire for knowledge caused a breach in their contract with God. Constance found herself relating the story to her own life. Had it been her desire to help other women, to give them a better life, which had formed a breach in her relationship with Barnard? Perhaps if she had been more docile, had not desired to grow and learn, she could have been content … or at least not in her current situation.

She shook her head, unable to accept this answer. Barnard had been cold to her for years, had violated the vows he claimed they had shared in word and deed. She had tried to show Christian charity, and had been disrespected and abused for her troubles.

The Abbess's words cut through her thoughts. "We are told by the male church leaders that the story of Adam and Eve is one of female weakness. They justify many of their actions with the words from Genesis. Because of the one line, 'in sorrow you shall bring forth children', they insist women have no salve or balm during childbirth and many die as a result. Where holy warriors and Templars are allowed medication and succor, women bringing new Christians in the world are allowed to languish in pain and die."

She took in a breath, her eyes sweeping the room of quiet women. "Still, was Genesis a recitation of fact? Was it rather an important story for us to learn and take guidance from, as rational adults? Take, for example, the case of the snake. Now, those of you sisters who come from Ireland might not know about snakes …" She looked fondly at a trio of young women who sat to one side, and they chuckled quietly at her jest. "The snake in this story talks to Eve about the forbidden fruit. The snake tells her it is fine to consume. He says her eyes will be opened."

She pursed her lips in consideration. "Why did he do this? The fruit represented knowledge – the basic, mature understanding of right and wrong. Up until then, Adam and Eve are said to have been unable to judge good from evil. They were like animals, simply doing what their instincts drove them to do without any moral sense. The eating of the fruit gave them that moral sense."

Her eyes shone with passion as she continued. "We pride ourselves on having that ability in modern times. Should we not rejoice that we have that moral compass? It is only because we choose good that we have proven our worthiness. If we have no choice, we are no different from a trickling mountain stream, or wayward sheep."

Constance pondered the thought for a moment. It was true, she valued her ability to make a choice, to decide on a path which was correct for her. She would not want a life where she was trapped in a rutted path, forced to go in one direction only.

The Abbess's voice carried strongly across the room of attentive listeners. "So how could Eve be faulted for choosing the apple, when she did not yet know right from wrong?"

She smiled, her eyes twinkling. "Also, God surely knew that this would happen. He is omniscient. He knew this was the inevitable result. Her growth up to that point was complete. She – and Adam – needed to take the next step, to grow as rational human beings. The Lord knew he would need to turn them out of the garden, into the world."

Constance always found the sermons of the Abbess to be fascinating. The priest at her local church merely recited the gospels, instructing the laity to memorize them without thought or comment. Every time she attended one of the offices here at the nunnery, she found herself fascinated by the Bible, more curious to read it for several hours after the discussion – often right until the next office was about to begin.

The lesson was coming to an end, and the women began standing, gathering in groups of two or three to discuss the message before moving on to breakfast or other morning duties. Silvia spotted Constance in the corner and came over to join her.

"Well met, niece!" she called out in pleasure, taking her arm. "The abbess would like us to have breakfast with her in her office. Shall we go?"

Together the two women walked out to the main hall. A bustle of women surrounded them, walking over to the main dining area. Constance and Silvia turned left, going up the long flight of stairs to the second floor. The door at the top stood open, and they walked into the room beyond.

Abbess Agnes was waiting for the pair in her sparse, stone room. A polished oaken desk stood to one side, her quill and inkstand neatly arranged in the corner. A fireplace sat cold on one wall, and a trio of windows opened up over the main courtyard, letting in a gentle summer breeze.

A table had been set at the center of the room with three stools tucked in around it. Agnes gestured toward the table and they took their seats. A pair of sisters moved in at once, laying down trenchers and cups for each woman. When they were sure that all was set, they left the room, closing the door quietly behind them.

The Abbess gave a short prayer in her low, raspy voice. Constance listened dutifully with folded hands and downcast eyes. She echoed the "Amen", and then the group was passing around the toasted bread, apple tarts, and sausages.

The Abbess smiled fondly at Constance, drawing her in with a ready smile. "Did you know that the Bible never names the forbidden fruit as an apple?" she asked her young friend with a raised eyebrow, serving out the tarts. "The poor apple has been maligned for centuries, when it was never even involved in the story. Most scholars believe it was the pomegranate that Eve consumed."

"It figures," chuckled Constance with a smile. "A mistranslation somewhere along the line, and millions of people scorn a completely innocent fruit. How can we go about clearing its name?"

"Ah, once a reputation is formed, my child, it is nearly impossible to undo," offered the Abbess with mock sadness. "The apple will simply have to bear the weight, and know in its own heart that it is innocent."

Constance nodded, taking in a bite of the apple tart. "It is very tasty," she commented with delight. "That is some consolation."

Abbess Agnes took a long drink of her herbal tea, letting the women eat for a few moments. She then looked over with a calm warmth. "Our long talk yesterday afternoon was very enlightening, and I hope we now understand the state you are in. I imagine after a night of reflection that you have some questions for us. Please ask anything – we will do our best to assist you."

Constance thought on her offer for a while, nibbling on her bread. The older women ate in contented silence, in no rush to move the conversation along. After a while, Constance brought up the question which had occupied her thoughts that morning.

"Would I be welcome as a novice here?"

Agnes and Silvia exchanged glances holding more understanding than surprise. Agnes nodded her head readily. "Yes, certainly, we have had several married women join our ranks. You know that many of our sisters are widows. Your aunt Silvia here joined us after her husband died. We do also have a few who took their vows while their husbands were alive, each for her own reasons. All that matters is that the woman has a sincere desire to serve God."

Constance looked down at the bread in her hand. Barnard swore he had unquestionable proof they were married. "Does she need the permission of her husband?"

A smile quirked at Agnes' mouth. "A commitment to God is of far higher precedence than any worldly concern," she intoned smoothly. "Any man or woman who chooses service to God is fully supported by the Holy Church – and the Pope himself – in their aim." Her smile deepened. "Especially if there is any material benefit to the church, as you might imagine."

"The land at Beadnell," replied Constance, her eyes harried. "However, I undertook this union to keep the people in that land safe. If Barnard cannot manage that responsibility, am I doing any better in turning it over to the church?"

Agnes looked over at Silvia, her eyes twinkling. "Oh, the church is far from a passive victim," she pointed out. "The crusades and the activities of the Templar Knights have made that quite clear."

Constance shook her head. "That is all thousands of miles away, in lands much desired by the Pope and his ilk. What concern would they have for a small patch of land in northern England?"

"The church needs more educated members – missionaries, priests, monks, and nuns," pointed out Agnes, her wrinkled face creased with thought. "We need a place in a protected area to educate our members. It would not be safe to set a school up in a contested area like Jerusalem. The Pope has asked all heads in England to keep an eye open for land that is well suited to creating a center of education. A nunnery – or monastery – dedicated to reading, writing, illumination, and transcription."

Constance's heart kindled with hope. "A training center?" she repeated, enthusiasm filling her. "To train the laity as well?"

Agnes nodded in understanding. "Yes, certainly, I know well of your efforts with women in your area. We would help them learn what skills they had an interest in. We would teach them of philosophy and critical reasoning, of numbering and reading. Also, as with all our sisters, we would include practical training – self-defense, herbal lore, and basic healing."

Constance was sorely tempted. This was more than she had imagined to be possible. She did so much enjoy her time here, the quiet lifestyle of the sisters, the opportunity to think and learn and grow. She would adore working with the women of the neighboring villages, helping them expand their horizons.

Still, her dreams ...

She looked down, not yet willing to close the door completely on any hope for the future, on any hope to be with Gabriel. "Would I need to take permanent vows immediately?" she asked, her voice low.

Agnes shook her head. "No, we want women to fully understand all that is involved in a life here before they take that step. We need to ensure they are at peace with their choice. Each novice begins with a year of postulancy, a trial period as it were. After that there is another year of novitiate. During this period the woman cuts her hair and dons the habit. Only then is she asked to profess a desire to take her vows. Even then, it is another three to five years before she takes the final step and becomes a bride of the church. This ensures that each woman wholeheartedly chooses her lifelong commitment here."

"Women who marry should be counseled to go through the same stages," muttered Constance under her breath. "For that commitment is no less important."

Agnes looked at Silvia and smiled. "Indeed, we have often said that they should," she agreed, nodding. "It is the wise and rational choice. However, many couples are neither wise nor rational when they decide to tie themselves together for life. They are thinking with more base emotions."

"Well, then, seven years," mused Constance. "That is a long time, certainly enough time to sort out these issues, to come to terms ..." she took a long drink of her chamomile tea. "Think, to work at a center of learning ... to help educate the women of this area ..." Her voice became wistful.

Agnes patted her hand gently. "There is no need to rush," she commented quietly. "The best decisions are made over time, after much thought, contemplation, and prayer. We are here to answer any questions you may have, to help you in any manner we can. In the meantime, as always, feel free to take advantage of our hospitality. You are a welcome and most helpful guest."

The bells of the church rang eight o'clock, and Constance looked up, her heart beating quickly.

"You run along," waved Agnes, sitting back with a smile. "Silvia and I have things to discuss now."

Constance curtsied, then tripped down the stairs with flying feet, heading for the main gate. One of the doors was open wide, and there, in the opening, stood Gabriel.

The sun shone down fully upon him, his leather armor fitting him like a second skin, highlighting the strength in his arms, the leanness in his form. His sword hung at the ready on his hip, and her eyes swept to the short blond hair she longed to run her fingers through. He was the very vision of masculine strength to her. Her heart thundered in her chest as she crossed the courtyard in a mere moment, pulling up on her side of the entryway with a smile.

Gabriel swung his arm down into a courtly bow, greeting her with warm eyes. "Good morning, My Lady," he welcomed with elegant charm. "How are you on this fine day?"

Constance glanced around the area with caution. A wide meadow stretched out before the gates of the nunnery, and a pair of guards stood alertly on either side of the door. Down the long slope began the outskirts of the village, and on the far side, the ocean was a distant hint of salt in the air.

Tentatively, she took a step across the threshold, the invisible demarcation of the nunnery's boundaries. She slid her hand through Gabriel's proffered arm, and walked with him the few steps over to the carven stone bench which sat to one side of the gate. She sat down on it and gazed upwards, reveling in the warm sunshine.

"I am doing well," she sighed, her shoulders relaxing back against the wall. "Very well. I spent most of last night and this morning with the Abbess and my aunt. They are very wise and learned women."

Gabriel nodded in agreement. "Abbess Agnes can always be counted on to see straight to the heart of any matter, and to offer wise council," he agreed, his eyes distant.

Constance glanced sideways at him, wondering when he would have spoken with the Abbess. On their trips to visit her aunt all those years ago, he had escorted her to the gates, but no further. "When have you discussed issues with her?"

Gabriel glanced up, his eyes shadowed. "My travels take me here and there," he replied vaguely. "The abbess is not always confined to the nunnery. She goes out on business, and our paths cross."

Constance thought on this for a moment, then nodded. Generally the sisters remained within the walls for their own safety, but some did choose to travel to nearby nunneries or shrines, either to make a pilgrimage or to learn from a respected teacher.

"I spoke with them about staying here for a while," she began, moving the topic to the one closest to her heart. "It appears it is very much an option for me."

A shadow crossed over Gabriel's face. "Staying at the nunnery?"

Constance put her hand over his. "For now, it is only a temporary solution," she consoled him, giving his fingers a squeeze. "Even if I did start down the path to becoming a sister, it is a long voyage – seven years. A lot can happen in that time. It would keep me safe from Barnard."

"*I* can keep you safe from Barnard," muttered Gabriel under his breath.

Constance shook her head. "You know this is a far larger matter," she commented quietly. "It is a matter of politics, of land ownership, and of military might. If we go against the law, then the force of the King's army will be against us, and we cannot withstand that."

She leant against him slightly, the warmth of his strength flowing through her. She was steadied by his presence. "We will find a way," she vowed to him, twining her fingers into his. "Together, we will find a way."

She soaked in the simple pleasure of sitting by Gabriel's side, of bathing in the comfort radiating from his body, of being beside the man she adored with all her heart.

They sat that way for an hour, not talking, not having any need for words. When the chimes tolled nine, Constance blinked as if awakening from a dream. She stood slowly, and Gabriel rose at her side, not releasing her hand. He walked her over to the gates, lowering his lips to her hand for a kiss.

"Until tomorrow, then," he offered quietly, holding her gaze.

"Yes," she replied, then turned to head inside.

She joined the group in the chapel for terce. The sermon this time was on Pentecost – on the holy spirit descending on the apostles, sending them out into the world to educate and uplift the farmers and fishermen. Constance felt that the sermon was directed at her, towards the formation of a school. She did feel the lure of the idea, the fulfillment of many of her dreams. Still, at what cost ...

The day moved through its phases. She helped Silvia for a while in the herb garden, pruning and tending to the dill and sage. Lunch was a quiet affair with a reading from the Bible as the women ate quietly. There were more periods of office, embroidery to be done by a sunny window, a dinner of fresh vegetables and fish. She basked in the warmth of the community around her, the benefit of the good deeds the nunnery provided for the poor in the community. The hospital held a child injured from a fall, as well as a local farmer who had cut himself while chopping down trees. Women came in to ask a share of the herbs for their home cabinets. A group of girls from the local village studied at embroidery and illumination. The sermons were never dull, always insightful and full of wisdom to glean. Yes, Constance felt that she could become very used to this way of life, and very content.

Content, but … as she climbed into the simple bed in her room, and blew out her candle, she found herself staring out the window for a long time. She knew that, in her heart, a middle ground would be much better suited to her dreams. Several women from the village came to the nunnery by day to volunteer their time, to help with training and copying tasks – but returned to their homes, their families in the evening. As much as Constance knew she would treasure the friendships with the sisters, a part of her still yearned for a family of her own, a husband at her side, children to raise. She knew that she would always feel something missing, incomplete if she ensconced herself within the nunnery's walls without having that experience.

She laughed wryly to herself that she was discounting her time with Barnard. To her, it did not count at all as time with a partner. It was more a penance with a captor, a penance she had done with full knowledge of the cost – but one she felt should come to an end. That had been done selflessly, for others. She wanted just one brief time for herself, for her own dreams.

Lost in thought, she drifted slowly off to sleep.

Chapter 18

Constance fell fully into the gentle rhythm of the nunnery, waking at dawn for Matins. She loved these early hours, loved the glistening of the dew on the blades of grass, loved the gentle tendrils of light which edged over the horizon and lit the world with a soft glow. This was one of her favorite offices – the simple praising of God for what He provided to the world. She counted again her blessings that she was fed, clothed, provided with friends who cared for her. Considering the hardships that many around the world faced, she had a lot to be thankful for.

Once again she was invited to a private breakfast with the Abbess and Silvia, and once again she sat in the simple stone room around a low table, sharing bread and eggs with the pair. The women did not press her for her thoughts, or bandy about any casual conversation. Instead, they ate quietly, emanating relaxation, and allowed Constance her time to speak or not speak. Constance found herself lulled by the peaceful atmosphere and ready acceptance of patience.

"I have been thinking on what we spoke of yesterday," she began at length, and the two women looked over with calm eyes to show they were paying attention. "As you know, the idea of setting up a school appeals to me greatly. There is a lot of good we could do."

She took in a long drink of her peppermint tea. "Still, I must admit I am still concerned about issues of security. The nunnery here is strong and well protected. It could withstand a concentrated attack. However, the structure at Beadnell would have to be built from scratch, of course. With the bandits, I do not know how you would hold the land in order to do that in safety. It would take years to complete the work."

"We would have the protection we needed, never you fear," reassured the abbess in a smooth voice. "That would not be a problem."

"Do you mean the bishop would recall some Templars back from the holy land, just to safeguard this project?"

The abbess held her gaze steadily. "We have no need to go that far to find men more than a match for the bandits."

Constance was caught by the wise face, and her mind skipped back to her arrival. The mercenaries had been respectful of the abbess, and she had greeted them almost as equals. Then there was their name ...

"Angelus?" she said suddenly, pieces sliding into place in her mind. "That is Latin for *angels*. I never thought about it; I always assumed it was the surname of the person in charge of the mercenaries. They are somehow associated with the church?"

"Our paths cross often, yes," agreed the abbess easily.

"I thought they were hired by the wool-making guild," rebutted Constance in confusion. "They are based in Shoreston, formed up due to the high level of piracy on coastal shipments. That has always been their focus."

"Has it now?" asked the abbess with a light tone, looking to Silvia with a smile. "Is that what you have observed?"

Constance frowned. "I suppose I never had first-hand knowledge of them, until recently," she admitted slowly. "It was only rumors brought in by Barnard from his travels. I only met them when ..." She looked down guiltily. She had dutifully revealed her evening activities to both women, holding back nothing in her telling, but she still felt embarrassed at them knowing about her teaching the local women. It was not proper for a woman in her position to be so rambunctious.

"Yes, when you were training the villagers to defend themselves," agreed the abbess, taking a bite of her egg. "The Angelus, as you might recall, were there on a protective mission as well."

"So you feel you can depend on them, to help with this task?" asked Constance, still not quite reassured.

The abbess nodded firmly. "I would trust them with my life," she replied easily. "As should we all."

The bells chimed, and once again Constance made her quick farewells, scampering down the long stairs and out into the sunny courtyard. Her eyes flew to the gate ...

She pulled up short, heart caught in her throat. The guards stood blocking the gate entrance, with Gabriel to one side, joining in the protective barrier without entering into the nunnery's grounds. Facing them was a man on horseback wearing the burgundy of her husband's livery. He eyed the guards with hostile disapproval, and his eyes sharpened as he saw Constance's approach.

"Well, there she is," he called out shortly, his displeasure evident. "I will see this parchment into her hands, and then I will be off."

One of the guards stepped forward. "I will take that to her, if you please," he insisted, holding out his hand.

The messenger huffed out his anger, but he removed a roll from the pouch at his side, holding it for a long moment. "I must see it placed into her hands myself," he warned, then passed the scroll down to the guard.

Constance halted a full ten feet from the scene and waited with trepidation as the guard brought the parchment back to her. She took it with trembling hands, fingering the wax seal which held it shut. She looked up at the messenger, her gaze dismissive.

The man took her meaning at once. "My Lady," he saluted her, his tone snide. Then he wheeled the horse around and started off at a gallop back up the road.

Constance stood still while he rode off, running her finger beneath the seal, loosening it. She did not move until the sound of hoofbeats faded away into silence, leaving behind the quiet birdsong of a nearby robin. The parchment came open under her hands, and she glanced down at it, then moved forward.

Gabriel stood there, watching her, and she fell into step beside him, walking over to the stone bench. He did not speak as she sat down, only standing above her, protectively, his eyes scanning the nearby road for any sign of movement.

Constance slowly read through the precise writing, her face relaxing as the words flowed past. "He has accepted a trip of two weeks," she told Gabriel finally, relief infusing her. "He says he will be here in full force at the end of a fortnight – but until then he will not invoke the law against my flight. That is a start at least."

"It does give us some time," agreed Gabriel, "Still, we must still find a solution here. Have you talked further with the abbess?"

"What do you know of the Angelus?" asked Constance by way of an answer.

His eyes flared with surprise, and then his face shuttered, went blank. "What do you mean?" he asked coolly.

Constance creased her brow in confusion. "Surely you must be at least somewhat associated with them, given how easily you knew to trust them by the bridge," she pointed out. "Had they been sent by the Abbess to help us on our journey?"

"I do hear that they are on good terms with the Church," agreed Gabriel quietly. "So the Abbess feels the Angelus can be of help with this situation?"

Constance shrugged. "I am not really sure yet. I think she feels, if I were to pledge myself to the nunnery and turn over the lands to the care of the Church, that the Angelus would help to protect the land until a new structure could be built there."

Gabriel turned at that, gazing far down the road. "That is certainly a possibility," he replied, his voice tight.

Constance reached a hand up to take his, to draw him down to her side. He came reluctantly, seeming on edge, his gaze scanning the distant reaches, watching for danger. She felt his restlessness, and again the salty aroma of the sea reached her, calling to her.

"I so wish we could ride down to the ocean," she mused wistfully. "It has been so long since I have seen it ..."

Gabriel's voice was tense. "That is a dangerous risk," he pointed out. "We still have no guarantee that Barnard is going to behave himself, or that the bandits have not made plans to capture you if they can."

Constance's shoulders tightened. "Just for a little while, it would be enough. If you and Ralph came with me, surely it would be safe."

Gabriel looked to meet her eyes, and she saw his rigidity lessen, his face soften. "You do want it badly, Connie."

"I adore the sea," she whispered, turning to look off to where she knew it waited for her. "Even a few minutes would sustain me for a long while."

Several minutes passed, and Gabriel finally let out a sigh, nodding.

"I will bring a horse tomorrow, and Ralph. You shall have your visit."

"Thank you," murmured Constance, a sense of serenity easing over her soul.

She folded her hand into his. They sat for a long while, soaking in the sunlight. A drifting peace drew close around them, surrounding them, enveloping them in its warmth

Chapter 19

Constance poured her heartfelt energies into the dawn service of Matins, recounting her blessings with a devout soul. She was so uplifted after the service was complete that she wondered why this was not a part of every person's waking ritual. It was so cleansing, so focusing, to remember just how much there was to be grateful for in each new day.

She helped her aunt weed the herb gardens for an hour, lost in the beauty of this quiet life. Every service here was a treat, a new awakening of her mind, a new set of thoughts to ponder and discuss.

The bell tolled for Prime, and she put away her garden tools, walking quietly with her aunt towards the chapel. The women filed in calmly, taking their seats in silence.

A figure in a long, white robe moved up towards the pulpit. Constance was intrigued. A Cistercian brother had come to give a guest talk at the Abbey? She knew the Cistercians had rebelled against the Benedictines, had challenged the "black monks" for their desire for wealth and power. In comparison, the Cistercians focused their energies on helping the poor, protecting the weak.

The white robed person stood at the podium for a long moment, and was met with an expectant hush. He looked around the chapel for a long moment, then pushed back his hood.

It was Abbess Agnes, a wide smile on her face.

The room broke out into amused laughing, as the sisters prodded each other, caught by the joke. She waited for the noise to settle down again before she began.

"We have been talking about Genesis this week, about appearances, expectations, and responsibilities. Let us talk this morning about the way we hide our nature from one another, how symbols can sometimes be more powerful than you might think."

She gave a tug on the edge of her white hood. "For example, just now you made assumptions about my background, my motives, and even my level of honor, all based on a simple robe I wore. How much of this same guesswork goes on every day? Who do we take for granted? Who do we judge based on their facade?"

Her eyes moved across the group of women. "Let us take, for example, the snake in the Garden of Eden. This story tells us of a reptile who lured Eve into crossing from ignorance into knowledge."

She tilted her head to one side, and her voice carried easily across the room. "Let us ponder the snake. Was it Satan? If it was Satan, merely in a snake disguise, why would God then curse *all* snakes for all time? Surely he should have punished Satan, not the poor animal whose form he had chosen."

The corners of her mouth turned up into a smile. "If Satan had decided to appear as a horse, would all horses have been cursed forever? That would not seem likely."

The women listening chuckled softly to themselves in agreement.

"Similarly, if a thief shows up in our midst disguised as a healer, do we condemn all healers throughout history to degradation as a result? A rational person would not assign blame so haphazardly. That is the key here, to consider what we read and perceive it rationally."

Constance's mind leapt to the Angelus. They were men in disguise, men she had seen only in shadows. Who were they really? Had she judged them based on their disguises? Were they really mercenaries? Or were they actually agents of good, men she was misjudging simply because of their outer appearance? She, after all, put on a disguise when she went out to help the local villagers learn self-defense. The Angelus had taken her for a bandit for that very reason.

She took in a deep breath. What of other disguises? What of her attempt to convince Gabriel that she had never loved him? What of her hiding her feelings from him?

The thoughts swirled in her mind long after the talk was done, occupied her during the quiet breakfast with her two friends. She made a decision to put aside all disguises, all deceptions. It was time to embrace what life presented, to appreciate every day as it came, and to no longer hide.

As she headed down the stairs to the front gate, her mind was on the sea, on its quiet peace, on the low rolling steadiness of the waves. She walked contentedly to the courtyard, and her heart leapt with pleasure when she saw Ralph and Gabriel waiting there for her, three horses tethered up nearby.

Ralph kept back a discreet distance as Gabriel and Constance walked their steeds through the quiet town, taking the familiar path across meadow and lane towards the ocean. Constance held back at the final turn, then allowed herself to be overwhelmed with pleasure as she moved forward, came over the crest, and was finally able to see the long horizon, the stretch of turquoise, the gulls soaring high on thermals. She looked over at Gabriel, stretched out her hand, and he took it tenderly, sharing in her joy.

Together they dismounted and left the horses to Ralph, moving down onto the sandy shore. The sun shone brilliantly on the water, almost blinding them, and Constance laughed aloud with pleasure. She sat on a tuft of grass and pulled off her shoes and stockings, then ran down to the surf, lifting her skirts as she chased the waves. Gabriel was at her side in a moment, running with her, lifting her up and spinning her in a circle.

They soaked in the ocean breezes for hours, sitting on the beach talking, walking along the surf, holding hands. Constance almost managed to convince herself that she was nineteen again, that her life stretched before her, that Gabriel was the only man in her world.

An afternoon breeze sprang up, and she shivered slightly, staring out at the sea. Gabriel moved up behind her, wrapping his arms around her, holding her close. Constance's mind went back to that fateful day and she leant back against him. Suddenly tears began streaming from her eyes. He saw them at once, but did not say a word, just held her close, pressing his cheek against her head tenderly, soothing her with his presence.

"You must be hungry," he offered softly after a few minutes. "Shall we walk in for some food?"

Constance nodded quietly, and the two headed back into town, Ralph following along quietly until they reached the main street. He motioned to Gabriel, then turned to take the horses down to the stables by the inn.

The innkeeper welcomed the pair with warm smiles, coming over to give Constance a tender hug. "My dear, I am so glad you are all right!" He stepped back to look her over. "I would never have forgiven myself if you had been killed. To think I was right there in the room with your kidnappers, and never realized it!" His face became wreathed with smiles. "I am just so thankful that you had the presence of mind to give me that message for Gabe here. I was wondering, at the time, just what you were thinking. After all, you left him abruptly all those years ago. Still, I did not question it, I just -"

"Pete," cut in Gabriel abruptly, his voice low but firm.

The rotund man stopped short, his face flushing crimson. "Oh," he burst out in confusion, "but, of course, I mean ..." He wrung his apron in his hands for a moment. "That is all in the past, my dear," he stammered finally, looking down at the floor, "and it is best not to dwell on past harms. Come, have your table, and let me find you some food!" He half ran into the back room, leaving Gabriel and Constance standing in the center of the room.

Constance was in a fog, and made her way over to the chair without a word. Was she in a dream? Here she was, sitting in the corner, and there was Gabriel, across from her, his tentative gaze laden with caution. The innkeep moved in silently, putting down two bowls of lamb stew and two large tankards of ale before vanishing again into the back room.

Constance did not even look down at the food or drink, only gazed at the man across the table from her. It was several long moments before she could speak.

"He … he told you about my message?" she finally whispered, her cheeks flaring with shame. It had been an act of desperation, a plea from the depths of her heart that night. To sit in front of him, to know he had heard of her weakness …

He put his hand across the table, placed his strong fingers on top of hers, comforting her. "Of course I heard," he confirmed, his voice low and rich. "I heard that you called for me, and for no other. Not for your brother, not for …" his face flushed, and he bit out the words. "Not for your husband."

Constance shook her head. "Never for him," she vowed quietly, her face grim. "There was no one else for me to turn to. I was desperate." Her voice dropped down, and she looked at the table. "I thought you hated me, I thought you were a world away. I had heard you returned to the Holy Lands."

He picked up his tankard of ale, took a long pull, then nodded. "I had, for several years. I hooked up with my old group, fell into my old routines. I tried to stay away, to let you lead the life you had chosen. Then, when Sir Templeton fell ill, and the new crop of recruits came in to watch over the trade routes …" He finished off the tankard in a long swallow, putting it down carefully on the table.

Constance's face flushed. He had answered the question of where he'd been, but not the other – if he had hated her for what she had done. She could not bring herself to ask further. She turned her attention to the stew, savoring the warm meal, drinking down the ale with studious attention. After a long moment, Gabriel joined her in eating, and Pete brought over a fresh tankard of ale for him without comment.

Constance did not speak another word during their meal. The wound had been re-opened, was too raw to mention. Every time she looked up, she was reminded again of that day six years ago, of the things she said, of the pain she caused.

When they were done, she got up and headed outside. Ralph was already there with the horses, and she mounted up easily. She needed to put some distance between her and that inn, between her heart and that long-past day, when her life changed forever … she had to get back to the nunnery. She felt its draw almost as desperation.

She headed off at a fast pace, the two men following close behind her. She took a short-cut through the woods, her feelings a turmoil. She had turned her back on Gabriel, had cruelly lied to him – and he had been the one she called out for in her darkest moment. *She had called for him.*

She cantered through a dense stand of trees, suddenly caught by a thought. Barnard had not sent help. Nor had her brother. Still, *someone* had. She had been moved in a rush, late at night, perhaps because trackers were closing in on her. Then, only days later, the mercenaries had broken her out of prison, rescued her by force.

They had taken her straight to Gabriel.

She pulled hard to a stop, and Gabriel and Ralph spun their horses in surprise, scanning the small clearing in alarm. Her mind was awhirl in confusion, the pieces falling into place one after another.

She turned her horse to face Gabriel's, her eyes meeting his. His look held concern, and he continued to search the area around them.

"What is it?" he called out sharply.

"Why not just tell me?" she shot out, pride and bafflement mixing within her. "Why this whole mystery?"

Gabriel's face became more serious, and his lips compressed into a thin line. "Tell you what?" he asked more cautiously.

Constance chuckled. "Gabriel. Angel. Angelus. Why did I not see it before? It was right in front of me the entire time." She looked up into his eyes, the smile growing. "With all the good you have done, why not shout it to the hill tops? Why not take credit for your deeds?"

Gabriel's eyes flicked around the clearing before returning to hers. "It is getting late, Connie. We can talk about this later, when we get you back to the nunnery."

A shadow separated itself from the edge of the clearing, resolving itself into a horse and rider as it approached.

Frank flashed a toothy grin. "No, Gabriel," he commented smoothly as he approached, "Why not talk about it now?"

Gabriel dropped his hand to his hilt, then froze. A dozen more shapes emerged from the woods around them, surrounding the group. He brought his mount in closer against Constance's, with Ralph moving in on the other side.

Frank smiled even more widely. "Just where are the Angelus men now, I wonder? Could it be they are along the main route you should have taken back to the nunnery, on the lookout for attack there? It seems they were not alerted to your change of plans. Luckily for me, I chose a more direct method of following your path."

Constance bit back the panic which was infusing every bone of her being. "Barnard said that he would not take me home for two weeks. When he hears that you have disobeyed him -"

She was cut off by loud laughter. "My dear, he said that after two weeks you would have no choice but to return to him," corrected Frank merrily. "If he could get his hands on you earlier, all the better."

Constance swallowed hard. She realized just what a precarious position she had put Gabriel and Ralph in. Barnard might yet have qualms about killing her, but these two …

She took a deep breath, forcing herself not to tremble. "Then I will go with you," she announced, "as soon as you let these two men go. Barnard would not have any reason to see them."

Gabriel's cry was immediate. "No!" He drew his sword in one smooth movement. "I will not let them take you to him!"

Frank made a motion, and one of the soldiers brought up a crossbow, aiming it at Constance's heart.

Frank's voice became chill. "My dearest Constance, maybe you should not be worried about Barnard," he commented. "Maybe you should be thinking about the bandit troop who could demand a hefty ransom from Charles. I think your brother will be more willing to pay, now that you have regained your family connections." His gaze moved between the two men. "Let us try to keep the lady safe. Your swords, please?"

Gabriel held his gaze for a long moment before tossing his sword down onto the ground with a snarl. Ralph followed suit, and Frank's men moved in quickly to tie their hands together, to gag them. The group headed out at a fast trot, wending their way deeper into the woods.

It seemed to Constance that they rode for hours. The night grew pitch black, and still the men threaded their way by starlight, moving along valleys, across a streambed, along a small pond. She was near exhaustion when they finally reached a low compound surrounded by mossy walls.

She had no strength to resist when Frank came over and roughly pulled her from her horse, leading her away into the crumbling building. She looked wildly about for Gabriel, but two guards were holding him back, pressing him with swords in another direction. Then he was out of sight.

She was brought up through the darkened main hall, up a long flight of stairs and into a bedroom. The small room was sparsely furnished, and the window was shuttered, but there was a clean bed there, and a low fire burned in the fireplace. She was released in the room, then her captors closed the door firmly behind her. She did not hear any retreating footsteps; they were standing guard outside the door.

Exhausted, she staggered to the bed and collapsed.

Chapter 20

Constance awoke to streaming sunshine dancing through the half-open windows, the dust motes creating a sparkly glow in the air. She sat up slowly, stretching her arms out languidly at her side. My, but she was hungry. The room seemed to shimmer as if she were immersed in a dream. The comforter on the bed was an intriguing shade of burnt orange, like a puffy, soft sunset. She pushed it off gently, swinging her feet to the floor.

A simply carved dresser sat next to her bed, and on it smoke wafted from a small bronze brazier. It had a floral scent, almost sickly sweet, but she found she liked the aroma. She stood and inhaled a deep breath of its perfume. Running her fingers through her long hair to bring some semblance of order to her person, she made her way to the door and pulled it open.

A sturdy guard with stubby salt-and-pepper hair was there waiting for her. He seemed vaguely familiar, and she nodded at him congenially. He smiled toothily at her in return, running his eyes up and down her with interest. "Breakfast is ready, M'lady," he commented at last, leading the way down the hall.

Constance became awash in keen pangs of hunger. She followed him with docile obedience towards the stairs. He courteously offered an arm to her as they reached the top, and she gratefully took it. She was feeling awfully wobbly this morning! Together they made their way down the stairs and to a large table.

A hoarse voice called out, "Constance!"

A smile wreathed her face – she would know Gabriel's voice anywhere! She saw with pleasure that Gabriel and Ralph were both already at the table, each flanked by a sturdy guard.

Neither man stood as she approached, and she smiled more widely. No need for such formalities amongst friends.

"Good morning, Gabe," she responded in a friendly tone as she sat across from them, settling onto a stool. She waved as her escort bowed to her with a smirk, then headed out towards the front of the structure.

A well-built man with dark, curly hair settled in next to her, and she turned to greet him. "Good morning to you too, Frank," she added, nodding to him as well. "Is Barnard here?"

"He will be soon, not to worry," Frank soothed her with a wolfish grin. "I have brought you some mead, and some eggs with bacon. You must be famished!"

The aromas of the food were heavenly, but Constance felt a strange lassitude in her arms, as if she just did not want to eat. Still, she forced herself to slowly reach for her mug, to bring it carefully to her lips and drink down some of the mead. It was ambrosial. She could feel the liquid move down her throat, trace its way down her insides, coat her stomach. She chuckled at the sensation.

Gabe's voice came from across the table. "Constance, are you all right?" His blue eyes were on her, sharp with concern.

She smiled tenderly at him. "I am quite fine, Gabe," she murmured. She turned her attention to the eggs before her, cooked to perfection. She took one mouthful, savoring the flavors.

"How did you spend the night?" pressed Gabriel, looking her over with a critical eye.

"I have a very nice bed," offered Constance between mouthfuls. "The comforter is this gorgeous orange color. I will have to show you later on."

Gabriel rounded on Frank with a snarl. "What have you done to her?" he snapped, straining forward in his chair.

"Patience, patience," advised Frank with a calm smile. "You can see for yourself that the lady has not been harmed. I have received news that her darling brother is quite amenable to the terms presented, and is making payment as we speak." He looked over at Constance, and his eyes sharpened with desire.

He slowly ran the back of his hand down her cheek, caressing her neck. Constance did not react at all, but Gabriel went extremely still, the muscles in his arm tensing with the effort.

"Take your hands off her," hissed Gabriel, his voice ringing with challenge.

Frank's smile widened, and he let his hand linger on Constance's breastbone for a heartbeat before languidly removing it. "I think you are not in a position to insist on anything," he reminded Gabriel with a grin. "Remember, we can do this the hard way, or the easy way."

The front doors flung open, and Constance looked up in curiosity. There he was! Barnard strode in, elegantly attired as always, flanked by … who was that now … ah yes, Jacob! That was the guard's name, it came to her now! The pair strolled to the end of the table with casual ease. Barnard looked over the assembled group with a satisfied grin. He held his gaze on Constance for a long while, and she smiled up at him contentedly before returning to her meal.

Barnard's face became wolfish, and he patted Jacob on the back in satisfaction before coming around to the chairs. He settled himself on Constance's left side, taking up her left hand in his, running a finger along the gold band encircling her fourth finger.

"How are we this fine morning, my wife?" he asked, his voice exultant.

"This food is delicious," responded Constance. "We must really talk this cook into joining us back at the keep."

Barnard brought his lips down to her hand, holding them there for a long moment. "What a wise idea, my darling," he agreed merrily. "After our little vacation here, we may do just that."

Gabriel's face was white with fury. "What have you done to her?" he challenged. "Let her go!"

Barnard sat back with a smile, stretching his arms out wide to either side, allowing one to casually rest across Constance's shoulders in a possessive manner.

"I suppose as leader of the Angelus that you are used to giving orders and having them followed. Perhaps having your friend, Ralph, spying in my house, gave you some sense of security. However, I am afraid here you are the guest, and I am in charge."

Barnard traced circles on Constance's shoulder, looking over at her with a smile. "As far as letting her go, as you can see she is under no duress. She is being treated quite well."

"Why not loose the bonds which hold me and Frank then, if this is such a friendly gathering?" snapped Gabriel shortly, pulling at his arms in demonstration.

Barnard gave a meaningful shrug. "It pleases me to have *your* senses clear. You two have caused more than enough trouble for me over the years. I consider this proper recompense. It will bring me inordinate amounts of pleasure to have your mind fresh and alert to witness this."

Gabriel's face went pale. "What is it we will be witnessing?"

Barnard brought his right hand up to rest against Constance's neck, his grin growing as Gabriel tensed in response. "This is my wife, after all," he reiterated with pride. "My property. She is mine to do with as I please."

"You would not dare kill her," whispered Gabriel, his voice hoarse.

"Why ever would I do that?" asked Barnard with sweet innocence. "My darling bride? The mother of my next generation?"

"You do not have any children," pointed out Gabriel warily, his eyes watching carefully Barnard's.

"Ah, that is true," agreed Barnard with mock sorrow. "As much as I would like to blame Constance, and have in the past, there comes a time when a man takes stock of his surroundings and makes a plan for the future. I cannot seem to create an heir from my seed. Still, my lands *need* an heir, a child I can shape and mold in my own image. Therefore ..."

He looked meaningfully over at Frank, who smiled back at him with greedy enthusiasm. Frank took up Constance's right hand, which was now resting idly on the table, her breakfast done. She smiled at him in an unfocused manner as he lowered his lips to her palm, kissing it with open desire.

Gabriel blanched. "You cannot be serious," he croaked. "Not even you could conceive of something so monstrous."

"Who will be there to say the child is not mine?" asked Barnard idly, sitting back contentedly in his chair. "The child will be born in my bed, in my home. I will swear that I had marital relations – repeatedly – with my wife during the conception period. It will be looked on as a blessing, a miracle, after all these years of hoping."

Gabriel looked between the two men. "I will not call it such," he insisted.

Barnard smiled. "You are with the Angelus, a group soon to be revealed as responsible for the bandit attacks. You – and your followers – will be tracked down and hung long before the child is born. The proof of your thievery is ready and incontrovertible. None will believe your wild ramblings. You would say anything to escape the noose."

Constance looked up in confusion. "Someone is to be hung today?" she asked, turning to Barnard with quizzical eyes.

"No, no, my darling," soothed Barnard, patting her hand with his. "That comes later. First I want this man to know what he has lost, to know his world has come to an end."

Gabriel's eyes flashed. "*She* will know," he ground out in anger. "She will remember the truth of what went on today."

Barnard raised an eyebrow. "Will she?" he asked with bright curiosity. He turned to his wife. "My dear, tell us about those flowers in the vase."

She turned her gaze toward the bouquet. "They are beautiful!" she called out, surprised that she had not seen them before. "Daffodils, and daisies, and are those tulips? Crimson roses … ivory roses … chartreuse roses … violet roses!" She turned her eyes back towards Barnard. "What a lovely bouquet of flowers you have brought for me."

Gabriel's face fell in dismay, glancing between her and the bouquet with a look of growing confusion.

Constance pursed her lips – surely he enjoyed the flowers as much as she did? She reached out to stroke one of the rose petals, and to her surprise it felt dry, perhaps even crunchy. She chuckled at the odd inconsistency and went back to enjoying her delicious food.

Gabriel drew in a long breath, and it almost seemed as if his voice had a tremble to it.

"Flowers are not the same as memories ..."

Barnard chuckled. "Let us talk about memories, then, shall we?" He put a finger under Constance's chin, and Constance obediently turned her face to look at him. He gazed into her eyes with fixed attention.

"My dearest, I think it is time we had a talk. I know you came to me pure of body – but there was in fact a man in your life before me. I can tell by the way he reacts when I do things such as this ..."

Barnard put a hand behind Constance's neck, pulling her face in to press his thin lips hard against hers for a long moment. He smiled widely at the rigid tension which immediately shot through Gabriel's body. Chuckling, he sat back slightly, staring at Constance with wide eyes.

"Tell me the truth, now," he pressed her gently. "There should be no secrets between us."

Constance looked over at Gabriel, the man who had watched over her, who had protected her for so long. The sound came out of her as a half whisper. "Yes," she admitted softly. "Gabriel was very special to me."

"I am sure you miss his kisses," prodded Barnard, running a finger idly down her neck.

Constance looked over to Gabriel, and suddenly desire billowed within her, the force of it taking her off guard, the longing of years threatening to overwhelm her. Her throat nearly closed with emotion.

"We never kissed," she vowed hoarsely, lost in his gaze. She could remember vividly the warmth of the stables, his closeness as she slid down from her steed. She would turn, pressed between the warm steed and his toned body, and she would see the passion in his eyes ... it had taken every ounce of her self-control, every day, to step away from what she craved most in the world.

Barnard gave a choking cough, and took in a long drink of mead. His eyes flew to meet Gabriel's. "You cannot be serious. You never even kissed her?"

Gabriel's eyes shone strongly with conviction. "I take my vows seriously."

Barnard smiled even more widely at this. "Oh, this is grand!" he laughed. "All those years of unrequited passion, of wanting each other but not being able to do anything about it, all because of a vow she took when she was ten years old?"

He leant forward and kissed Constance again, drawing it out, savoring it. "She has very sweet lips," he chuckled finally to Gabriel as he sat back.

"What are you playing at?" ground out Gabriel, his eyes flashing fury.

"Oh, this is not a game," promised Barnard with a smile. He turned to the woman at his side. "So you do love him?" he prompted.

Do I love him?

The emotions in Constance's heart were threatening to overrun all her carefully constructed defenses. For so many years she had resisted this topic, had known the immense danger which lay within. Constance could almost feel the heat of Gabriel's presence, breathe in the soul-searing beauty of his being. He was so close, so close to her and yet impenetrable walls separated them. Her voice eased out in the faintest of whispers.

"We have never spoken of it."

Barnard laughed out loud at that. "This gets better and better!" he chortled. "You have never even pledged your love to each other? I had no idea my vow was so powerful!"

He leant forward, taking both of Constance's hands in his own.

"My dear, look at me," he ordered gently.

Constance reluctantly brought her eyes up to meet Barnard's, wondering what punishment awaited her for her confession. An abyss opened before her, dark and foreboding.

His face became serious. "My dearest, I feel this torment has gone on long enough," he murmured. "You have strong feelings for Gabriel, and apparently he does for you as well. You have had these longings in your heart and body for far too long. It is my duty as a husband to help make you happy."

Barnard nodded at someone behind her, jerking his head to the right. He then looked back to Constance.

"Close your eyes, and stand up," he instructed Constance. She obediently complied, her heart pounding in her chest. Barnard stood with her.

A pair of hands took hers within them. They were stronger than Barnard's; sturdier. Her heart hammered nearly out of her chest . What was going on?

Barnard's voice was solemn. "Constance, I hereby release you from your vows of chastity. I am giving you permission to be with, to love, another man. That man is Gabriel. It is only right, seeing how you two feel about each other. I give you both my blessing."

He paused for a long moment. "Open your eyes, and look on your love."

Constance's world shimmered into a new realm of unreality. If it had been a dream before, now it was some higher level of fantasy. Slowly, ever so slowly, Constance opened her eyes to look at the man before her. She felt as if she were seeing him through heat waves. His face shimmered and resolidified, his hair seeming curly at times, sometimes short and straight. The lines of his face wavered.

She hesitantly spoke. "Gabriel?"

There was a shouted "no!" from behind her, cut off abruptly, but in front of her Gabriel smiled, nodded, held both of her hands in his own, bringing his lips tenderly down to them for a kiss. Then he brought her hands in to his chest, pressing them against the center of his breast.

She could feel the shape there, feel the circle beneath his tunic. With shaking hands she sought out the leather necklace, pulled the medallion from beneath the fabric. She sighed in relief, in pleasure, running her fingers over the familiar design. His face and features shimmered again, solidifying into the ones she knew from her dreams.

"Oh, Gabriel," she breathed, caught up in the medallion. "Look, the dragon faces to the right."

"Because you are always right by my side, my love," responded Gabriel tenderly.

He leant forward to kiss her, but despite her husband's statements she turned her head to the side, taking the kiss chastely on her cheek. It was still too much to draw in, too much to absorb.

Gabriel chuckled at her shyness. "Maybe we should go somewhere that we can be alone, to … talk," he suggested with a smile. "Come with me, my dearest."

Slowly he began to lead her back towards the stairs, and she followed at his side, her heart thumping in nervous excitement. Could it be true? Could Barnard really be allowing her to share herself with Gabriel, as she had always dreamed?

Behind her, she heard muffled shouts, but she paid them no mind. Gabriel was guiding her up the stairs, back towards the lovely room with the burnt orange comforter. She twined her fingers into his, feeling the answering warmth of his grip. She had waited so many years, suffered so many indignities, to reach this day.

She led him into her room almost shyly. They had been alone together countless times in the past, and he had seen her in various stages of undress while he tended to wounds and scrapes. Still, there had always been a strict line of conduct between them – nothing more intimate than a tender kiss on the forehead or hand. That was about to change.

She shivered in anticipation as he closed the door behind him. She took in a deep, full breath, inhaling the pungent smoke from the brazier. It was so soothing, almost intoxicating. The sensation thrilled through her, seeped out of her pores, spiraled out from her fingers and toes.

"Is that not the most delicious scent ever?" she asked in abandon, raising her hands to rest them alongside Gabriel's face.

"Yes, my darling," he responded, his voice thick with passion. "That is why the other guards remain downstairs, to stay clear-headed. It is just you and I alone in here." He removed the dagger from his belt, placing it carefully alongside the brazier on the dresser.

"Alone," she breathed, her head swimming. "We are finally alone."

She trembled as he knelt down before her, grasped her outer dress layer, and slowly, carefully lifted it over her head. She dutifully put her hands up over her head to help him, and in a moment it was off, laid gently in a corner of the room. She turned and faced him in her thin white chemise, drawing pleasure in the way he looked up and down her body.

Wanting to return the favor, she moved up against him, taking the hem of his tunic, pulling the heavy material up and over his head, tossing that into the corner on top of her dress. He stood before her, strong, steady, the medallion hanging around his neck over his thin shirt.

She put her hand instinctively to her own chest, to where her medallion had hung. That they had worn matching medallions for all those years … tears sprang to her eyes. She took a step forward to press against him, to trace a finger along the guardian dragon, gazing to the right …

The tiniest seed of hesitation lodged in her brain, like a grain of sand in a delicate silk stocking. It poked there, pushed at her as an irritation. "You stand to my right," she murmured, "So your sword arm is free. So you can protect me."

"I will protect you always," vowed Gabriel, his voice heavy with desire. "I will be at your left, your right, on top of you. I will be everywhere." He pushed her gently back towards the bed.

Constance took in another deep breath, and the room shimmered and sparkled. The dragon seemed almost to curl and coil, to turn and look at her. Its eyes held a look of caution, of warning.

A tremor of uncertainty echoed deep in her soul. She had dreamt of being with Gabriel for years. She pulsed with desire in every part of her body. It was an ache in her heart, a throbbing in her loins. Even so, she knew this was wrong.

She put her hand tenderly against his chest, against the medallion. "I cannot do this."

Gabriel pushed her back to sit on the bed, his body inexorably moving against her. "Barnard has given his approval. It is all right," he soothed her, his eyes bright with passion.

Panic rose in Constance as Gabriel continued to push her down onto the bed, to press his body full length against hers. Confusion mingled in her voice. "I have waited for you for over ten years," she insisted. "I will not taint our love by being with you in this manner, not when we are unwed -"

"Our love is all that matters," insisted Gabriel hotly, pressing his lips down against her neck, her chest, and then lower. "You and I are all that matters. Vows are meant to be broken. Honor is meaningless. We are here right now, and that is all that counts."

Constance's world shifted and shattered; she watched the sparkling diamonds fall around her and crash onto the ground, burst into a million shards. Gabriel shimmered, his hair became curly, then straight, his eyes became the brilliant yellow of a wolf, then the thin black slits of a snake.

She breathed in deeply in shock; the smoke raced through her veins, exploded out through her fingers and toes, and now it was a demon who loomed over her, with red hot eyes and fiery, smoke-laced wings, the heat of his breath blasting her, melting her.

"You are mine!" he extolled, his arrogance echoing around the room in waves. "How I have dreamed about this day!" He reached a hand down to grasp at her chemise, preparing to rip it down the center.

His touch was the searing edge of a hot poker, and Constance let loose with a banshee's scream of anguish. The demon started back for a moment, then drove down hard against her, wrestling with her chemise in earnest. Constance kicked out her knee hard against him, heard him bellow in pain, saw one clawed fist swoop down out of the sky and smash her on the side of the head. Pain exploded through her skull, and hot blood coursed down her face. She howled in agony, then instinctively rolled and flung herself to the other side of the bed. A strong arm grabbed her leg, dragged her backwards hard, flinging her down face-first onto the mattress. A heavy body landed on top of hers, pinning her down with its weight.

"Help! Help!" she bellowed at the top of her lungs, thrashing beneath the demon's bulk.

"God's teeth, you harpy!" cursed the fiery demon, and another blow rained down on her head, temporarily stunning her. She shook her head to clear it. The hands were at her knees, roughly pushing her chemise up to her waist. She thrashed again, bucking with every ounce of strength …

The door to the room was flung open, slamming into the wall and rebounding again with a tremendous clap of thunder. An imposing figure in shining white stood there, a flaming sword in his hand, fury and vengeance glowing on his face. Constance could see a pair of full white wings unfurl behind him.

"The angel Gabriel," she whispered in awe, spellbound by his presence.

The demon let loose with a roar of fury, then rolled to grab his dagger from its resting place. With a howl he launched himself at the angel. Constance knew she should do something – run for help, take cover – but she could not move. She was transfixed, curled up on the bed, watching the two entities slash at each other, circle each other, thrust and parry, dodge and leap. There was a scarlet ribbon on the demon's arm, and then a matching one across the angel's chest. She was mesmerized by the ballet, the sliding feet and clanging metal creating a music, a song, and she found herself wondering how it would end.

Then, suddenly, Ralph burst into the room, and in a whirl of motion the demon spun into smoke, blew out the door and vanished. Constance looked up to Ralph with a confused smile, curious what new oddities might occur.

Ralph took one look at her, one look at the smoking brazier by the bed, and let out a low oath. He grabbed up the comforter from the bed, used it to swaddle the hot burner and then lobbed the entire bundle out through the closed shutters. Shards of wood flew everywhere, and Constance watched them fall in slow motion. A deliciously cool breeze tickled her face and arms, and took a long, deep breath of the liquid air.

Ralph's voice was panicked concern. "Gabe, we have to get her out of here."

Constance looked up in alarm. Gabriel had gotten back into the room? Her eyes spun around the area – and she froze in fright. Gabriel was somehow standing in the center of the room! His sword was covered in blood, and there were several gashes on his arm and midsection.

Gabriel took a step towards her, and she shrunk back in fright, her eyes wide. She would never let him touch her again!

Gabriel froze at her reaction, his face blanching.

"Constance …"

Ralph pushed past him impatiently, and Constance eagerly wrapped her arms around him in relief, the one sane person in her world. She clung to him as if to a life raft. Ralph easily slid one arm beneath her, the other behind her back, and pulled her up to him. Once he had her, he turned and quickly carried her from the room. It seemed they took the long staircase down to the main hall two steps at a time.

At the bottom of the stairs Constance gasped in shock. The table was overturned, the chairs broken and scattered. The two guards who had sat alongside Frank and Gabriel lay dead, their bloodied daggers still gripped tightly in their hands. Constance looked wildly around as Ralph hurried through the large room, but she could not see her husband or Frank anywhere.

"What happened?" she cried out in confusion, leaning in against Ralph in fright.

Ralph pulled her more closely to him, settling her securely in his arms, racing towards the front entrance.

Jacob stepped into the large archway, sword and dagger out at the ready. He grinned with pleasure. "Hand over the lady," he instructed. "She is worth a pretty penny to me, and you seem to have your hands full right now."

Constance smiled with delight. "Jacob!" she called out, happy to find another friendly face in this chaos.

Ralph instantly took a long step to his left, and Jacob's cock-sure smile vanished as he realized Gabriel was right behind. Jacob swung fiercely with his sword, diving in to slash with his dagger, but Gabriel was in no mood to brook delays. He drove in hard, forced Jacob to the wall behind him, slamming his fist repeatedly against Jacob's sword hand until the man released the weapon, screaming in pain. Gabriel pinned Jacob's left hand down with his knee, then rolled with his sword, driving it hard into Jacob's chest. He held it there for a long moment before pulling it free, springing to his feet and looking around for fresh threats. His face was a mask of absolute focus.

Constance was shocked beyond belief. "You killed Jacob!" Had Gabriel gone mad? What happened to the man she had loved?

Gabriel gave a quick nod to Ralph, and in an instant they were back in motion, skimming down the front steps, running across the main courtyard in a blur. To her surprise, Constance saw that a pair of Angelus mercenaries waited at the far end with a group of steeds.

Ralph eased Constance to the ground by one of the horses, and all of her previous concerns vanished in a flash. They were going for a ride! She dutifully climbed onto the mount, eager to get started. She turned, then pouted as Ralph vaulted up behind her, grabbing the reins out of her hands.

"I can ride quite fine!" she argued petulantly, wiping the blood from her eyes. Her eyes skimmed the group. "Hey, I want to ride that gorgeous unicorn over there, instead!" She pointed to a shimmering beauty with skin the color of rich cerulean which stood to one side. Suddenly Gabriel moved to the unicorn and climbed on. Seeing her attacker so near, Constance cringed back against Ralph.

Ralph did not wait another moment. He kicked his steed into action, and the group thundered away from the building, heading out into the forest. Constance thrilled in the ride, and leant low over the horse's neck. A pair of ebony angels flanked them on either side, and she could see the wings on the Pegasus they rode folded in alongside the beasts' flanks.

She glanced back behind her and shivered. "Gabriel is gaining on us!" she called out in alarm to Ralph.

"You hold on," he responded in a low, tight voice. "Everything is going to be all right. Just hold on."

Constance wrapped her hands more tightly into the horse's mane, letting herself enjoy the exhilaration of the race.

It seemed hours, or days, or maybe seconds, but suddenly the nunnery was ahead of them, its long grey walls and high main gate an imposing barrier in the dark night. Constance winced as they thundered towards the wooden doors, her head suddenly beginning to throb. Ralph uttered a low curse as he saw the closed doors, reluctantly pulling hard on the reins to draw the horse in to a clattering stop. He called up to the guards.

"We have Constance here, let us in!"

A row of torches appeared instantly along the top of the gate – and an answering line of torches flared into existence in a semi-circle from the surrounding forest, approaching slowly. Ralph spun the horse in surprise, the two Angelus men drawing close on either side. Gabriel put himself in front of the group, drawing his sword.

"You shall not have her, Barnard!" he called out in hoarse challenge.

A trio of riders separated from the surrounding line. Constance smiled as she saw Barnard and Frank in the group, nodding to them in welcome. The third man she could not place. He seemed in his mid-forties, lean and rugged, with graying hair and beard.

"I am Sheriff Tristan," he called out to the group huddled by the nunnery's gates. "I order you to put down your arms and submit quietly."

Gabriel did not lower his sword, and his voice was hot with anger. "On what charges?"

"You have kidnapped the lawful wife of this man, and by your own admission now are refusing to return her to him. You are in league with the Angelus, as we can see here with our own eyes. The Angelus are responsible for many of the bandit attacks."

A clear voice pealed out from over their heads. "This nunnery is a sanctuary for all who request it," called out Abbess Agnes, her voice steady and calm. "Constance, the woman in question, had been granted leave to visit with us for another ten days yet. We will take her in now for her stay."

Barnard raised his head, his face flushing with anger, but the Sheriff put out an arm to forestall him. The official turned his searching eyes on Constance's face.

"My Lady, is this your free desire?" he asked calmly.

Constance turned to look up at the Abbess, so high on the wall, seeming like an angel watching over her. Yes, she had come to the Abbey to stay for two weeks, and the time was not yet up. While she had no qualms about going back to Barnard, it would be rude to leave her friends so quickly.

She turned back to the Sheriff with a smile. "Yes, I would like to finish my stay," she agreed merrily.

The Abbess' voice rang steadily across the plain. "My offer of sanctuary extends to all of the men at my door," she stated without inflection.

Barnard stood in his stirrups immediately, his face mottled with fury. "She cannot do that!" he trumpeted. "They are ours!"

Gabriel turned and gave a long look at the Abbess, nodding formally to her. "Your offer means more to me than you can imagine," he stated quietly, his voice rich. "However, I will not draw you into this set of machinations. Watch over Constance, and keep her safe. That is all I ask."

He turned then to look at Constance. She drew back against Ralph, but was caught by the look of tenderness in Gabriel's eyes, of regret. When his voice came, it was rough and weary.

"Let her go, Ralph."

Ralph put out an arm, helping to lower Constance to the ground. A small door in the main gate opened behind her with a long creak, and a pair of the nunnery's guards came out to flank the opening. Constance looked uncertainly between Gabriel and Ralph, then turned and walked through the doorway.

She was immediately embraced by her aunt, who hugged her as if she had been gone for years. "You poor thing," sobbed her aunt, looking over her disheveled state and bruises in one long gaze. "We need to get you inside right away, and clean you up."

For some reason Constance expected to hear the sounds of fighting as she was led to the main keep – shouts, clangs, the neighs of horses. To her surprise, it seemed as if silence echoed around her as she crossed the courtyard and was swept into the main building, the doors closing firmly behind her.

Chapter 21

Constance awoke wearily, her head throbbing. It took a few moments for her to realize where she was. The familiar cell at the nunnery took shape around her. Her face pulsed with pain, and she raised a hand to it, surprised at the bandages she felt there. She struggled to remember …

The door to her room swung open, and she pulled back in bed, alarmed. Her aunt rushed in without preamble, holding a green dress in her arms.

"They came for you far more quickly than we had thought," she muttered under her breath as she moved. "We have to get you dressed."

"Dressed for what?" asked Constance in confusion. "Where am I going?"

"You are not going anywhere," insisted her aunt stoutly, seemingly to reassure herself as much as Constance. "Still, they do need to talk with you, of course. Here, put up your arms."

Constance obediently let her aunt help her with the dress, and stood while Silvia brushed out her hair with long strokes. Her aunt's voice had a slight tremor to it. "Now remember, my dear, this is extremely serious. Be truthful in everything you say – but think long and hard before you say anything."

"What do you mean?" Constance pressed, baffled about what was going on.

"I am supposed to say nothing to you," replied Silvia tightly. "Come on, now, we have to go."

She led Constance down the long network of hallways and chambers to get to the main meeting room. A large table had been placed at the center of the room, and a collection of people were sitting around it. The Abbess was at one end, serene and steady. Opposite her was the Sheriff, his eyes sharply moving from face to face, watching for reactions. Down one long side were Barnard and Frank, and then a guard who held a dagger on Gabriel. Ralph was alongside Gabriel. Another pair of guards stood behind the two men. Constance could see that Gabriel and Ralph's hands were tied in front of their bodies.

Gabriel started as she came in, his eyes going to the bandages on her head and arms. The guard instantly pressed the dagger in against his neck, holding him down. Constance found herself freezing in place, but at her aunt's gentle urging, she made her way to the lone chair opposite the four men.

The Sheriff ran his eyes warningly down the line of men. "You have all had ample opportunity to make your statements," he told them sternly, "You are here to hear what this witness says – but not to affect or suggest anything at all to her. If any of you speaks, or influences her in any manner, I will have you removed immediately. Do you understand?"

The four men nodded quietly, their eyes fixed on Constance.

The Sheriff turned to hold her fast with his gaze. His look softened slightly as he took in the injuries, still fresh and swollen. "I know you have been through a lot," he stated, "However, we need to hear your side of the story now, while it is still fresh. We want to know the truth, as you see it, when it is as clear as possible in your mind – and as unadulterated." He smiled wryly. "In short, I want to hear – in your own words – what took place after you left the village inn yesterday afternoon."

His look became more steady. "Keep in mind that you are in a holy place, and that you must tell the entire truth. Do not fall into the sin of a lie of omission. Tell us fully, honestly, what transpired."

Constance wished that she had time to get her thoughts into order, to figure out what was going on. Still, she would do the best she could. She settled herself into the chair, folding her hands before her on the table.

"We rode from the inn ... Gabriel, Ralph, and I ... to come back to the nunnery where I was staying. We took the track through the forest."

"Why did you take that path?" asked Tristan, his tone neutral.

Constance flushed. "I was angry ... upset ... at the memories the inn brought up. I wanted to get back to the nunnery quickly, and the main road seemed too long to me."

"What made you upset?"

Constance's face burned as she realized that Barnard and Gabriel were sitting almost side by side, hearing her confession. She lowered her eyes. "Six years ago, at that inn, I lied to Gabriel. I told him that I never loved him, and that I was eager to marry Barnard. A week later, I was hand-fasted to Barnard."

"So you and Gabriel were lovers?"

Constance's eyes shot up in fierce rebuttal to meet the Sheriff's. "No!" she shouted hotly. She took in a deep breath, and her mind suddenly filled with the memory of standing on the beach, Gabriel's cloak wrapped around her, his arms tenderly holding her ...

"Yes," she admitted more softly, her hand absently pressing against her chest. "Only in our hearts, though. I was untouched when I went to Barnard's bed. After that day at the inn, I put Gabriel into the past."

"Hmmmm, but did he do the same?" murmured Tristan under his breath, making some notes on a parchment at his side. He looked up. "So you were riding through the woods?"

"Yes," agreed Constance. "Then we ran into Frank." She motioned towards the dark-haired man who sat opposite her.

"So Frank stopped you three, by himself, as you were riding to the nunnery?" asked Tristan mildly.

Constance shook her head in confusion. "No, we were already stopped," she replied, thinking back.

"Why was that?"

"Because I had just realized ..." her voice trailed off, and she looked up at Gabriel. His eyes were weary but resolute.

"Had realized?" prompted Tristan calmly.

Constance swallowed. Gabriel had seemed to feel it so important to keep this information hidden. While she could not guess at his reasons, she wished it was in her power to not have to reveal his secrets. Still, she could not lie, and she saw in his eyes that he understood.

Her voice was a hoarse whisper. "I realized that he was the leader of the Angelus."

Barnard and Frank exchanged looks of triumph, and Tristan scribbled a few more notes on his parchment. "How had you realized that?"

Constance felt as if she were being lead down a path she could not escape. "He was the one who rescued me from the bandits, when I had been kidnapped, and the others reacted to him as they would to a leader. The Angelus had taken me immediately to his home. Later, when I was out at night with Ralph, Gabriel and two other Angelus ran into us, thinking we were bandits. Then, when we were heading to this nunnery, a group of Angelus were waiting to escort us, again looking to him as a leader."

Tristan wrote for several minutes, then looked up to meet her eyes. "So you were stopped in the woods, discussing this, when Frank came along? What then?"

"Frank said that Barnard wanted me back, and that the bandits would try to ransom me again, now that my brother would be more likely to pay."

Tristan's eyebrows quirked up slightly. "Did Frank say *he* was with the bandits?"

Constance furrowed her brow, trying to remember his exact words. "No ..." she responded slowly. "He said they should not be worried about Barnard ... he said, 'Let us try to keep the lady safe.'"

Barnard nodded smugly to Frank, and Tristan shot them both a warning look. "Pray continue," he prompted.

"Frank and his soldiers escorted us to a keep deeper in the forest. It was late when we got there, and I was given a room to sleep in."

"Were you locked in?"

Constance thought back to that night. She had been so exhausted …

"No, there were simply guards outside my door."

Tristan nodded. "You slept until morning? Then what?"

"I woke up, and went down for breakfast," recited Constance slowly, focusing on the memories.

"Who was there?"

Constance automatically brought her eyes up to the men who sat across from her. "Frank was there, and Gabriel and Ralph. A few guards stood by as well." Her eyes flitted to Barnard's. "Barnard came in a little while later, while I was still eating."

"What happened next?"

It seemed to Constance that her memory flitted and flowed. There were colors, sensations, and a dense fog that swirled around everything. "I … I went back up to my room?"

Tristan lent forward, his arms on the table. "Alone?"

Constance felt hemmed in, as if all eyes were on her, as if all the men present waited for what she would say. She felt the tears fall before she knew she was crying. In that whole dream-like morning, his face stood out in perfect clarity, pressing down on her, hitting her …

She looked up to meet Gabriel's eyes, her eyes streaming. His eyes were rich with anguish.

Her voice was a hoarse whisper as she bit out her answer. "I told him I would *not* dishonor our love by sleeping with him unwed," she growled. She saw the pride shine in Gabriel's eyes, and her fury rose at his reaction. He was proud of his attack on her?

She flung herself to her feet, staring down at the men around the table. "Do you know what he said? He said 'vows are meant to be broken'! He said 'honor is meaningless'! This from the man I trusted with my life! How could he say these things? Then he forced me down on the bed … he punched me when I resisted him …"

Gabriel's eyes instantly filled with raw shock, his face going pale. His voice was ripped from his soul, anguished. "Constance, I swear -"

The dagger was pressed hard against his throat, drawing a ribbon of red along it. Gabriel was pulled up hard against it, his voice cutting off, but his eyes pleaded with her to believe him.

She turned away sharply, her breath coming in heaves, refusing to see his face, to listen to his lies. She heard Tristan's voice coming as if from far away, concerned but insistent.

"It was Gabriel who did this to you? Who inflicted these wounds? Not Barnard?"

"It was Gabriel," she cried out, moving away from the table, away from the man she had trusted, had loved. Her eyes went back to meet his again, unwilling to believe her own memories, and then she was in motion, running … running …

She collapsed on her bed, her breath barely pulling into her lungs between the heart-wrenching sobs. It felt as if her world were collapsing around her. In a short while the gentle arms of her aunt were around her, and she lay in her embrace, a river of sorrow coursing through her. It seemed that hours went by, draining her.

She was completely exhausted, and two pairs of hands helped her sit back up on the bed, leaning against the side wall. Her aunt pressed a mug of mead into her hands, helping her raise it to her mouth for a long, grateful swallow. Constance finally looked up, emptied of all energy, looking between the two women.

The Abbess sat beside her, taking Constance's hands in her own. "My poor dear, you have been through more than any woman should have to bear. I want you to know you can stay here as long as you wish. You have the full support of our abbey behind you."

Constance's voice was a hoarse whisper. "Thank you."

Abbess Agnes patted her hand comfortingly. "Let us get some food into you. I am sure you are starving. Then we can see how you feel."

Silvia went to the door, and in a few minutes a sister brought in a tray with fresh eggs and spinach. Constance did not feel hungry, but she dutifully made an attempt to eat the food. She did feel slightly better once she had, and gave a weak smile to her hosts.

Agnes waved for the tray to be brought away, and offered Constance another mug of mead.

"My dear," she murmured, once Constance had settled back against the wall again, "I know you have been through a lot – but if you feel up to it, I would like to talk a little."

Constance nodded, her shoulders tightening. "I will do my best," she promised.

Agnes folded her hands together, keeping her gaze down at her hands, her tone neutral. "I have known you since you were a little girl, Constance, and I know that you are honest and dependable. I would trust you in any situation."

The Abbess interlaced her fingers together slowly. "I have also known Gabriel and Ralph for many years," she added quietly. "Both men have proven their courage to me many times over."

She looked over at Sylvia for a moment, then returned her gaze gently to her hands. "Your aunt and I are not saying that you are false in any way. I hope you understand that. I just want to feel more secure in what went on. Things will begin to move very quickly. The bandit accusation is a serious charge. The ..." she paused for a long moment, then took in a breath and continued. "The executioner has been called for. Arrangements are being made for the judgment to be carried out less than a week from today."

A shiver ran through Constance. It was all too much to take in; so many events had occurred so quickly. She wished she could have several weeks to hide out on an island, to recover, to think about what had happened, what it meant. She knew she did not have that luxury.

"What do you want to know?"

Agnes spoke quietly, calmly. "Was there a brazier by your bed?"

Of all the questions she expected, Constance was thrown off guard by this one. It seemed so neutral, so free of emotion. "Well, yes," she agreed, thinking back in time. The words began to come more easily to her, with such an innocuous topic to discuss. "A bronze one, quite pretty, actually. It had this deliciously fragranced incense in it. I suppose Barnard must have put it there for me, maybe to cover the scent of lingering mildew. The keep did not look as if it had been occupied before we arrived."

Agnes nodded neutrally. "Now this next question may seem a little odd. During your time at the keep, did you see anything ... unreal? I mean, besides people who treated you poorly. Was there anything you saw or heard which seemed fantastical?"

Constance shook her head at the question. What could Agnes possibly mean? She thought back through the day. Everything had gone from calm and happy to terrifying in the blink of an eye. What was *not* unreal about the day? Still, she tried to remember ...

She blushed deeply. She looked up hesitantly at the Abbess, unsure about sharing her thoughts. "You will never believe me," she cautioned quietly.

"You would be surprised," replied Agnes with an encouraging smile. "What did you see?"

"When Ga-" Constance dropped her eyes, finding she could not bring herself to say his name. Her voice dropped to a whisper. "When I was being hit, I must have received a serious blow to the head. Suddenly it seemed like ... my attacker ... turned into a demon, complete with wings and fire. Then, suddenly, there was an angel in the room, with a sword, protecting me."

Agnes nodded in understanding. "What happened to the demon?"

Constance was surprised that Agnes was taking this so calmly. "He evaporated – floated out of the room – when Ralph showed up."

Agnes waited a few moments. When she spoke again, her voice was coaxing. "Constance, the brazier on the dresser was stocked with opium. This is a drug made from poppies – a type of flower. Inhaling the smoke causes unreal visions."

Constance looked up in surprise. "So I really did see those things? Even the cerulean unicorn?"

A smile quirked the corner of Agnes' mouth, but she nodded in agreement. "Yes, even the cerulean unicorn. Your mind would be completely certain that it saw those things. Ralph said the room was a dense fog by the time he got up there."

Constance sat up. "Someone drugged me?"

Agnes nodded again. "I think Barnard was looking to make you more compliant. So let us think about breakfast. Where was everybody sitting at the table?"

Constance relaxed a bit. Breakfast had been calm, happy. There were no dangerous memories there.

"Barnard was on one side of me, and Frank was on the other. Gabriel and Ralph sat across the table."

Agnes again kept her focus on her hands, allowing Constance to take her time. "Then Barnard suggested you go upstairs, with Gabriel."

Constance nodded uncertainly, knowing that the dangerous ground was coming. So far, the memories were still safe. "Yes," she agreed.

Agnes kept her voice neutral. "So you took his hands across the table?"

Constance shook her head, her memories suddenly tangling. "No, he was standing beside me," she responded, speaking slowly. "He was on my right."

"You said he was across from you …?"

"Yes, he was, but then …" Constance suddenly realized where the men had been, and froze.

"That was where … Frank was," she whispered hoarsely.

Agnes pressed forward gently but firmly. "Then the man who held your hands showed you something?"

Constance refocused her attention, grabbing onto something solid. "Yes, his medallion," she agreed, glad that a memory was making sense. "It is how I knew he was Gabriel. I mean, I thought I knew, but I seemed unsure. He seemed like he was … wavering."

"You noticed something about the medallion," suggested Agnes.

"Yes," confirmed Constance, her eyes sharpening on Agnes, suddenly curious about how well the Abbess knew the details which she could barely latch onto. "I commented that it was looking to the right, and ... the man ... said that I was right by his side."

"However ..." encouraged Agnes quietly.

"Gabriel's dragon points to the left," stated Constance, her world suddenly coming into sharp focus. "It keeps his sword arm free. He always kept me on his left."

"So whose medallion pointed to the right?"

Constance replied without hesitation. "Mine. My medallion. The one that had been ripped off my neck by the bandits, when I was kidnapped."

Silvia offered Constance the mug of mead. Constance took it gratefully, downing a long draught, thoughts swirling in her head. She had been drugged, had been immersed in fantasies. Gabriel had been sitting across the table from her – *not* at her side. It had been Frank who had brought her upstairs, not Gabriel.

It had been Frank who attacked her.

She stood up suddenly, looking between the two women with alarm. "I have got to go see Tristan!" she insisted in panic. "The things I said! They will think Gabriel -"

"Sit, sit," soothed Agnes gently. "I know the assault on you was very serious. However, in terms of the law, the murders and thefts associated with the bandits are what carry the death penalty. We need to find a way to prove those charges are false."

Constance sat down slowly. "How can we clear them? I know Gabriel *is* with the Angelus," she admitted. "He is the leader of those mercenaries."

"The mercenaries are *not* part of the bandits," countered Agnes with certainty. "They are explicitly here to help protect us, and the innocents of this area, from the bandit menace."

"How do we prove that?" asked Constance, sitting forward.

Agnes shook her head. "Barnard and his crew have been busy. The brazier which was in your room has vanished. The study was stocked with papers supposedly linking the bandits with the Angelus. There were one or two inexpensive items from the burglaries there as well." She paused. "However, all of the more valuable items are still missing"

Agnes looked over at Silvia for a moment, nodding her head.

Silvia sat alongside her niece, taking her hand. "Constance, we need to find the true identity of the bandits. We need substantial proof. Otherwise, the Angelus will be put to death – and many innocent people will be without protection."

A surge of energy filled Constance. "What can I do?"

Silvia looked down. "Frank had your medallion. We received a full report on what the men had said from Tristan, before we brought you down to him. It was part of our conditions for him talking with you so quickly. The dialogue that Gabriel and Ralph heard would seem to indicate ..." she hesitated, then looked tenderly at her niece. "It seems to show that your husband is involved with the bandits."

For some reason, Constance was not surprised at all. She seemed beyond shock at this point. "It would certainly explain many things," she mused. She took in a deep breath. "So you want me to go back home ... with Barnard," she continued with resolution.

Silvia held her hands, her eyes serious. "This involves a great deal of risk, and if there were any other way, we would not even think of asking you. However, there are a lot of lives at stake here – innocent lives. We do not want you to do anything at all which might bring you to harm. Just keep your eyes open, and if you find something, get word to us."

Agnes sat forward. "We can arrange for Vera, your friend from North Sunderland, to join you at the keep. That way you will have someone else within the walls to support you."

Silvia looked to Agnes with concern. "However, we two cannot go with you. That would be suspect."

Constance looked to her two friends with renewed conviction. "I will do it. I just wish … is there any way I can see Gabriel before I go? I know time is short, but …"

Agnes nodded decisively. "I am sure we can arrange it. There is not a moment to lose." She looked up at Silvia.

Silvia was standing before Agnes said a word. "I am on it," she agreed. She hurried out the door and was gone.

Agnes smiled fondly at Constance, patting her on the knee. "You are a brave woman," she praised her friend. "You carry the hopes of many on your shoulders."

Constance shook her head, looking off into the distance. "Gabriel is the brave one," she responded softly. "He put his head into the noose to protect us all. He is sitting in that cell, facing death, for crimes he did not commit. He should be earning a medal for his efforts, rather than being held prisoner."

Agnes nodded in agreement. "Together, we will free him," she vowed. "Just you wait and see."

Silvia slipped back into the room. "It is all in motion," she let them know with a tentative smile. "Barnard and Frank will undoubtedly be here in an instant when they hear you are willing to return with them. Tristan would not miss the reunion for the world. I get the sense that he is still not convinced he knows the whole truth here."

Constance nodded, and brought her hand to her chest, to the hollow space there. She closed her eyes, and for a moment she could almost feel Gabriel's love wrap around her, nestling her in its warmth.

She opened her eyes in determination. Whatever it took, she would set him free.

Chapter 22

Silvia and the Abbess took their time helping to make Constance presentable. When all was ready, they walked down to Abbess Agnes' office to prepare for their visitors. Silvia headed out to the main hall to wait for the arrivals. Constance did not have long to pace the floor. Within moments, Silvia slipped into the room to let them know that Tristan had arrived.

"Ladies," he greeted them cordially, walking into the room, his eyes sharp on Constance. "Are you sure you are ready to return home so quickly," he added with curiosity. "You seemed quite shaken by the events, and rightfully so."

Constance gave a small smile. "I am upset," she agreed. "That is why I want to go home. Everything is upside down and confused. I want to be in my own bed, in my own surroundings."

A haughty voice came from the door. "As well she should be." Barnard strode in, flanked by Frank. "My wife belongs in my home, under my protection." He stopped by Constance's side and nodded slightly to Tristan. "Sheriff."

"Barnard," answered Tristan coolly.

Agnes spoke from her position behind her elegant wooden desk. "There are two conditions on my releasing her from my care here," she interjected evenly.

All three men's heads swiveled to meet her gaze. Barnard's features creased with anger, but he held his tongue with visible effort.

"First, I would like for Vera to join Constance, to care for her. Given her injuries, Constance will need an attentive nurse for the first week or two. Vera is a childhood friend of hers."

Barnard's face relaxed. "Done. I will send a coach for her immediately," he replied. "The second condition?"

Agnes flicked her eyes towards Constance for a quick moment, then looked back to meet Tristan's. "Constance would like to face Gabriel again, to address him personally about what he did to her."

Tristan looked cautiously at Barnard. "I am not sure that is the best of ideas, to -"

Barnard beamed with joy. "I think this is fantastic," he interrupted, rubbing his hands together. He realized suddenly that all eyes were on him, and his features became more tender. He lowered a hand to pat his wife on the shoulder. "My darling should of course find resolution for her anger, retribution for what was done to her," he added with firmness. "If this will help her recover, then I am all for it."

A sharp look flitted past Tristan's eyes, but he masked it quickly behind a neutral nod. "Of course. We can head over to where they are being held now, if everyone is ready."

Constance nodded, wrapping her arms around herself. "I would appreciate that," she agreed, looking up hesitantly. "The sooner I am home, the sooner I can start feeling more like myself again."

Barnard tucked a conciliatory arm around her, guiding her from the room, and the others followed behind. Together they reached the horses and coaches in the courtyard. In a few moments, the coaches were slowly making their way to the center of town.

It seemed a mere heartbeat to Constance until she was being helped back out of the coach. The dark, drab building loomed above her, a solid structure built of grey stone. A shiver ran down her spine. Gabriel was somewhere in here, trapped, facing death. She sturdied her resolve. It was up to her to prove his innocence, to rescue him, as he had been her savior so many times.

She followed behind Tristan and Barnard, her nervousness growing with every step. They moved across the main floor, with a meeting hall and private chambers, its décor functional and plain. At the back wall they reached a thick, metal-banded door. A stout, serious guard stood at attention before it. He nodded to Tristan before turning the key in the lock and pulling it wide. The dark stairs down filled her heart with trepidation.

Tristan looked to Barnard as they took up a pair of torches and descended. "We have captured ten of the Angelus already," the sheriff explained with some pride. "According to our investigations, there are only two left. We should have them in another day or so."

"Good, good," agreed Barnard, his eyes sparkling. "Very soon this will all be over."

They reached the bottom of the flight. Dark cells lined either side of a long hallway, torches flickering in between each pair of rooms. Shadowy forms lurked in the back of each cell, far from sight. Constance peered in at each one, half afraid it would be Gabriel, that she would be met with eyes full of accusation and scorn.

To her relief, each man was a stranger. They were each well-built, either doing simple calisthenics or sitting, cross-legged, staring at a wall in calm silence.

They came to the last cell on the left, and Tristan stopped without a word. He motioned for Barnard to step back, then waited, his face neutral.

Constance's heart pounded against her chest. Multiple sets of eyes were watching her every word, her every look. She put it all out of her mind. Only one thing mattered – Gabriel.

She stepped forward slowly until she stood at arm's length from the bars. She stood there, silently, looking in, allowing her eyes to adjust to the dismal light. A man was kneeling in the back corner, still, his eyes closed. There was a long moment of silence while he sat motionless, pressing a hand meditatively against his chest. At last he opened his eyes and swiveled his head.

He stood instantly, locking eyes with Constance, striding forward to press himself against the bars. Relief washed over her. His hands were steady and strong as his fingers wrapped around the metal rods. His eyes were clear, and they held a pleading intensity.

"Connie – I swear I would never lay a hand on you," he vowed vehemently without preamble, his words coming as if they had been recited over the hours as a litany. "Whatever else happens, I need you to believe that."

Constance's world crystallized into this one moment. She put every ounce of love and tenderness she possessed into her eyes and face. In the dark surroundings, with the other men behind her, only Gabriel would be able to see her features clearly. In contrast, into her voice she burnt the sharpest disdain she could conjure. She visualized that her words were aimed towards Barnard, who stood behind her. She hoped against all hope that she got the balance right.

"I now know the truth of what transpired at the keep," she hissed. "I will not allow that to happen to any other innocent person."

Gabriel straightened up slightly, flexing his fingers on the bars. His head cocked to the side, and his gaze sharpened on Constance's eyes with careful attention. "What you went through, no woman should have to endure," he agreed slowly, running one hand down the bar absently, searching her face.

"They will shortly have all your men rounded up, the *Angelus*," she continued, her eyes tender, her voice rough. "However, they have only found a few trinkets in your hideout. The bandits have taken far more than that over the past few years. Where are all the valuables?"

Gabriel's voice came ripped from within him, as if he had been pleading this issue for hours. "My men, the Angelus, have fought the bandit presence from the start," he reiterated, his eyes flashing to Tristan's for a moment. "These men are honorable and are guilty of no crime. Together we exist to protect the innocents of the area." His eyes moved towards Tristan again. "You find that stash of jewelry and stolen items, and you will find who is truly behind the bandit raids."

Constance gave the slightest of nods, the merest flicker of her eyes in acknowledgement.

Barnard's voice was preemptory. "Enough," he called out. He strode up to stand alongside Constance. "My dear, this man shall trouble you no longer. In a week he will be dead, and his vermin friends shall hang alongside him." He slid his arm around Constance's waist, smiling at the resulting flinch that flashed through Gabriel's shoulders.

Barnard held Gabriel's eyes with his own, triumph glowing in them. "Come, my wife, it is time for us to return to our home."

Gabriel's hands instinctively tightened on the bars. "Home?" he cried in shock, his eyes flickering between Bernard and Constance. Then, after a long moment he started, all blood draining from his face. Connie knew that he had realized her plan, had put together her willingness to return with Barnard and the challenge of finding the hidden treasure.

Her heart began hammering wildly in her chest. She was suddenly infinitely aware of Barnard's thin arm around her waist, of Gabriel's strength and loyalty only an arm's reach before her, and how the situation balanced on the point of a knife. If Gabriel said anything to raise Barnard's suspicions even a hair, Barnard's rage would know no bounds. He could lock her in her room, hold her captive, and all hope of saving Gabriel would be gone.

Gabriel could be lost to her forever.

Gabriel's gaze flashed through fierce pride, bitter frustration, and then shimmered into an emotion Constance had never seen on his face before – fear. Constance could see the tenuous hold he had on his self-control in the ice-white knuckles which gripped the bars. His voice, when it came, was low, guttural, almost a whisper of a plea.

"Connie, no ..."

Constance had chosen her path, and she clung to it as a shipwrecked sailor on a tempest-tossed lifeboat. She leant slightly into Barnard to distract him, to reassure him of her loyalty, while she held Gabriel's eyes with her own, reassuring him that he could trust her, that he had to let her go. There was no other choice. If he gave any indication of her plan, it would spell doom for them both.

"Vera is coming to stay with me. With her help, I will find what I seek." She gave Barnard a pat on the hand, but her gaze was only for Gabriel, only for the man who stood before her, the man she had depended on for so many years. Now she would be there for him, no matter what it took.

Her voice trembled, and she fought to hold it firm. "Soon my life will be exactly the way it should be."

"Oh, Con …" he whispered, his voice laced with agony. His shoulder muscles rippled and tensed. Constance half expected the bars to bend beneath his exertions, to melt as butter in the summer sun, and for him to press past them, come to her side, the consummate, loyal guardian she trusted with her life.

She nodded softly to him. This time he could not. This time it would be her who risked all to save him from death.

Gabriel closed his eyes for a long moment, pressing his forehead against the cold metal, taking in a full, deep breath. Then he opened his eyes and gazed straight into her own.

"I love you," he breathed, his eyes serene, the depths going on for an eternity.

Constance's world froze in a shimmering of torchlight and the echoes of those three words. In the many long years they had been together, they had never given voice to their feelings, never pledged their love out loud. It had been an undercurrent which had flowed around and through and within every action they had taken, every glance, every word spoken. But never once had she heard the words pass his lips, not even in her dreams.

The moment etched itself on her mind with crystalline clarity. She knew she would never forget the sound of his voice as he said those words, would never forget his eyes as he released all pretense and opened his heart fully to her.

With the watchers around her, Constance knew she could not respond in any way, not give Barnard the slightest hint of how profoundly Gabriel's words had affected her. She found she could not trust herself to speak, and she grasped desperately at her self-control, to keep even the slightest hint of her reaction from Barnard and Tristan.

Gabriel's eyes held hers for one last moment, and then, with an effort that caused his hands to tremble slightly, he carefully unlaced his fingers from the bars. He turned his head and retreated back into the shadows of his cell. Gabriel settled himself down to sit against the back corner, closed his eyes, and became still.

Constance's world started up again, her shoulders sagged in relief, and she half slumped against Barnard, only partially feigning her weakness. He chuckled, patting her on the shoulder. "That was well done, my dear," he reassured her, and then in a moment they were turning, walking back down the dark aisle, climbing the stone steps and emerging once more into the sunlight. Constance found there were tears streaming from her eyes, and she shakily used her sleeve to wipe them clear, keeping her eyes lowered.

Barnard clapped her on the back, smiling with pleasure. "I know that was rough on you, my dear, but I must admit that you have more spunk in you than I give you credit for sometimes." His grin widened. "That was, in fact, quite impressive," he commented with a tone of pride in his voice.

"You not only laid out the certainty of his impending doom, but you left the man without a hope in the world." His eyes twinkled with delight.

Tristan came up behind the couple, his eyes attentively moving between them. "Yes, that was eye opening," he agreed with an even voice. His look moved to hold Constance. "You are returning home with Barnard now?"

Constance nodded, wiping away the remaining tears, a knot of nervousness twisting in the depths of her stomach. The overwhelming danger she was about to willingly step into suddenly shimmered into reality for her. She would be beyond help, without protection …

"Would you care for an escort?" Tristan offered mildly.

Relief swept across her, and immediately she shook her head, fighting to control her features, to keep her look calm and serene. She could not let it be shown that she had any qualms, any concerns about being with the man known as her husband.

"I am sure we will be fine," she demurred, forcing herself to look up to Barnard with a gaze of trust.

"Of course we will," agreed Barnard expansively, puffing up with pride. "We will be home just after dark. No problem at all."

"As you wish," agreed Tristan with a nod, his eyes cataloguing silently.

Barnard's eyes moved to his second-in-command. "In fact, Frank, you will stay here and help Tristan with his tasks. Arrange for a room at the inn until these men are hung and dead."

Frank opened his mouth to object, his eyes going quickly to Constance with a flash of desire. He promptly pressed his lips together, frustration vanishing behind a mask of resolve.

"Of course," he agreed smoothly. "We would not want to disturb Constance at all with her memories so … fresh." He glanced sideways at Tristan. "I mean, we want to resolve this for her as soon as possible. I will do my part to ensure all of the Angelus are caught and hung as quickly as possible. Their reign of terror must be brought to a swift end."

"I appreciate that," agreed Tristan with an even look. His eyes turned to gaze again at Constance. "Speaking of which, I assume you will be back for the ceremony on Tuesday?"

Constance responded instantly, without a second of hesitation. "Yes. Absolutely." Her throat tightened up at the realization that she was planning to attend Gabriel's hanging.

Barnard beamed with pleasure. "You are quite the girl," he lauded her, patting her on the arm. "Of course you should be able to witness that sight. I would not miss it for the world."

Tristan's voice was neutral. "Maybe you might wish to say a few words, before the crowd," he added. "Sometimes it helps a victim to have that … catharsis."

"I would like that," agreed Constance, looking at Tristan with sharper interest. What was that behind his professional eyes? The officer only nodded in acceptance and showed the couple out the main door.

Constance stepped into the bright light of day and drew in a deep breath. Gabriel, the man she loved with all her heart, was locked in a dark cell. He faced the certainty of a hangman's noose. She would do everything in her power to prevent that from happening.

A Sense of Duty

Chapter 23

Constance leant against the window of the coach, staring at the dense woods as they scrolled past her gaze. If she had been told three days ago that she would be voluntarily riding home with Barnard, back to the purgatory of his home, back to his control …

She shook her head, focusing her thoughts. There was no retreating from her chosen course now. She knew the abbey would do what it could to help, but she was certain in her heart that the stolen goods were stored somewhere in the keep she had lived in these past six years. Barnard was too arrogant, too jealous, too untrusting to allow his possessions to be far from his grasp. Not only would they be within the walls of his home, but they would be somewhere he could easily visit, to fondle and admire.

She ensured her answers to him were low and weak as they rode, emphasizing her poor health and inability to cause trouble. Barnard looked even more pleased as the journey progressed. By the time they arrived at the main gates, a cloud-covered moon was high in the sky and Constance was well and truly exhausted.

She was thrilled beyond words to see Vera waiting for her in the courtyard as the coach pulled to a stop. Barnard was unusually gracious, greeting Vera as a welcome guest and helping guide Constance up to her room.

He even deigned to wait for a moment while Constance was settling in to bed. "We are glad you are here, Vera," he commented, his voice resplendent with the warmth of a proper host. "You have been provided with a room to your liking?"

"Yes, thank you very much," she agreed quickly. "My room is right next to Constance, so that I might tend to her easily."

"Good, good ..." replied Barnard absently, already turning from the room. "You two rest for as long as you need to. I have many things to attend to, as you might imagine. I will have food sent up to you in a while."

He was gone in a moment, but Vera waited alertly, ensuring his footsteps went far down the hall, and then down the stairs, before quietly moving to firmly shut the door. That done, she ran back to the bed to envelop her friend in a warm embrace, holding her close.

"Oh Constance, what has happened? When I heard you wanted me to come tend to you here, I packed immediately – but what are you thinking? Your brother told me you were to be safely in the nunnery for several weeks yet!"

"Please keep your voice low," responded Constance, glancing towards the door with caution.

Vera looked about her, then snuggled even more tightly against her friend, pressing her face against the pillow.

"It is as if we are children again, whispering secrets and hiding from our parents," she joked gently, her eyes sparking with merriment despite the gravity of their situation.

Constance allowed herself to smile. "Yes, and we will have to use all of the skills we learned back then to get through the next week."

Vera's eyebrows raised with interest. "So this *is* going to be something more than bringing you soup. I thought as much. Tell me everything."

Constance kept her voice low and hushed, and carefully laid out everything that had happened since she had left her brother's keep. In addition to needing Vera's help, she also wanted another witness able to speak on her behalf should something happen. She had given most of the details to her aunt and the Abbess, but now, with the luxury of time and Vera's undivided attention, she went through the events step by step, item by item.

It was several hours later by the time she had finished, and Vera's eyes were wide with surprise. "I cannot believe you are still sane after all of that," she whispered in amazement. "You *should* be taking bed rest for several weeks, or even months, you poor thing!"

Constance shook her head resolutely. "There is no time," she reiterated. "In five days they will be killing the only men strong enough to stand up to the bandits – men of courage, of honor. It is time for us to do our part, to make that same stand."

"I am ready," stated Vera promptly. "Just tell me what to do." Her hand went absently to the bruises on her face, now faded, but still fresh in her memory. "I am willing to do anything to ensure those bandits are stopped permanently."

Constance gave a tender smile to her friend. "We both are," she agreed. "I imagine we will leave here Monday evening to ensure we are there for the Tuesday ceremony. Today is already over. That leaves us three full days in the middle for our searches. We will have to be careful, but diligent. Barnard would not have left his contraband anywhere obvious, anywhere that a servant might accidentally come across it. We will have to think as he does, and be watchful."

"We can do it," swore Vera firmly. "We must."

The women sat for another hour, discussing each room in the building, weighing its likelihood. When the knock came on the door with two trays of steaming stew, the women were grateful for the break, and lingered over their meal with pleasure, renewing their strength, preparing themselves for the task ahead.

* * *

The next day dawned bright and sunny, and a lightness eased into Constance's heart. The lovely weather meant most of the staff would find reasons to be outside, in the fresh air, and their searching efforts might be unhindered.

She lay in bed quietly for a long while, creating her own personal time of Matins. She gave thanks that Gabriel was still alive, was safe, if only for today. She gave thanks that Vera was here to assist her with the search. She closed her eyes, summoning the image of Gabriel, sending him her strength, her prayers, her love.

A firm knock came at the door, and Barnard pushed his way in.

"My dear, how are you feeling this morning?" he asked jovially.

Constance blinked wearily, working to ensure her movements were as feeble as possible. "I am still so tired, Barnard. I think it best I stay in my room for the day."

"Of course," he agreed. "I will be out riding with some of my friends, but Vera will see to your every need, I have no doubt."

Constance allowed herself a quiet smile. "Yes, please, put us out of your thoughts. We will be fine here. You go enjoy the sunshine."

Barnard did not need urging. "Until tomorrow!" he called out, and in a heartbeat he was gone. The door had barely closed when it opened again and Vera slipped in. "It seems he was in a good mood," she commented, going to her friend's side.

"We could not hope for a better start," stated Constance with a smile. "Let us work on the upper floor today. It is only the bedrooms and guest chambers. He might be using one of the empty bedrooms for storage, I might imagine. It seems unlikely to me. Still, it is the easiest place to start. None would question our poking around in the bedrooms up here, and it is most likely that nobody will see us. Once the maid finishes with her morning sweep, they will all be out and about, and should not return to our floor until evening."

"I will go let the cook know that I will fetch food when needed," suggested Vera with a nod. "We will have the floor to ourselves!"

Constance dressed while Vera went on her mission. Her friend returned shortly with an assortment of cheese and bread. The two ate a quick breakfast, then got started.

They moved slowly, carefully through each room. Most were empty guest rooms, but there were several storage rooms as well. They pulled at floor boards, pushed at chimney stones, peered out windows. They used a stool to get closer to the ceiling and press at the timbers there.

As the long hours dragged on, Constance kept the image of Gabriel trapped in that dark cell before her. She pressed a hand to her chest, where her medallion should be, where her connection to Gabriel was lodged. It was absolutely imperative that she find the stolen items in the next three days.

She crawled under beds, holding her breath against the dust. She went to the bottom of each cupboard, to the top of each cobwebby corner. There was nothing.

Constance even braved the long, rickety stairs which led to the open roof. Only servants went up here, to patch leaky holes and to clean the chimneys. There was nothing on the faded stone platform but stray branches and an ancient bird's nest.

As the afternoon faded into evening, there was only one room left on the floor to look through – Barnard's. This was the riskiest room on the floor to search. None would question Constance being in any other room of the day's search – there were simple enough excuses which would make complete sense. Explaining her presence in Barnard's bedroom would be far more problematic.

Constance gave a wry grin as Vera stationed herself out front as a lookout, then she slipped into the chamber. It was ironic that the one room a wife should not be expected in was her husband's bedchambers. She took in a deep breath. She would have to be as quick as humanly possible – and as thorough as she could be. Out of all the rooms on this floor, this was the only one where she expected any chance of success.

She stood for a long moment, allowing her eyes to sweep around the room, refamiliarizing herself with its contents. There were inlaid wood boxes on his polished oak dresser, their lids open, each holding a selection of gold and silver rings. Gold embroidery ran down his deep burgundy curtains and matching blankets covered his large bed. The headboard was inlaid with several rubies. Twin wardrobes on the back wall stood open; each holding a wealth of dressing gowns and slippers. Constance had already gone through his many other outfits in the spare room closets.

Constance focused on her task with pinpoint precision. Every board was tested and sounded. Every location on the wall was prodded and mentally compared with the adjoining rooms. She looked under the dresser drawers and ensured they slid back to meet the wall. She looked for compartments beneath the bed.

Finally, she just stood in the center of the room, gazing around with a sense of completion. She was now sure that the cache was not on this floor of the house.

The silence pulled at her, and she began to look at the room not as a location to search, but as an actual bedroom. She remembered the earliest days of her stay, when she was nervous about being with Barnard, when she had hoped to bring a child into the world. This had been a room of expectations then, of fresh beginnings. What had happened?

A hurried knock came on the door – Vera's warning signal. Constance gave one last look around the room to ensure everything was exactly as it had been, then sprinted to the door, slipping through it, closing it gently behind her. There was the sound of footsteps on the stairs, and then Barnard came up to the landing, stopping in surprise as he caught sight of her.

"Constance? What are you doing out of bed?" he asked with concern.

Constance dropped her eyes as her mind raced through her options. She kept her eyes lowered, her voice weary. "I was lost in old memories," she admitted truthfully, her voice echoing her regret. "I was thinking of when I first came home with you."

"My dear, of course you are lonely," responded Barnard as he walked to her side. Constance looked up, surprised to hear a note of tenderness in his voice. "Come, I have a few moments. Lay with me for a while."

A shiver of nervousness ran down her spine. "I do not know if I am up to -"

Barnard smiled gently, patting her on her shoulder. "Just to rest and talk," he expanded. "It has been a long while since we did that. After all you have been through, I think it might help."

Constance nodded at Vera, then allowed Barnard to lead her through the door into his room, the room that, until today, she had not entered in these past five years. He guided her around to the bed, helping her to sit back against the pillows. Then, true to his word, he laid down next to her, not touching her, simply being there.

Constance slowly relaxed, and found herself remembering those early days. Barnard had been patient and understanding as he exposed his new partner to the intimacies of conjugal life. What had happened?

Apparently Barnard's thoughts were drifting in the same direction. "We have been through a lot, you and I," he commented quietly, his eyes closed. "There was a time that I blamed you for our problems in creating a family. I was furious with your failings. I railed against you for wasting ten years of my life."

He let out a long sigh. "I want you to know, you are not responsible. I am sure, with the right man, you would be a wonderful mother. It seems it is *my* line which is flawed."

His voice was so dejected, so drenched in utter despair that despite all her myriad feelings Constance felt drawn to respond. "Barnard, there is always hope. Maybe -"

Barnard shook his head. "No, I think it is time to face the simple facts. If I was meant to father a healthy child, I would have done so by now." He hesitated for a moment, then looked at her with eyes shadowed by pain. "You know that I have had other women in my life. I do not apologize for it. Creating an heir is all important for what my family has handed down to me." He chuckled bitterly. "However, in addition to this land and wealth, apparently they also handed down a defect. I must accept the good with the bad."

He closed his eyes again. "It was my one dream in life to be a father. I waited ten long years for you to come to my side, to turn that dream into a reality. When one child died, and then two, my rage and frustration nearly drove me mad."

Constance almost felt pity in her heart for the man by her side. He had indeed waited a decade to join with her. She had seen firsthand the pain and fury he felt after each stillborn birth.

His voice was quiet. "Did I ever tell you how my mother died?"

Constance looked over at him, honestly curious. "You said she came down with an illness when you were three or four."

Barnard shook his head. "I did not want to frighten you; I did not want to curse myself." He took in a deep breath, looking down at his hands. "My mother was a healthy woman, like you, coming from strong stock. My father was sickly but also very wealthy. She had one miscarriage, and then I was born. The doctors worked night and day to ensure I survived my infant months. Thrilled with the success, my father pushed my mother to bear another child. She had five more miscarriages, one after another. It sapped her health and damaged her spirit. I remember her being so sad, so lost."

He twisted his fingers together. "I think in the end she just gave up. She stopped eating, stopped sleeping, and let herself die." He looked over at Constance, his eyes finally meeting hers. "I did not want that to happen to you."

Despite her swirl of emotions, Constance found that a small part of her heart did sympathize with the man by her side. Rationally she knew that this did not make up for his actions, could never excuse his many injustices and illicit activities. Still, somewhere in the depths there was still a small boy, watching his mother waste away, knowing the same fate could await any woman he chose to marry. There was some cause for pity.

She patted his hand gently. "I am grateful that you thought of me," she responded, and found that in a way she did mean it. His affairs over the past few years had been very painful, very hurtful to bear – but in his own way he was trying to protect her. He did not want to drive her to death with repeated miscarriages and stillborn children.

Constance did not agree with the liaisons, but she could understand a small part of the underlying motivation. He had desperately wanted a child of his own blood to continue his family line, to inherit the family lands.

Barnard let out a deep breath. "Time to get you back to bed," he commented, shaking himself slightly and climbing to his feet. "I imagine you are tired and ready for sleep."

Constance went with docile calm back to her room, and looked at the door for a long while after he left. She wondered how differently things might have been if Barnard's parents had remained content with one child, if he had been raised by a loving, doting couple. She knew it did not excuse his misbehavior, but still, she wondered ...

Chapter 24

Constance drifted to wakefulness with the fullness of Thursday's sun shining warmly across her bed. She gathered herself into a seated position, drawing in a deep breath. She focused her thoughts, envisioning that Gabriel sat across from her, quietly waiting in his cell, trusting in her, depending on her strength and courage to see this through. She could almost feel his presence there with her, almost see as he pressed his hand to his chest, and of its own volition her own hand moved to echo the action.

Her mind moved to Barnard, and she nodded her head in determination. Yes, he had experienced a rough life. Yes, some hurdles had been placed before him. But other people had dealt with far worse circumstances and had risen above them. If Barnard was now a man of dishonor and deceit, he had allowed himself to sink to those depths, and she would ensure he could not hurt innocent people any longer.

She swung her legs over the edge of the bed, standing and moving to choose a dress. There were still two more days left for searching. Today had been set aside for the lower, basement rooms. This area held the storerooms and a few of the servants' quarters. Constance thought how this would also undoubtedly serve to be fruitless, but they were also rooms she would not be questioned about visiting, and she was still building up her strength. She wanted to leave the most likely rooms – the ones prone to cause the most suspicion – for the last day. If she got Barnard or the others nervous about her activities right now, she would never be able to finish searching the entire house.

Barnard came in to see her shortly after breakfast had been brought to her and Vera. "I am glad to see you up," he offered with a smile. "You seem to be feeling better?"

"A bit," agreed Constance, nodding her head. "In fact, Vera and I were thinking about going through the fabric stores in the basement today, to find some sewing to work on. We thought it might keep me occupied while I recuperated."

"Good, good," encouraged Barnard absently, his eyes glancing at the large window, the sunny landscapes beyond. "I will be heading out on a ride for the day with some friends. I am glad to hear you will have something to fill your day."

His eyes dropped slightly to gaze at the gardens barely visible through the window, and his brows narrowed slightly. "It is just as well that Ralph was caught in that trap," he added, a pensive tone layering into his voice. "I never did approve of him pulling you into his martial pursuits. Far better that you focus on sewing and other wifely duties."

Constance's spine stiffened at the casual reminder of her friends' approaching deaths, but she forced herself to smile, to maintain a neutral look. "Of course, you are right," she agreed quietly. "I am sure this is for the best."

"Well, I will see you later tonight," he called out with an offhanded air as he left the room. Once he was gone, Constance sent up a fervent prayer for both Gabriel and Ralph, and then finished her meal as quickly as she could. They waited by the window until they saw Barnard ride out, flanked by a trio of women. Then she and Vera made their way quietly down to the basement.

There was nobody to disturb them as they went from room to room, setting up torches and lamps to light their way. With the beautiful weather, and the lord away, the keep was almost deserted. Servants found excuses to escape for a few hours on whatever errand they could invent. Constance and Vera set up their plan and searched in earnest. In room after room they found nothing but dust, cobwebs, and a small nest of soft-fuzzed baby mice.

Constance kept at the search, holding the image of Gabriel tenderly in her mind. He was in a dark room, much as this one, trapped by lies. Only the truth would set him free – and it was up to her to find that answer for him. He had come for her when she was captive. He had rescued her from the dark when nobody else lifted a finger. She would do everything in her power to save him now.

She moved on to another trunk in the dingy storeroom she was searching. It was an old construction, oddly familiar. She pulled up the lid with a creak.

"Oh, Vera, come here," she called in a hushed whisper.

Her friend was by her side in a moment, kneeling in the dust. "What is it?"

Constance reached into the dim recesses and pulled out a large bolt of fabric. It was soft to the touch, and as it came out into the torchlight it shimmered with a sea green / blue color that captivated her eyes.

"This was part of my dowry," remembered Constance, her eyes gazing with fondness at the fabric. "My father knew how much I adored this color and sent it with me." She ran a hand slowly down its length. "Barnard wanted me only in his family colors – burgundy and gold. He redirected the chest into the storeroom and I have not seen it since."

"It is beautiful," agreed Vera quietly. She waited a long moment, then added softly, "Those are the colors Gabriel wears."

Constance caught her breath. Vera was right. The tapestries in Gabriel's home, the tunics they wore, they were all this same hue. While he had served at her family home he had worn her family colors, but after he returned …

Constance gathered up the fabric in her arms, closing the lid with a bump of her hip. "I am going to make myself a dress of this fabric," she stated tersely. "Not only that, but I am going to wear it to the ceremony." She could not bring herself to name the actual event – the execution – which was going to take place there.

Vera's face turned pale.

"Are you sure that is a good idea?" she asked with worry.

"I will tell Barnard that this fabric was part of my wedding dowry – that I want us to start afresh, anew. I think he will appreciate the symbolism and encourage me." Constance took one last look around the dingy rooms. She was certain that nothing else remained to be found down here. Together they made their way back up the stairs.

Evening was descending in velvet hues. The staff had returned to the keep to finish up their chores, and the rooms bustled with activity. Constance and Vera brought the fabric into a side room, and to their surprise several of the maids came in to bring thread or a selection of sliced apples. Apparently the staff was also making an effort to start over again.

Constance smiled. The staff's acceptance would help make tomorrow's investigations easier. Also, the new dressmaking task would give her and Vera a handy excuse. They could now go poking into various rooms in search of whatever dressmaking implements they might invent a need for.

Chapter 25

Sunday morning dawned with fierce thunderstorms pelting rain down in sheets. Gloom settled over Constance's heart – there were only thirty-six hours left to search. A mere two days from now Gabriel would be slain, his Angelus troop with him, and all would be lost.

Her resolve steeled. She would not let that happen.

She dressed quickly, making her way downstairs. The household was gathered to head to the church and Barnard solicitously put an arm out to escort her. Constance took it with exaggerated weakness, allowing him to help her down the submerged path to the stone chapel.

She focused every fiber of her being on the mass, on her desire for help, on asking God for forgiveness and understanding. She had fallen short of the Lord's requirements. She had allowed desire and longing to enter her world. Whatever she had done wrong, she would not allow Gabriel to suffer for it. She needed every helping hand, every grace the Lord could send her now.

The priest, a middle-aged, portly man with thinning hair, finished the mass and turned to the congregation for a more personal comment.

"I know some of you have gone through hard times recently," he began in a strong voice which echoed off the back walls. "This may have caused you to question God; to wonder what kind of deity would allow such tragedies in our lives. I am here to tell you that life is not always smooth – and this is a good thing. You must take the long view on your life.

"Think of a child, learning to walk. The child falls often. She skins her knee, she bruises her hand. This is what helps the child learn. Over time, she improves, she masters walking – and then running. The bruises heal, and the skills she learns become critical to her daily life."

He swept the room with his eyes. "Think of the soldier practicing his art. If he is lazy or slow, he takes a blow on the shoulder. This encourages him to improve. Over time he becomes skilled at his craft, and can use his talents to protect the weak and the helpless. His strength grows."

His eyes seemed to Constance to target hers; he seemed to be speaking right to her heart. "Sometimes what seems to be a hardship is really a sign from God. It causes you to focus on what you had not seen before; it causes you to take action where you had been passive. The great benefit that results will make the hardship seem a triviality. The great joy that results will wash away any memories of the pain which came before."

His eyes moved back to encompass the entire group. "Focus on your goals, every day, and make steadfast progress towards them. Focus also on the steps you take to achieve your goals, ensuring that each one is in and of itself honorable, true, and right. There is no moral goal which is achieved by immoral means. There is no right aim which is achieved by lying, destroying others' lives, or taking what was not earned by your own two hands. It is far better to be contented and poor than to build wealth on the backs of others."

He swept his arms wide in emphasis. "Make every day your legacy – and use every day to increase that legacy."

Constance was enlivened and renewed as they returned to the main house. Now she only had to wait out the traditional hour of visitors – not that their home ever saw any – and then she could continue her work on searching the main floor with Vera.

To her surprise, there was in fact a man waiting for them in the hall as they returned from chapel, his yellow and white outfit proclaiming who he was long before he turned to look at her in concern. Constance ran into her brother's arms, comforted by his warm and welcome embrace. He held her for a long moment before holding her at arm's length to look down into her eyes.

"Oh, my dear Connie," he rasped in concern. "How are you doing? I cannot believe -"

"Everything will be all right," Constance interrupted quickly, turning as Barnard came up behind them. "Look, my brother has come to visit for a while," she added brightly in a louder tone.

Barnard frowned slightly, but he nodded. "Of course, welcome, Charles." He shook hands brusquely with Constance's brother. "I imagine you are concerned about your sister's injuries at the hands of Gabriel," he commented, his face smug.

Constance gave Charles' hand a warning squeeze, and his lips thinned as he bit back a comment. "I still cannot believe it," he finally replied tersely.

"Oh, believe it," responded Barnard with a chuckle, relaxing. "A few more days and the nightmare will be over." He moved over to a sideboard which held decanters and glassware. "Some wine?"

Charles shook his head no, and Barnard shrugged, poured himself a large glass and strode off to his office. Constance waited until he had left before drawing her brother over to a corner bench. Vera brought them mugs of ale before leaving them to their own counsel.

"Constance, what is going on?" asked Charles in a hush. "You cannot have me believe -"

"No," agreed Constance, cutting him off, "but I cannot go into it any further. We are running out of time, and I need help." Her mind flew over the plans she and Vera had discussed over the past several nights. "You have contacts in all the local villages. Can you get for me a list of what the bandits have stolen – a description of the more valuable items, and who they belonged to?"

Charles nodded. "Yes, of course. That has all been gathered as part of the documentation against Gabriel and his group. It would be a simple matter for me to get a transcription."

"Please bring it with you to the ceremony on Tuesday," asked Constance, her throat growing tight as she realized just how little time was left to her. "I think it will prove useful."

"As you wish," agreed Charles. His hands held hers gently. His eyes went to the bruises still visible on her face. "Are you sure you are all right? Is there nothing else you need?"

"I need more time," sighed Constance, a half smile flitting across her face. "But that you cannot give me."

Charles stood at once, finishing his ale and putting the mug on the bench besides him. "Then I will not delay you further," he stated with a nod. "I will see you in two days' time. God speed."

Constance stood as well, giving him a tender hug. As soon as she released him, he turned and strode from the room. Almost instantly, Barnard was in the doorway, looking at her curiously. He came over to stand beside her, picking up her mug of ale and glancing at its untouched brew.

"That was a quick visit," he commented wryly.

"I asked him to compile a list of what the bandits had stolen," admitted Constance frankly, sure that servants had been set to overhear her conversation. "I thought I might read some of it at the ceremony, so that all present would be aware of just what harm the bandits had done."

Barnard's grin grew wide. "What a delightful idea!" he crowed. "That will stir up the crowd's emotions even more strongly. Well done, my dear."

Constance steeled herself not to show any emotion, not to flinch as he patted her on the back. "Now that he is gone, I can get back to working on my dress. I want to look my best, to show I have survived recent events, and that I am ready to make a fresh start."

Barnard beamed with pride. "Of course you do. I will leave you to it," he agreed. "You just let any of the servants know if they can assist you in any way." He took in a deep breath, smiling. "If you will be so occupied, I will go for a ride out to visit a friend. It looks like the sun is beginning to peer through the clouds. You and Vera enjoy your afternoon." He gave her a brief bow, then turned and left.

Constance waited several moments to ensure he had really gone, then waved Vera over and headed for the side study. This sitting room had been unused for several years. They took a few minutes to set up a table with benches and lay the cloth upon it. Once the room was prepared for dressmaking, they huddled to one side to discuss their plans for the afternoon.

Constance had left the main floor for last for several reasons. To begin with, it was by far the most frequently used of the three. She assumed that Barnard would want to keep his activities secret. Few would have seen him moving around in the basement at night, or in the back storage rooms. If he had tried to sneak around the pantry area, it was likely someone would have come across him no matter what time of day or night he was using the room.

The same would be true of her search. She and Vera had never been interrupted in their two days of investigating the other floors. However, they could not imagine spending five minutes in any room on this floor without a maid coming in to dust the furniture, a servant asking if they would like some wine, a steward lighting a fire or opening a window. The rooms were a bustle of activity.

Constance could not really imagine Barnard secreting his purloined treasures in the main hall, in the pantry, or in any common place. She knew deep in her heart where she would most likely find the items. However, that room held the most danger, and if she was caught there she would be preventing from searching further. Therefore, she and Vera would eliminate all other possibilities first. Only then would she take that great a risk.

They worked step by step. First they went in search of cutting tools to lay out the fabric. Using that as an excuse, they moved through the entire pantry. They were not able to do a thorough sounding of board and tile as they had in the unoccupied rooms, but even with people moving in and out they were able to look through each cupboard, each trunk, to satisfy themselves that the room held no secrets.

Back in the sewing room, Constance worked on the dress while Vera searched the walls, ceiling, and floor. It was easy enough to turn from the task when a servant came in, and to return to the search when the room was quiet again. An hour passed, the dress was ready for sewing, and the room was declared clear.

For the main sewing task, they took the fabric into the main hall, finding a sunny spot at one end of the room. Over time, they were ignored by the servants who came and went through the area. Constance focused on the sewing, and on distracting any maid who happened into the room. Vera, under the pretense of seeking out new thread, something to drink, or a snack, went from area to area in the room. It seemed highly unlikely that Barnard would use such a public room as a hiding place, but they went about their work nonetheless. Soon it was clear that there were no secrets hidden here either.

The light began to fade, and the foot traffic in the room eased to nothing as the staff settled into a Sunday evening quiet. Constance gathered up a pair of lamps and set up a work area next to the door to Barnard's private study. She had rarely been in there, and even now her heart hammered furiously as she prepared for her incursion.

Vera took over the sewing for her, working on attaching the sleeves, on doing a first hem of the neck and bottom. She set up her station before the door. Constance took a long, careful look around the hall before pulling open the door to the study and slipping in quietly.

      * * *

Constance stood in the semi-dark room for a few long minutes, allowing her eyes to grow accustomed to the gloom, to work out the general layout of the furniture. There was a heavy desk and leather chair to one side, and a long couch positioned before the fireplace. Small side tables stood on either end. Over the fireplace hung a pair of portraits – Barnard's mother and father. The father was thin and hunched, looking down with watery eyes. The mother ... Constance had always thought she looked sad, and young – so young.

There was a long set of shelves down the left wall, filled with parchments, scrolls, and other documents. The top of the shelf held a number of decanters of varying sizes along with glassware.

All remaining wall space was filled with Barnard's trophies. He had racks of antlers, a wolf's skin from a trip to Germany, a stuffed badger, and a large trout. When Barnard had visitors he often took them on a tour of this room, explaining in detail how he had achieved each victory. His trophies were his life, and he spent many long hours in this room reliving his past accomplishments.

Constance took a deep breath, then let it out again. She had felt all along that Barnard's acquisitions from any bandit activities would be in here as well.

She started, methodically, to the left of the door. Working slowly and carefully she moved along the shelves, lifting every memento, moving every codex. She checked the decanters, pulled at the shelves themselves. All was sturdily in place. It was tedious work, but she held the image of Gabriel sitting in the deep darkness of his cell as a beacon in her mind. Gabriel could do nothing but wait and pray. She would be his salvation.

She moved along to the low bench beneath the windows. The moon was beginning to rise outside, and she paused for a moment to look out over the grounds. For six long years this had been her home. She had resigned herself to living here forever, coming to accept the harshness of her life as normal. Now that she was exploring the option of leaving, she realized just how much she did not fit in here. The grounds were dusty and bare, with little sign of life. The soldiers moved about with lackluster energy. The only spot of beauty was her gardens. She would miss them – but she was sure she could start anew in whatever corner of the world her new home happened to be.

Shaking herself, Constance moved on to the desk. She put focused effort into every last area of the desk – every drawer, every leg, the wood beneath the desk, the walls behind it.

In the back of the main drawer she came across a small oak box. She lifted it out, setting it on top of the desk. She opened the lid with curiosity.

A velvet display held a dozen rings in it. She had seen these rings on Barnard's fingers occasionally during their years together. They all had oval faces, each with a small gemstone embedded in its center. She picked one up at random, a ruby-adorned ring with a dull sheen. As she turned it in her hand, she noticed a small ledge running around the oval face. She pulled up at the ridge with her nail.

The top of the ring hinged up, and she realized there was a small compartment within – and it held a curled lock of bright blonde hair. She stared at it for a long moment, awareness sinking in. Helga, the cook's sweet, slim helper, had hair of just that color.

Constance had known Barnard was routinely unfaithful, but for him to wear tokens of his dalliances, to keep them lined up in his trophy room ...

Constance replaced the ring and shut the box lid with a snap. She swallowed the bile which rose in her throat, taking in long, deep breaths. She was on a timetable, and it would do no good to get upset about things which she could not change. She had to move on.

She pushed the box back into the drawer and pressed onward, her thoughts even more focused. She would find Barnard's secret stash. She would free Gabriel and bring an end to this for once and for all.

She made her way to the fireplace, to the sofa and tables which stood before it. The fireplace occupied the wall to the left of the door. She stared at the fireplace for a long while, pondering it.

Constance had become intimately aware of the keep's construction over the past few days – far more aware than she had been in the six years she had lived here. The keep had four chimneys, located in the center of each of the four sides of the building. The chimneys rose straight through the lower and upper floors, rising through the roof. Each floor had a pair of hearths per chimney. The hearths faced opposite each other, warming adjoining rooms. She knew this helped to maximize the heat that could be gained from each chimney.

She looked again at the fireplace before her. Above her she knew this flue was shared by her room and Barnard's. On this floor, though, there was no matching flue on the other side of this chimney. There was only the pantry – but that room had its own separate chimneys. Also, she would not have said that the pantry's wall was adjacent to this one. What was behind here?

She looked more closely at the chimney's stones, at the mantle and the trinkets which adorned it. Then she looked up at the pair of portraits. She lifted the father's portrait cautiously. A large, furry spider scurried out of the depths and into a far corner. She turned to look behind the mother's portrait ...

There she found a lever, hidden behind the sad face of Barnard's doomed mother. Constance hesitated for a moment, then she carefully pulled down on the lever.

There was a soft click, and the wall panel to the left of the fireplace swung open a few feet. Constance's heart began pounding in her chest. She replaced the portrait and approached the opening. Cautiously, she peered inside. The room was small – maybe six feet by four – and the walls were lined from floor to ceiling with shelves. There were no windows, but a small candle with flint and tinder waited on a stand in the center of the room. Constance peered into the darkness, but without a window it simply was not possible to see. Finally, she gave in and lit the candle. She hoped that this evidence of her being there would not be noticed.

The candle bloomed into light, and she looked around her, eyes growing wide as the room came into view. Barnard had indeed been amassing trophies. She had always thought of the bandits as scroungers, immediately selling whatever they found. Barnard apparently had different aims in mind. It would seem that every item taken over the past years must be accounted for on these shelves. There were golden hair ornaments, richly wrought silver bracelets, bags of loose coin, carved ebony boxes, and much, much more. Constance could just imagine Barnard standing in this room, basking in his power, remembering each victory as a separate triumph in his life.

Her mind quickly rifled through her options. She had to bring proof to the ceremony – but she had to be discreet. Undoubtedly, Barnard knew his stash well and would notice if anything obvious was missing. On the other hand, if she just brought random coin as her proof, how would anybody know that this was really from the bandits' plunder?

She knelt down to view the lower shelves, where missing items would not be so obviously missed. She looked along the back of each shelf, seeking out items which were unique and memorable. A golden necklace with a lion's head. A cane top of silver with a hawk's talon. An ivory hair comb featuring a cascade of roses. Each was far enough back in the shadows that it should not be missed right away. She might have a chance of getting away with this.

She tucked the items carefully into the bag at her belt, then stood, looking around to ensure she had not dislodged anything else. Satisfied, she snuffed out the candle with a quick movement. She blew at the wick, hoping the smoke would dissipate and quickly blend in with the fragrance of the room's accumulated dust and ash. Then she left, pulling the panel closed behind her with a soft click.

The study looked exactly as it had when she had entered it; she had been extremely careful to precisely replace each item she moved. Nodding in satisfaction, she slowly eased open the main door, peering out. To her relief, only Vera was in the room, sewing studiously by the lamp light.

Vera exhaled in relief as her friend closed the study door behind her and joined her at the table.

"So?" Vera asked softly, her eyes bright with curiosity.

"I think we should finish this task in my room, where we will not inconvenience others," replied Constance with a grin.

Vera's face lit up with delight, and in moments the two had gathered up their supplies, relocating to the security behind the barred door in Constance's bedroom.

Constance pulled the stolen items from her bag, laying them out on the bed. Vera lifted each one, gazing at them in amazement. "So he saved these items for himself?" she asked with wonder. "Will he notice them missing before tomorrow evening?"

Constance shook her head. "These were only a few of the *many* items Barnard has in his trophy closet," she clarified to her friend. "These were minor items on lower shelves, blocked from sight by other jewels."

Vera looked up in shock. "Why would he just keep all of these things? What is he doing this for?"

Constance shrugged. "I hear he did not eat the wolf meat from the skin he has in his study. With his lovers, he will take on a new conquest, then abandon her after a few months. It seems that it is the achieving he enjoys – the thrill of victory."

She sat looking at the items for a long while. "I imagine, too, it is hard to sell some of these stolen goods – they would be recognized as the bandit's take. Perhaps he was waiting to find a seller who could purchase the lot, then take them far away for sale. It might not be worth it to do that in smaller increments."

Vera ran a finger along the delicate roses in the ivory comb. "So now what do we do?"

Constance picked up the dress and began working on the hem. "The safest place to transport them is down in the lower hem of this dress" she decided. "The hem will never be touched by anyone, and certainly not inspected. That will enable me to bring them to the ceremony. Once there, I will simply rip the hem open to display them."

Vera nodded in agreement. For the next few hours the pair worked diligently to finish the dress construction, to tuck in every corner so that the outfit was as seamless as possible.

A Sense of Duty

Chapter 26

Constance felt as if she had barely slept. Today was the day she would leave with Barnard for the nunnery. Tomorrow was … the ceremony. She still refused to think of it as an execution, even to herself. There would be no execution. She would publicly expose Barnard, and Gabriel would be saved. Ralph would be saved. Only one more day and it would all be over.

Vera knocked at her door, and they gathered up the dress to bring downstairs with them. They set up an area to one side of the main hall, and Vera brought over a bowl of fresh fruit. She sat quietly by her friend as Constance began embroidering.

Constance did not begin with a plan, but as she worked she found that she was tracing the curling, elegant designs of dragon smoke along the hems of the sleeve, the hems of the skirt, and along the waist and neckline. Gabriel had come to rescue her with that tracery on his helmet. She would stand before all in her dress of deep blue, embroidered with her own symbolism, his symbolism. The hours drifted by in the quiet meditation of sewing, and always before her she saw Gabriel's deep blue eyes, his steady faith in her. She would see this through.

She was just about finished when she heard footsteps. Barnard strode into the room, turning to smile as he saw the women quietly sewing in a corner. "So you are up and about!" he called out jovially. "That is wonderful. Are you feeling ready for our journey this afternoon?"

"Yes, I am ready when you are," agreed Constance quietly, taking in a deep breath.

"Well then, it is a long trip! Let us get started," encouraged Barnard with a smile. It seemed that only minutes passed as servants carried trunks to the coach and soon they were rolling through the main gates.

Constance's heart hammered a thousand beats a minute as the coach made its way steadily through the evening dusk. Barnard and his men rode escort outside; only Vera sat beside her in the enclosed interior, their fingers tightly entwined. The dress sat on her lap, safely folded.

Constance resisted the urge to run her hands along the hidden treasures, to reassure herself they were there. Only one more day and everything would be revealed. She only had to hold onto her sanity for one more day. She could not raise any suspicions. She must be perfectly blameless, perfectly composed, a paragon of docility.

Every halt of the vehicle, every comment from beyond the coach caused her heart to double in speed. She was exhausted by the time they reached the bridge, and when they pulled up in front of the inn she could barely make her way from the coach. Vera helped her inside, up the stairs to their room. Both climbed into the shared bed and fell into a deep sleep.

***

The following morning, Constance rose to find herself shaking, and could not seem to stop. Vera called for a bath, and Constance spent a long hour soaking in the hot tub, washing herself thoroughly, thinking through every aspect of the coming day. So much rode on her ability to execute her plan, to explain herself clearly, to convince those present that Gabriel was innocent. So many lives depended on her.

She finally stood and dried off, then unfolded the dress. She ran a hand tenderly over the swirling smoke embroidery, thinking of Gabriel being taken from his dark cell, then brought into the town square. He had come for her when she was imprisoned. He had set her free. She would do the same for him, whatever it took.

She dressed carefully, then sat to allow Vera to brush her hair into long, tawny waves. When she was done, Vera stood back for a moment, looking over Constance with satisfaction. "I know it is a serious day," she commented quietly, "but you are positively glowing. I am sure that every eye will be on you once we arrive."

"I hope so," responded Constance nervously. "I will only have one chance to convince them."

The two made their way down the stairs together, and all eyes turned as they reached the main hall. Barnard stood and arrived at their side in a single movement. "My darling, there you are! You are beautiful, as always! I will be quite proud to have you standing by my side as we kill the traitors. The world will see that my family remains untouched by this all."

"Yes, of course," demurred Constance quietly.

Frank came up beside her, his eyes raking in her beauty with greedy appreciation. "I cannot wait until this is over, until we are all back home again," he offered throatily, taking her hand in his, bringing his lips down for a long kiss.

Constance looked down, biting her lip, willing herself to remain still until he released her. She had to present steady calm and quiet until the ceremony. She could not give either man any reason to question her, to prevent her from having her chance to speak.

She put her hand on Barnard's arm, allowing him to escort her to a large table in the center of the room. She picked carefully at the apple wedges laid out before her, her stomach knotted and uneasy. She ate but a few bites before pushing away her portion.

"Can we go over to the square now?" she asked Barnard quietly. "I would like to be there early, if at all possible."

Barnard beamed. "Yes, of course you would," he agreed grandly. "You want to soak in every moment of pleasure, watching those vermin squirm. The sheriff has set up a covered platform for us to sit on with plush chairs. I insisted on that. I am sure we will be quite comfortable there." He extended a hand to her. "Come now, my dear."

A wiry boy went scurrying for the coach, and Barnard walked Constance out to the main steps. The coach was brought around, and Constance boarded it first, followed by Vera. Barnard and Frank mounted their horses and rode alongside as they covered the short distance to the main town square.

Constance's heart tripped in tense panic as they drew near. Yes, there were the covered stands Barnard had spoken of, with ten chairs lined up beneath a canvas awning. It had an almost carnival-like gaiety to it, with the burgundy curtain and the pillowed chairs.

Her eyes turned to the right. There, before the stand, was a large, square wooden platform. Fourteen ropes hung from a pair of long wooden beams, seven in front and seven behind. A squat wooden box waited beneath each rope. Constance forced herself to breathe, to take in, to release, to keep going. He was not dead yet. There was still time.

The carriage pulled to a stop by the covered stands, and in a moment Barnard came around to help her out. The small crowd of onlookers turned to watch as the foursome made their way up to the raised seating area, taking seats near the center. The platform was a mere ten feet away, facing out into the center of the town square.

"They should be bringing the men out shortly," promised Barnard with a smile, settling himself into his chair eagerly. "Still, it will be an hour yet before the main event begins. They want to give the crowd time to properly examine the culprits, of course."

"Of course," echoed Constance, her heart pounding. She wanted this moment to freeze forever. Gabriel was safe now; he was alive. At the same time, she wanted this time to speed through in an instant. She wanted to get past the uncertainty, past the waiting – to see Gabriel's face, to tell the world the truth.

People drifted into the square in ones and twos, standing to stare at the platform. To Constance's surprise, most did not seem the rough children and zealous clergy she normally associated with these types of events. Many seemed to have come from far away, judging by their dress, and seemed somber and serious. She recognized the innkeep from her flight to the nunnery, as well as Pete from the local tavern. Both men nodded quietly at her before resuming their solemn vigil. Many others in the crowd seemed here to honor, rather than malign, the men who stood accused.

A glimmer of hope shone into Constance's soul. Maybe this audience would not be as hard to convince as she had feared. Maybe others also felt that the Angelus had been unjustly accused.

There was a movement to one side, and the crowd stirred, murmuring. Five soldiers were escorting a red-headed man toward the square platform. His hands were tied behind his back, and his feet were shackled so that he could only shuffle slowly. The guards carried drawn swords and swept alert glances around them. They carefully helped the man up the stairs to the central platform, then worked him around to the furthest rear rope. With his hands and feet still tied they boosted him to mount the high box. Once he was steady, one of the soldiers expertly tied a noose in the rope. He looped it around the man's neck, cinching it tightly in place. Then he stood back, admiring his work.

Constance stared at the condemned man's face for a long moment. She did not recognize him, but she knew this man had laid his life on the line for her several times. She nodded, and prayed, honoring his past actions solemnly in her heart. He had been there for her when no others had lifted a hand. She would be there for him now.

Barnard smiled. "Ah, so it is beginning," he commented, sitting back and stretching. "This will be quite enjoyable."

Constance ignored him, all of her focus on the square. Two of the guards remained on the platform while the other three headed back out. In a short while they made their way back, prodding along another prisoner. Again, he was a stranger to Constance, but she stared at him as he moved, memorizing his face, gazing at him with compassion.

An aura of respectful silence descended over the square. Her heart filled with resolve as she looked around the courtyard. Apparently she was not the only one grateful to these accused.

Judging by the reaction of the spectators, she was sure that several others in the courtyard had also been protected by these brave men.

The square began to fill with more watchers, and it became a mix of those who gazed quietly at the condemned men, and others who exhibited a more raucous attitude. Her ears caught their voices - there was a stir of motion near the grand stands. Constance looked up as her brother neared her chair, coming up to sit alongside Vera.

"I brought that list you requested," he offered Constance quietly by way of a greeting. He handed her a rolled up scroll of parchment, tied with a blue ribbon.

"Thank you," breathed Constance gratefully, taking the scroll and quickly opening it.

Barnard peered over her shoulder. "My, those bandits were industrious indeed!" he whistled, grinning widely. "Look at all the valuables they made off with! That is quite an achievement, I should say."

Constance scanned the list rapidly. There − a third of the way down the list - a gold necklace, featuring the head of a lion. It had been taken from an elderly Crusader. Her eyes scanned further. The taloned cane top belonged to a priest in the next town over, a man Constance knew well by reputation. The rosebud comb was the wedding present from a mother to her only daughter. That had been stolen six months earlier.

Constance hoped that the three victims would be in the crowd, but even if they were not, she now had the proof that the items had been stolen by the bandits. The location of the stash made clear that the group was led by Barnard.

She carefully re-rolled the scroll and tucked it into the small bag at her hip. Taking in a deep breath, she looked back out at the main square. The back row of seven nooses was now full, and the guards began bringing in the front group. More guards filtered in to stand along the edges of the platform, and a few moved among the growing crowd, keeping a wary eye on the more rambunctious members.

Constance's heart thumped even louder as the soldiers slowly began to bring in the remaining members of the troop. The crowd became more full, more somber, as the minutes passed. A dark haired man, thick and burly, was brought out. A sallow man with a thin, wiry build. There were only four spots left ... then three ...

Constance's hands gripped the arms of her chair. The trio of guards were making their way through the crowd with Ralph at their center. He blinked in the bright sunlight, shuffling along carefully, focusing on the ground before him. Only when he got to the platform did he look around him, look over to the row of chairs. His gaze skipped past Barnard's and met with Constance's, his look tender and sad. Constance felt Barnard turn to watch her, and she steeled her emotions, pressed her lips together until they formed a flat line of concentration. She could not falter now, could not give Barnard any reason to distrust her, to drag her away from the proceedings.

Ralph held her gaze for a long moment, then looked down again, his feelings hidden from view. In a moment the guards were helping him onto his own box. It seemed only seconds before the noose was fitted around his neck.

Constance looked out across the platform. Only one empty box remained. Thirteen men ... thirteen brave, strong men ... stood resolutely, without complaint or outcry, waiting for their leader. The crowd quieted to an expectant hush, and all eyes turned in the direction of the town hall. Constance felt as if her heart would burst ...

There was a movement, and she could not help herself. She vaulted from her chair, pressed herself against the railing at the edge of the seating area, her eyes glued to the figure being guided towards the execution area. There were five guards around this man, as well as Tristan who moved immediately at the prisoner's right side. Gabriel was blinking in the light, much as Ralph had, and then his eyes swiveled around through the crowd.

They went immediately to Constance, standing on the raised dais above the crowd, and he stopped instantly, his eyes caught on hers. The entire crowd tensed, looking between the two, watching for any sign of emotion, any signal or word. Constance could not betray her intentions, not yet, not before all was ready. Still, without thinking, her hand moved of its own accord to press against her chest, to press the hollow spot where the pendant had hung for so many years. She held her hand there for a long moment, taking in a deep, steadying breath.

Gabriel's hands were tied firmly behind his back, but she saw the acknowledgement in his eyes, the steady resolve. Then he started moving again, his feet shuffling at a slow, regular pace, his eyes never leaving hers. Even as they fitted the noose around his neck, he soaked her in with his eyes, drawing in every last moment he could.

Tristan stepped forward to ensure the noose was properly tied, being gentle but firm with the rope. He nodded to the guards, then turned and strode towards the viewing stage. The remaining local officials had filed into their empty seats, and the courtyard was overflowing with spectators. Constance retreated to her chair as Tristan came to the center of the platform. He nodded in a quiet greeting to her and Barnard before standing against the railing, raising both hands. It was hardly necessary. Every eye in the place was glued to him.

"Today is a somber day," he began without preamble. "You see assembled before you the members of Angelus. The men are named as follows."

"Gabriel, of High Newton by-the-Sea. Distinguished in two separate campaigns in the Holy Land."

"Ralph, formerly of Swinhoe. Served with Gabriel in the Holy Land. Distinguished service."

"Richard, of Ellingham. Served with Gabriel in the Holy Land during both campaigns. Distinguished service."

Constance's eyes moved from man to man as their name and accomplishments were read. Each man had served with Gabriel; each man stood proudly at his side, his back straight, his eyes clear. Pride welled up within her, and she saw appreciation from most in the crowd as well.

Beside her, Barnard shifted his weight. "Is this an execution or a parade?" he muttered beneath his breath.

Tristan had finished with the roll call. "Now to the charges," he announced to the throng. "Evidence has been provided by Barnard of Swinhoe" – Tristan motioned with a hand towards the man sitting behind him – "that Gabriel and his Angelus guard are responsible for the bandit attacks. These attacks have led to numerous injuries, loss of possessions, and loss of life over the past few years. For these crimes, the men have been sentenced to hang by the neck until dead."

A cold shudder ran through Constance, and the crowd muttered and shifted. Several members of the throng stared at Barnard with open dislike. He tossed his head back with relish, wrapping an arm around Constance's shoulder with pride.

"Maybe it is time for you to speak, my dear," he encouraged with a grin. "That will help silence the crowd."

Tristan turned, holding her eyes with his own, his creased face neutral. "Yes, I am very interested to hear what you have to say, Lady Barnard," he agreed. "Are you ready to speak?"

Constance's legs wobbled, but she took in a deep breath, steeling herself. This was her only chance to stop the atrocity which was about to occur. If she fainted, if Barnard managed to pull her away, the brave men before her would be put to death. There would be none left to stand in the way of the bandits, none left to protect the weak and innocent.

Tristan moved back as she approached the railing. Hundreds of eyes were upon her, and a sense of panic swept through her. Then she turned her gaze to the platform and felt the strength, the trust, flow from the men who watched. In the center of them all stood Gabriel, his eyes steady, his face almost serene. She realized suddenly that he would not blame her if she failed. He had accepted his fate. She had only to do the very best she could.

She smiled, almost, then turned to the crowd.

"Good people, you have come here today to see justice for the atrocities practiced by the bandits over the years. I speak to you as one who has witnessed and experienced these heinous acts. My name is Constance. What I am about to say, I swear to you is the whole truth."

She let her eyes sweep across the crowd, connecting with each person in turn. "Several weeks ago I was abducted from the very inn in this town by the bandits and held for ransom. I was locked in a dark cell, beaten, cared for poorly, and a precious medallion of mine was stolen." Her eyes went to meet Gabriel's. "It was only due to the valiant efforts to this man here, Gabriel, that I was freed. He came for me – he and his band of Angelus mercenaries. They fought their way into my prison and took me out to safety."

Barnard's voice shot out. "Lies!" he called, leaping to his feet. "They only played at that to gain your trust!"

Tristan firmly held him back. "You may have an opportunity to speak after," he warned Barnard. "It is Constance's chance to be heard."

Constance did not turn, but kept her gaze on the crowd, on the men. "When I traveled to visit the nunnery, to visit my aunt, again it was the Angelus who came to my aid, to ensure I arrived at St. Francis unmolested."

She heard mutterings behind her, but apparently Tristan was actively suppressing them – none came forward to hinder her. Still, Constance had the sense that if she gave him the opportunity, Barnard would find a way to silence her. She quickly pressed on.

"When evidence of a few trinkets was found, and it was put forth that these had been stolen by the Angelus, I asked myself where the rest of the wealth was. Hundreds of items have been taken over the years. Only a few tiny objects were found in the 'Angelus cache'. I therefore did some research of my own this past week. I will show you just a small sample of what I discovered."

She took the knife from her waist belt and bent down. With a smooth motion she sliced open the hem of her dress, removing the three items secreted there. She stood again, putting two into her left hand. She held the remaining item up before the crowd.

"A lion's head necklace, made of solid gold. This belonged to a brave crusader who -"

An aging voice filled the air. "That – that is mine!" The crowd looked about, muttering in surprise. Slowly a way parted down its center. A white-haired man staggered carefully through the crowd, his eyes misting with tears. He spoke as he drew near the seating area.

"The bandits took that necklace from me, and killed my faithful servant of twenty years! It was given to me by my commander when I departed from the Holy Land. I had never thought to see it again."

Gentle hands helped him walk up to the edge of the railing, and Constance handed the necklace down to him. He held her hand for a long moment, pressing his lips against it in gratitude.

"I never thought to see this pendant again before I died," he breathed quietly. "Now I can pass it down to my son, and know he has his inheritance."

Hundreds of eyes swiveled up to meet Constance's, bright curiosity burning in them.

"The bandits were responsible for that thievery and murder," she reminded the throng in a ringing voice. She looked down for a moment, selecting the larger item for display.

"Next," she called out, holding up the silver cane top, its gleam catching in the light. "In the shape of a hawk's talon, this is -"

A man's voice rang out. "Thank the Lord!" Again, the crowd eagerly parted and made way as a middle-aged priest moved quickly forward, his face alight with joy. "My mentor gave that to me when I became a priest and took on my first assignment!" he called out with pleasure. "After the bandits ran off with it, I was sure it had been melted down and used to fund who knows what illicit activities! To think that it is safe ..."

He reached the railing, and Constance carefully placed it into in his hands. He gave both of her hands a squeeze, then crossed himself and looked up to the sky.

The crowd was eager now, and looked to see what other wonders she would reveal. "I only have one more item with me," she called out to them. "However, the storage cache I discovered was full to the brim with the rest of the objects. These are but a few tokens as proof of my story, evidence that what I say is true."

She held up the ivory comb. "This hairpiece is made from ivory, and is engraved with a cascade of rosebuds. It is also identified on the lists as having been taken by the bandits."

After the first two dramatic results, she half expected screams of delight to follow this unveiling as well. The crowd looked around with expectation, waiting for a grateful woman to come forward and claim it. Yet, a long minute passed, and there were no shouts.

"I will make sure Tristan returns this object to its rightful owner," began Constance, turning.

A woman's voice cried out, "Wait!" The crowd turned with a murmur, and Constance saw that a young, pregnant woman was slowly being helped through the throngs by an older lady. The ensemble made room for them, waiting patiently as they shuffled up to the railing.

The young woman reached up for the comb, tears filling her eyes. "This was given to me by my mother, on my wedding day," she explained, turning the piece over in her hands. "When the bandits came to rob us, my husband tried to stop them. They beat him within an inch of his life, laughing the whole time. Even now my husband is not fully healed and cannot walk well."

She turned to gaze at the men on the platform. "I came to see the bastards who had ruined our lives, to look them in the eye, to watch them die. I wanted that satisfaction." She let her eyes run along the line of men, then turned back to Constance. "However, studying their faces, I cannot believe these men are the ones who did such a thing to me and my family. Tell me, where did you find my comb?"

This was the moment. All eyes were focused on Constance, and her skin tingled with nervous energy. What would happen once she spoke? There was only one way to find out.

"I found all of the stolen bandit goods in a hidden room in my home in Swinhoe."

Her words echoed around the courtyard, and for a long moment there was shocked silence. Then there was a roar of anger from behind her, and Barnard was suddenly at her side, calling out to the crowd.

"I knew nothing of this!" he swore vehemently. "If what she says is true, then there is a traitor in my home!"

Constance's first and only aim was to get Gabriel free. Anything else could come later. If she could get Barnard on her side, if only for a moment ...

"Maybe Barnard is right!" she cried out, her voice carrying to all corners of the courtyard. "There was an item stolen from me when I was captured by the bandits. It was a pewter medallion with a dragon on it. That dragon was facing to the *right*," she added. "Gabriel wears a mirror image of that pendant; his faces to the *left*."

Tristan nodded to the guard near Gabriel, and the guard went over and pulled open the tunic at Gabriel's chest. The soldier drew forth the medallion, laying it on top of Gabriel's shirt so it would be visible to the crowd.

Constance's voice carried clearly across the throng. "Let us see if the bandit boldly stands amongst us. Does any man here carry the partner to that medallion?"

One by one men pulled open their tunics, proving to the world that they were not involved in the bandit activities. Barnard pulled open his own burgundy tunic with pride, proclaiming his innocence. Constance turned around, her eyes seeking out Frank. His face had gone as white as a sheet, and his hands strayed nervously to his neck. The others on the stand had pulled away from him and were eyeing him with suspicion.

A hush fell across the crowd as the gathered townsfolk realized what was going on. Tristan's voice cut across the silence, his order direct.

"Frank, show us your chest."

Frank hesitated, then in one quick movement reached up and yanked the medallion free from his neck, leaving twin stripes of red along the sides of his throat. He held the pendant out, wild eyed, to Barnard, stumbling forward.

"This was your idea," he pleaded, his eyes desperate. "You said this execution would go smoothly. You said we would be rich beyond our wildest dreams!" He lurched to a stop before Barnard, grabbing him by his arms. "Even when you wanted me to -"

He lurched suddenly, his eyes going wide in surprise. A bloody froth bubbled from his mouth. Barnard stepped back, the blade of his dagger drenched in blood. He gave Frank a push, and the man fell backwards against a chair, the medallion falling from his grasp, rolling to the floor.

Barnard held his bloody blade aloft as if he were a conquering hero. "I have identified the traitor, and I have slain him!" he called out to the crowd. "You are now safe thanks to my brave action!"

Constance dove for the medallion, her heart flooding with emotion as she knelt on the floor, cradling it again in her hands. It was safe. It was hers again. She would never let it go.

She rubbed the blood off the face of the dragon with her sleeve. Tenderly, reverently, she tied the leather thongs carefully around her neck, nestling the dragon against the front of her dress as she stood.

Barnard turned from his victory pose and saw her standing there, her face glowing, the dragon at her chest, the blue embroidered tendrils tracing out along her neckline and hems. He suddenly took in her entire outfit, and his eyes bulged with fury. He spun to stare at Gabriel. Even bound, Gabriel stood as if prepared for hand to hand combat, his head held high, his eyes bright with challenge. His own medallion sparkled in the sun.

Barnard's face boiled into the deepest crimson as he realized the sea of onlookers was watching him, judging him.

He twisted back to face Constance, his body shaking with anger. "*You take that damned thing off!*" he screamed at the top of his lungs.

Constance raised her right hand to the medallion, feeling its reassuring weight at her chest, feeling the familiar lines of it, pressing it against her. Her eyes met Gabriel's, and she smiled with complete certainty.

"Never."

Barnard roared with rage, and Constance drew back a pace in shock, turning as a sea change shook him to the core. Before her eyes his logical, rational mind lost control, and he was drowned in a tsunami of fury. After a staggering, tumultuous moment the ravenous flames of his inner inferno raced throughout his body, becoming his master.

He moved with a speed she had not thought possible. One minute he was towering over her, his eyes bright with rage, and the next he was holding her from behind, his dagger tight against her neck, his hot breath sending beads of sweat down her throat.

"I will not lose my trophies to that mob, and I will not lose you to that cur!" he snarled out, all semblance of civility lost. Constance felt as if she had been caught in a frozen tableau. Her brother and Tristan were both motionless, hands midway to their swords. Gabriel and Ralph, balancing on their boxes, had arm muscles taut and swollen as they pulled hard against their restraints.

Barnard spared a look of annoyance at his fallen right hand man, then turned to face the crowd.

"I know several of you are here today at Frank's order; he always told you he was the head of the bandits. This deception is no longer necessary. I am the one who controls the funds, and I decide all shares of the profits. As of today, the rules have changed."

He pulled his dagger tightly against Constance's throat, and a thin line of warm blood trickled down her neck. "Back off," he growled to the men on the stand. One by one they moved away, giving him the space he demanded.

"You too," he snarled at Vera, his eyes dropping meaningfully to the dagger she was easing from her belt. "I have heard about Constance's little adventures. You go join the others, or your friend here will face the consequences."

Vera's face darkened, but she nodded. She sent a look of strength to Constance before stepping down to stand with Tristan and the men.

Satisfied, Barnard turned to the mob again. "I will be relocating to Bordeaux," he called out to the unsavory faces he spotted here and there. "Any man who makes that trip with me will get a full share of the loot. A *full* share. Those men who are not here, they forfeit their rights. We leave immediately, and we take what we can carry. Who is with me?"

There was a long moment of hesitation as the crowd looked nervously around, wondering who would answer such a call. Then a burly man pushed back his cloak hood, revealing a head of curly red hair. Constance recognized him, recognized the scar that traced its way down his face. She looked coldly down on him as he pushed his way forward through the shocked throng.

Mark did not spare a glance for the fallen body at Barnard's feet. "I will go," he stated brusquely. He glanced over his shoulder. "Jack, c'mon."

A squat man with thick arms came up beside him. Soon another man joined them. After a few minutes there were a dozen men milling in front of the stand.

Barnard did not wait any further. He dragged Constance sideways from the raised podium, over to the coach waiting to one side. Constance looked around quickly for Gabriel, and met his eyes for a long moment. He still strained against his bonds, and Constance could see that a guard stood nearby, his dagger held at his side, ready to cut the ropes as soon as Barnard was away.

Constance felt the connection between them as a palpable force. Gabriel had risked his life to descend into the depths of the bandit-held keep to rescue her. She had submitted to the hands of an abusive tyrant in order to keep the hangman's noose from Gabriel's neck. She had no doubt that, the moment she was clear of this courtyard, that Gabriel would come for her.

Gabriel's eyes shone with love and determination. She knew with absolute certainty that he would track her down, no matter what it took, no matter where Barnard took her. She drew in that strength, a smile almost coming to her lips.

A harsh pull spun her head. She was jerked down by Barnard, who flung her face first into the coach. He climbed in after her, calling out harshly, "Away, quickly! Make sure you bring my horse!"

In only a moment the entourage was in motion, moving at faster and faster speeds through the town, and then out to the open road.

Constance brought a hand up to rub at her neck while Barnard took up ropes and tied shut both doors with sturdy knots. He then sat back against the opposite side of the carriage looking at his wife with weary disdain.

"Oh Constance, I had no idea you could be so troublesome," he growled finally, glaring at her in disappointment. "Here I thought there was potential for a truce between us."

Constance pursed her lips, saying nothing. She was alive, at least, and was being used as a hostage. They would want to keep her alive until they reached the coast. After that, who knew? She would keep her wits about her until then.

The miles rolled by in furious thunder, and Constance was not surprised when there appeared to be no sign of attack or trouble from pursuers. She imagined they would hold off until the group got to the keep, where they could mount an attack without her being at the center of the fight. After all, the pursuers knew exactly where their quarry was going.

She brought up the mental image of the Angelus girding up for battle, of them riding in a mounted phalanx to take down the bandits once and for all. Even if she was not saved, the threat would be over. The Angelus would be cheered as heroes. She could hope for nothing more.

Exhausted and relieved, she closed her eyes and allowed herself to fall into a deep and troubled sleep.

A Sense of Duty

Chapter 27

It was dark when the clatter of cobblestones woke Constance from her twisted dreams. She rubbed at her eyes, trying to remember where she was, what was happening. She knew she had to save Gabriel ...

Barnard twisted her arm hard and pulled her from the carriage. Around her, the bandits were reining in to a stop, the soldiers running to swing closed the main gates and bar them. She saw the word pass quickly about the pursuing troops, saw the guardhouse turn out as all available men moved up to line the walls.

Then she was being pulled brusquely, dragged to the main entryway, through the quiet hall, then up the back stairs towards her room. Barnard pushed her into her dark bedroom without another word, then the door was pulled shut with a slam. She heard the sound of a heavy bar falling across outside the door. It had never occurred to her that her room could be barred from both sides, but she did not hesitate for one moment. Two could play that game. She ran to her own bar and lowered it quietly into place. That might buy her some time.

Constance then turned and moved to the window. She peered out into the dark, looking for any sign of movement behind the walls. It was a mix of shadow and substance; she could not be sure what she was seeing. Only the white of a trio of birch trees shone in the moonlight.

Frustrated, she moved to her fireplace, using the flint and tinder to strike up a small fire. She lit a candle from the small blaze, then brought it to the window, waving it back and forth in a line. If only someone would see ...

There! From the line of trees a single rider rode forth, his helmet in his arm, his blond hair catching the moonlight. Her breath caught as Gabriel gazed up at her. A line of the mounted Angelus moved in behind him. Together they drew their swords and solemnly saluted her, holding for a long moment.

Constance's eyes teared, and she put a hand to her chest. They were free. It had all been worth it – they were free, vindicated.

As she watched, to either side, the force filled gradually with more men, both mounted and on foot. She could pick out the uniforms and garb of guards and townsfolk from the surrounding villages. Her brother was there with many of his best soldiers. Pete and several other innkeepers stood ready with dagger and cudgel. Tristan and Ralph sat on their steeds side by side, their aspect grim.

A shout went up from the guards on the wall as the force became visible in the moonlight, and the answering roar from Constance's saviors sent shivers through her spine. There was a long pause, a building of tension that felt as if her heart would burst – and then it was as if a floodgate had been unleashed. The attackers drove forward in a thundering motion, releasing a charge at the front gates.

The assault was on.

Constance pulled back from the window, driven into action. She knew she did not have much time. She was here as a hostage, after all, and once Barnard realized he was under siege he would make sure to use her to his best advantage. He would ward the attackers off with the threat of harming her. The bar she had put in place would not hold the door forever.

She grabbed the blanket off her bed and laid it down next to her heavy dresser. With a great effort she managed to lift one of the dresser legs, sliding the blanket beneath the post. She moved around to each other leg, straining hard to lift the leg even a tiny amount to slide the blanket under. Her heart was hammering after all four legs had been placed, but the task was complete.

Now that the dresser was on a slick surface, it was at least possible for her to nudge the dresser along towards the door, by throwing all her weight hard against the piece of furniture. She had no doubt that, if she survived this night, her arms and legs would be a mass of bruises. She did not care. She flung herself at the heavy wood again and again until finally it rested in front of the sturdy door.

Then came the task of pulling the blanket free again. She was utterly exhausted by the time she had gotten all four legs solidly on the floor. She slumped to the floor, leaning back against the dresser.

THUMP. The bar on the other side of the door fell free, and the door rattled on its hinges. A loud curse sounded from the hallway as Barnard realized what she had done.

"Constance, open this door right now!" he ordered. "It will only be worse on you if you make me break it down!"

"Maybe by the time you do your keep will be breached!" shot back Constance hotly, stepping up and away from the dresser.

There was the sound of running feet, and Constance knew she had only bought herself a few minutes. Still, they could prove crucial. The longer she stayed free, the longer Gabriel and his men could act completely unfettered, breaking their way into Barnard's keep.

She dug furiously through her trunks. Her sword was tucked into one; she pulled it out and flung it on the bed. She still wore her dagger at her belt, and there was no need to fetch the one safely beneath her pillow.

A loud thud sounded at the door. A fight was out of the question. Could she last more than ten seconds against a cadre of men who faced hanging? There had to be another way. She looked about in a panic.

Her eyes lit on the blanket heaped on the floor. There was another loud thud at the door. She sat down and began quickly tying knots in the blanket, every foot or so. She worked her way down its length, working it into a long rope. When she reached the end of it, she grabbed the top sheet off the bed and tied it on. Then came the lower sheet. The thumps against the door grew louder, steadier. She heard a crack as one of the hinges began to give way.

Her fingers moving furiously, she finished knotting the third length and then ran over behind the bed. With all her strength she shoved the bed over towards the window, the grating of the bed legs on the floor matching the low grinding as the dresser blocking the door was slowly, inexorably pushed back. She raced to the bed leg nearest the window and tied the sheet firmly around its base. Then she flung the shutters wide and tossed the length out. The rope went down to six feet above the ground. She gave one last look as a pair of guards ran just below her improvised ladder. Yes, it did seem doable.

The door gave one last groan, and she grabbed her sword, dropping to the floor, rolling quickly beneath the bed, tucking herself in the back corner by the wall. There was the sound of wood cracking, and the door flung hard against the far wall, splinters and metal pieces flying everywhere. Four sets of heavy feet burst into the room, and then someone was running to the window, cursing loudly.

"Get her!" he screamed in the night at his guards, and then the men were turning, running from the room, thundering down the stairs. The room was left in sudden silence, the curtains fluttering in with the summer breeze.

Constance remained pinned against the back wall, breathing heavily, uncertain that her ruse had really worked. If she was able to distract Barnard's guards and thieves with a fruitless search for her, all the better for the Angelus. Even so, she did need to get somewhere safe. Safe but visible, so that Gabriel would know she was all right. Otherwise he might be hesitant to attack an area, not knowing if she might be hurt.

The roof. If she could get up there, she could remain hidden, only showing herself when she was sure Gabriel was looking. That would give him the reassurance of knowing she was unharmed. Barnard would never think to look for her up there, and if he did find her, she was no worse off than she had been before.

She made her way warily out from beneath the bed, bringing her sword with her. She stepped carefully over the detritus and peered out through the open doorway. The hallway was abandoned, and she could hear no noise from below her in the keep itself. All shouts seemed to be centered at the front courtyard. She quickly made her way along the hall to the attic stairs, then up the rickety wood slats to the roof. In a moment she had closed the outer door behind her. There was no lock, nothing at all on this side of the door with which to wedge it closed.

She made her way carefully through the dust to the front of the building, looking over the low wall which lined the three-story drop. She could see that the main gate had been broken open, but that the Angelus stood arrayed along the outer side of the door, facing perhaps twenty guards and bandits. At the center of the defensive line stood Barnard, holding a cloaked figure over his shoulder. Mark was at his side, laughing at the reticence of the invaders to move.

Barnard gave a shake to the figure in his arms. "Not one more step," he called out in warning. "Drop your weapons, or she dies!"

Constance looked more closely at the face hanging over Barnard's back. Which of the maids would he have risked in such a dangerous gambit? With a surprised gasp she realized the figure was made of straw! Several bits of hay stuck out from the opening of the hood which pointed back at the keep.

"Gabriel!" screamed Constance at the top of her lungs. She climbed onto the low wall, waving her hands in the air. "Gabriel! That woman is made of straw! I am up here!"

All eyes turned to look up at her, and then a roar of attack bellowed from the townsfolk and the Angelus alike. A wave of men poured over the guards as a rough sea crashing onto breakers. Gabriel dove for Barnard, but Barnard managed to slip behind Mark, who roared in delight as he found himself facing the Angelus leader.

"I am the one who kidnapped Constance," Mark sneered as he brought his sword down hard against Gabriel's, circling him before jumping in again. "Her skin was as smooth as a babe's, although I found she bruises easily when hit. I shall be sure to take good care of her once you are dead."

Gabriel growled, spinning his sword into a higher position, moving in with a sudden attack. Constance watched, her heart in her throat, as the men lunged and parried, twisted and blocked. Gabriel ducked under a blow, then stood suddenly and threw a solid punch with his left arm, catching Mark hard on the temple. Mark staggered back, and Gabriel closed with him in a heartbeat. He swung his sword down, hard, slashing diagonally across Mark's chest.

Mark threw his hands back, his mouth open in a silent scream. He seemed to timber backwards in slow motion, his sword flying from his hand. His body landed heavily in the dirt, sending up a cloud of debris. He did not move again.

An arrow zinged past Constance's head, and she dove flat on the ground, suddenly aware of her surroundings again. She knew better than to make herself an easy target for Barnard's archers! She realized she should find another hiding place, but now that the full assault was set in motion, she could not tear herself away. There would be little she could do to help or hinder the attack now. She could only pray that the Angelus forces would be victorious.

She peered carefully over the edge of the wall. The grounds below were in chaos. The local guards had the advantage of knowing their home turf well, of knowing which alleys ran into dead ends, which windows could be wiggled through. Even so, the Angelus moved through their ranks with deadly efficiency. The townsfolk followed behind, wrestling survivors to the ground, tying them securely and throwing them into the stables for safe keeping.

The bandits were already outnumbered, and Constance watched as more townsfolk arrived on horseback, coming to help as news spread of the battle. The new arrivals carried whatever they had at hand – an axe, a large knife, a pitchfork. Every additional man quickly joined in the search for hidden enemies, or in watching the bound bandits.

The minutes passed, and Constance almost began to relax. The end was in sight. The sounds of conflict began to die out below her. With a relieved sigh, she stood and turned away from the wall. If the few remaining bandits were retreating into the keep to make a final stand, her current location might not remain safe. She could still be useful as a hostage to someone. She worked her way back to the door, running her mind over her options for a better hiding place.

The door flung open as she reached it, and she stepped back in surprise. Barnard's eyes blazed with delight as he grabbed hold of her arm, whipping her around to press up against him. The all too familiar dagger was quickly brought against her throat.

His breath came heavily against her ear. "Just who I was looking for," he rasped. "You will serve some use for me yet, my dear."

He dragged her back away from the door, and Constance moved with him in confusion. Why would he be going this way?

The answer barreled up through the door only moments later. Gabriel looked around quickly, then froze as he saw Barnard holding Constance. He still wore his heavy leather riding gloves, his sword held firmly in his right hand.

Barnard's voice was tight. "You know the drill," he insisted. "Sword. Down."

Constance's heart stopped. "Gabriel, no," she pleaded. Once Gabriel was disarmed, there was nothing to stop Barnard from killing him, from escaping justice. If anyone knew the ins and outs of this structure, with all its secret doors and passageways, it would be Barnard.

Barnard was long past playing. He pulled his knife hard against Constance's throat, creating a long, thin slice along her neck. "Go ahead, try me," he warned Gabriel in a guttural voice. "I have already lost everything else. I would gladly gut her just to watch the misery on your face, to know you would have to live with that agony for the rest of your life."

Gabriel crouched down, his eyes not leaving Barnard's, and he laid his sword down lengthwise before him. He rested a hand on its hilt for a long moment, then stood again. His body was tensed for action, watching for any opening.

Barnard motioned to the left. "Over to the wall," he ordered. Gabriel moved slowly, placing his feet carefully, keeping his attention focused on Barnard. At Barnard's gesture he stepped the two feet up onto the lip.

Barnard looked down at Constance. "Say goodbye to your hero," he sneered. "Perhaps it is fitting that you see him off in that accursed dress of yours, with the matching pendant. It will remind you, every time you see it, that you were the cause of his death."

Constance watched in panic as Gabriel looked down beneath him, then to her surprise he carefully took several steps to the left along the wall. She glanced out to her left. She knew those woods by heart; they were the area her window overlooked. There was the trio of white birch where Gabriel had ridden out from. It meant that her window was right below them ...

Her eyes rose to meet Gabriel's. He was pulling hard on the cuff of his gloves, settling them in against his fingers. His gaze was intent, serious.

Her heart thudded in her chest. "I still keep a dagger under my pillow, just as you taught me," she whispered.

The edge of his mouth quirked up into a wry smile. "I am more concerned with how well you tie your knots," he answered, his eyes holding hers.

Constance nodded, swallowing hard. "I swear, they will not fail."

Barnard gave her arm a hard shake. "Enough!" He leered at Gabriel. "You jump, and I let her live. If she is lucky, I will be able to take her all the way to Bordeaux with me. She will be kept as a queen. She always desired a life of wealth or so I have been told. You think on that on your way down."

Gabriel locked his gaze on Constance. "I will come for you," he murmured. "Trust in me."

Constance could not take it. She pressed forward against Barnard's hold, even though it cut the knife more deeply against her. "Gabe ... I love you," she whispered, releasing the fullness of her passion, her pride, her adoration for the man before her. He was everything to her, and she let the knowledge shine from her very soul.

He smiled then, a shimmering of peace washing over his features. He spared one final look down, took in a deep breath, and stepped off.

Constance screamed, pressing against the sharp blade to run forward, to see ...

A shout roared up from below, from the crowd of townsfolk and mercenaries on the ground level. Hearing that, Barnard turned instantly, pulling Constance hard toward the stairs, moving quickly. "You behave, and you might just survive this," he warned her as he kicked open the door with his foot. He pushed her brusquely down the stairs.

Her mind spun as she stumbled down the flight. Had Gabriel survived the fall? Had he been able to grab onto her blanket ladder one story below? Had it snapped at his weight? What if ...

Tears sprang to her eyes, and she brushed them away quickly. If he was hurt, maybe seriously, she needed all her wits about her.

Barnard gave her a hard yank as they reached the bottom of the stairs, pulling her close in front of him, maintaining the knife at a tight angle against her throat. He moved carefully down the hall, past closed doors, past ...

Constance froze as they got to the blown open remains of her bedroom door. This is where Gabriel would come lunging out of the room. He would fly in a blaze of glory, his eyes sharp, his right hand wielding her dagger. He was her avenging angel. She took in a breath ...

Nothing. There was no movement, no swirl of revenge, nothing but the gently blowing breeze rustling the curtains at her window. Her eyes traveled down to the bedpost. Her face went cold with shock, and she found herself staggering back against Barnard, all hope gone.

The bedpost was bare. Her knot had failed. The blanket tied to the bed was completely missing.

Barnard snarled at her weakness, pressed her onwards, forcing her forward down the hall. Constance no longer knew where he was taking her, or cared. She could see it clearly in her mind now. Gabriel had stepped off the roof putting his life into her hands. He had grabbed at her rope, had trusted her. He had held onto it, expecting it to save him.

She had failed him. She had caused the one man she cared for most in this world to plummet to his death.

Barnard pressed her down the main stairs into the great hall. Peripherally she saw a few of the Angelus mercenaries start in surprise, then pull back cautiously. As they moved their way across into the entry hall, out into the courtyard, the throng around them grew. Soon they were surrounded by a mob of Angelus and innkeepers, of soldiers from the town and common folk. All stood silently, cautiously keeping a distance, and it did not matter one bit to Constance. She would go where Barnard took her. When he was done, he would kill her. She did not care. Gabriel was gone … he was gone …

Barnard pulled up to a sudden stop. Constance roused herself to look at the main gates. Three men stood framed in the large archway, with a row of soldiers lining the wall above them. Tristan stood in the center, with Ralph on the left and Charles on the right. All three men held swords at the ready.

Tristan's tone was rational and quiet. "We cannot let you take her, Barnard," he stated in a low voice. "You need to leave Constance here if you wish to leave alive."

Barnard laughed. "You are joking, right? If I let her loose, you would eagerly tie my noose's loop yourself. No, I am giving the orders here. I want a fresh horse outside the gates, saddled and ready for riding. I want all of you inside these walls. I will mount up and take this woman with me. When I am sure I am not being pursued – and not one moment earlier – I will release her."

Tristan's eyes narrowed. "We cannot -"

Barnard was long past negotiating. He drove his knife downwards, cutting a long, vertical slice along Constance's chest. She cried out sharply at the pain, falling hard to one knee. She heard the cry of rage echo around her, and the group surged forward for a moment, only to pull back again as he reseated the blade at her neck, pulling her hard, raising her to her feet.

Barnard's voice was a growl. "Do not press me, Sheriff," he warned. "I have very little to lose here. I can torture her all day."

Tristan waved with his hand, and two soldiers ran quickly for the stables. He, Ralph, and Charles moved carefully into the courtyard. Constance could see the tension in their shoulders, the sharp focus of their gaze. She almost shook her head to warn them not to bother. It was over. Barnard would take her out of here, and later he would kill her. They might catch up with him eventually, but it did not matter. Gabriel was dead.

Still, the bandits had been found out. The Angelus were free. The townspeople were safe. It was almost all she had hoped to achieve. If her only role left in this world was to help ensure no more lives were lost before Barnard was finally brought to justice, she could do that much.

She held her head high, her eyes glistening, and watched as the sturdy brown horse was led to a spot outside the archway of the main gates. The wooden doors were pressed wide, and all of the soldiers pulled back from the area. Only a few men remained at the top of the wall to watch over the proceedings.

Tristan's voice was tight. "There is your horse."

Barnard smiled at that, his arrogant stance returning. He looked around him with haughty pleasure, at the men ringing him. His gaze landed on Ralph and Charles, at the Angelus who flanked them.

"If you thought it was to be me or Gabriel who was left standing this day, I wonder who you would have bet on," he called out in a challenging voice to the men. "I will be riding free, I will have my woman securely in my grasp. Think on that when you wipe down your swords tonight. You go look on the broken body of your leader and know who is the true master."

He pushed Constance across the remaining length of the courtyard, moving towards the waiting horse, toward his freedom.

Something came into Constance's vision as they approached the archway. It was a loose piece of rope, dangling from the archway top, hanging almost down to her shoulders. She glanced at it idly for a moment, then her vision sharpened as they grew closer. No, this was no random piece of twine. It was the sheet she had tied from her bedroom. It was solid, whole, and as she looked more carefully, she saw that one of her handhold loops had been added to the end of it. Her heart beat more quickly …

They were coming past it now. Barnard was laughing as he walked, scoffing at the men behind him, looking forward at the horse which would bring him to an easy escape. His knife hand moved back slightly …

She was at the rope, and she dove for it with a sharp twist, lacing her wrist into the loop, grabbing at the rope with both hands. Barnard cried out in surprise, and suddenly she was being hauled upwards, drawn into the sky. A pair of sturdy arms enfolded her, the scent of bergamot and sweat and blood pulled her in. She was crying, laughing, wrapping her arms around Gabriel in a whirling rush of emotions. Below her she could hear the yells as the Angelus raced in at Barnard, driving him to the ground, forcing him into submission.

Constance was torn between disbelief and joy. "You are alive!" she cried out. "Tell me this is not a dream!"

Gabriel pulled her close, holding her against him in a powerful embrace. "This is real," he vowed in her ear, not turning, not letting her go. "I will never leave you again. I swear it."

Chapter 28

Constance stood staring out at the ocean, watching the waves draw in and recede, listening to the soft cries of the gulls as they soared far overhead. She pulled her cloak closer around her. There was only a gentle throb now from her injuries and bruises; the week of healing and rest had done her good. Still, she had been hounded by Audrey to take it easy. She knew she should go in to the keep behind her, return to her room, but she could not leave the beauty of the sea. It soothed her soul, it calmed her restless heart. She could stay here for hours.

Footsteps sounded behind her, but she did not turn. In a moment a pair of strong arms gently wrapped around her, pulling her in close. She turned her head and nestled against Gabriel, closing her eyes. She found her throat closing up; she could not bring herself to speak.

He let out a long breath. "It is done," he murmured against her hair. "The messenger just came. Barnard has been executed for his crimes."

The final vestiges of tension drained from of her shoulders. It was over now. All ties to her past had been severed.

She brushed the hair from her eyes. "The Beadnell lands?"

Gabriel smiled. "Charles has agreed with your wish to turn them over to the nunnery," he responded. "The region will be developed into a center of learning, just as you wished. The villagers have given their enthusiastic blessing."

"A new beacon of hope - guarded over by the Angelus," added Constance, turning to look up at Gabriel with warm eyes.

"If that is your desire," he confirmed with a nod. "You are a free woman now, after all. You can make your own choices."

He looked away, out to the sea, his eyes distant. "This is your first chance to be on your own," he mused quietly, his voice hoarse. "Many men have stopped by in the past days, wishing to congratulate you, to court you. Now that you are freely able to marry, I imagine you could have the pick of any noble around. You could take your time, enjoy your freedom."

Constance shook her head, gently taking his face in her hand, turning his eyes down to meet hers.

"Is that what you think I want?" she murmured softly.

"What *do* you want?" he asked, his voice half anguish.

She smiled gently. "I want to say ..." her voice dropped down into a soft whisper. "I love you." She leant forward to kiss his cheek, and he closed his eyes in surrender.

"I love you." She kissed his other cheek tenderly, and he brought his arms more tightly around her.

"I love you," she vowed with all her heart, and she brought her lips to a whisper's length from his, holding there. He opened his eyes, let out a ragged sigh, and then he pulled her hard in against him, pulled her lips in against his. They were kissing, kissing, kissing, the ocean waves crashed down around them, the timeless reaches of the sea filled their senses as they gave themselves fully to each other.

Dedication

To my mom, dad, siblings, and family members who encouraged me to indulge myself in medieval fantasies. I spent many long car rides creating epic tales of sword-wielding heroines and the strong men who stood by their sides. Jenn, Uncle Blake, and Dad were awesome proofers.

To Peter and Elizabeth May, who patiently toured me around England, Scotland, and France on three separate occasions. Elizabeth offered valuable tips on creating authentic scenes. Visiting the Berkhamsted motte and bailey was priceless.

To Jody, Leslie, Liz, Sarah, and Jenny, my friends who enjoy my eclectic ways and provide great suggestions. Becky was my first ever web-fan and her enthusiasm kept me going!

To the editors at BellaOnline, who inspire me daily to reach for my dreams and to aim for the stars. Lisa, Cheryll, Jeanne, Lizzie, Moe, Terrie, Ian, and Jilly provided insightful feedback to help my polishing efforts.

To the Massachusetts Mensa Writing Group for their feedback and enthusiastic support. Lynn, Tom, Ruth, Carmen, Al, and Dean all offered detailed, helpful advice!

To the Geek Girls, with their unflagging support for my expanding list of projects and enterprises. Debi's design talents are amazing. I simply adore the covers she created for me.

To the Academy of Knightly Arts for several years of in-depth training and combat experience with medieval swords and knives. I loved sparring with Nikki and Jo-Ann!

To B&R Stables who renewed my love of horseback riding and quiet forest trails.

To my son, James, whose insights into psychology help ground my characters in authentic behavior.

To Bob See, my partner in love for over 16 years and counting. He enthusiastically supports all of my new projects.

Glossary

Ale - A style of beer which is made from barley and does not use hops. Ale was the common drink in medieval days. In the 1300s, 92% of brewers were female, and the women were known as "alewives". It was common for a tavern to be run by a widow and her children.

Blade - The metal slicing part of the sword.

Chemise - In medieval days, most people had only a few outfits. They would not want to wash their heavy main dress every time they wore it, just as in modern times we don't wash our jackets after each wearing. In order to keep the sweaty skin away from the dress, women wore a light, white under-dress which could then be washed more regularly. This was often slept in as well.

Drinking - In general, medieval sanitation was not great. People who drank milk had to drink it "raw" - pasteurization was not well known before the 1700s. Water was often unsafe to drink. For these reasons, all ages of medieval folk drank liquid with alcohol in it. The alcohol served as a natural sanitizer. This was even true as recently as colonial American times.

God's Teeth / God's Blood – Common oaths in the middle ages.

Grip - The part of the sword one holds, usually wrapped in leather or another substance to keep it firmly in the wielder's hand.

Guard - The crossed top of the sword's hilt which keeps the enemy's sword from sliding down and chopping off the wielder's fingers.

Hilt - The entire handle part of the sword; everything that is not blade.

Mead - A fermented beverage made from honey. Mead has been enjoyed for thousands of years and is mentioned in Beowulf.

Pommel - The bottom end of the sword, where the hilt ends.

Tip - The very end of the sword

Wolf's Head – a term for a bandit. The Latin legal term *caput great lupinum* meant they could be hunted and killed as legally as any dangerous wolf or wild animal that threatened the area.

About Medieval Life

When many of us think of medieval times, we bring to mind a drab reality-documentary image. We imagine people scrounging around in the mud, eating dirt. The people were under five feet tall and barely survived to age thirty. These poor, unfortunate souls had rotted teeth and never bathed.

Then you have the opposite, Hollywood Technicolor extreme. In the romantic version of medieval times, men were always strong and chivalrous. Women were dainty and sat around staring out the window all day, waiting for their knight to come riding in. Everybody wore purple robes or green tights.

The truth, of course, lies somewhere in the middle.

Living in Medieval Times

The years in the early medieval ages held a warm, pleasant climate. Crops grew exceedingly well, and there was plenty of food. As a result, their average height was on par with modern times. It's amazing how much nutrition influences our health!

The abundance of food also had an effect on the longevity of people. Chaucer (born 1340) lived to be 60. Petrarch (born 1304) died a day shy of 70. Eleanor of Aquitaine (born 1122) was 82 when she died. People could and did lead long lives. The average age of someone who survived childhood was 65.

What about their living conditions? The Romans adored baths and set up many in Britain. When they left, the natives could not keep them going, and it is true they then bathed less. However, by the middle ages, with the crusades and interaction with the Muslims, there was a renewed interest both in hygiene and medicine. Returning soldiers and those who took pilgrimages brought back with them an interest in regular bathing and cleanliness. This spread across the culture.

While people during other periods of English history ate poorly, often due to war conditions or climatic changes, the middle ages were a time of relative bounty. Villagers would grow fresh fruit and vegetables behind their homes, and had an array of herbs for seasoning. The local baker would bake bread for the village - most homes did not hold an oven, only an open fire. Villagers had easy access to fish, chicken, geese, and eggs. Pork was enjoyed at special meals like Easter.

Upper classes of course had a much wider range of foods - all game animals (rabbits, deer, and so on) belonged to them. The wealthy ate peacocks, veal, lamb, and even bear. Meals for all classes could be flavorful and well enjoyed.

Medieval Marriage
Marriage choices were critical for both sons and daughters. Wealthy families would absolutely arrange for "proper" marriages for their children. This was about the transfer of land far more than a love match. Parents wanted to ensure their land went to a family worthy of ownership, one with the resources to defend it from attack. It was not only their own family members they were concerned with. Each block of land had on it both free men and serfs. These people all depended on the nobles – with their skill, connections, and soldiers – to keep them safe from bandits and harm.

Yes, villagers sometimes married for love. Even a few nobles would run off and follow their hearts. Even so, they would have first seriously considered the potentially catastrophic risks which could result from their actions.

Here is a modern example. Imagine you took over the family business which employed a hundred loyal workers. Those workers depend on your careful guidance of the company to ensure the income for their families. You might dream about running off to Bermuda and drinking martinis. But would you just sell your company to any random investor who came along? Would you risk all of those peoples' lives, people who had served you loyally for decades, to satisfy a whim of pleasure?

Medieval Women
In pagan days women held many rights and responsibilities. During the crusades, especially, with many men off at war,

women ran the taverns, made the ale, and ran the government. However, as men returned home and Christianity rose in power women were relegated to a more subservient role.

Still, women in medieval times were not meek and mild. That stereotype came in with the Victorian era, many centuries later. Back in medieval days, women had to be hearty and hard working. There were fields to tend, homes to maintain, and children to raise!

Women strove to be as healthy as they could because they faced a serious threat - a fifth of all women died during or just after childbirth. The church said that childbirth was the "pain of Eve" and instructed women to bear it without medicine or follow-up care. Of course, midwives did their best to skirt these rules, but childbirth still took an immense toll.

Childhood was rough in the middle ages – only 40% of children survived the gauntlet of illnesses to adulthood. A woman who reached her marriageable years was a sturdy woman indeed.

To summarize, in medieval days a person could live a long, happy life, even into their 80s – as long as they were of the sturdy stock that made it through the challenges of childhood. This was very much a time of 'survival of the fittest'. Medieval life quickly weeded out the weak and frail.

So medieval women were strong - very strong. They had to be. Still, would they fight?

Women and Weapons

Queen Boudicia, from Norwalk, was born around AD60 and personally led her troops against the Roman Empire, quite successfully. She had been flogged - and her daughters raped - spurring her to revenge. She was extremely intelligent and quite strategic. Her daughters rode in her chariot at her side.

Eleanor of Aquitaine, born in 1122, was brilliant and married first to a King of France and then to a King of England. She went on the Second Crusades as the leader of her troops - reportedly riding bare-breasted as an Amazon. At times she marched with her troops far ahead of her husband. When she divorced the King of France, she immediately married Henry II, who she passionately adored. He was eleven years her junior. When things went sour, Eleanor separated from him and actively led revolts against him.

Many historical accounts talk of women taking up arms to defend their villages and towns. Women would not passively let their children be slain or their homes burned. They were able and strong bodied from their daily work. They were well skilled with farm implements and knives, and used them with great talent against invaders.

Many of these defenses were successful, and the victories were celebrated as brave and proper, rather than dismissed as an unusual act for a woman. A mother was expected to defend her brood and to keep her home safe, just as a wolf mother protects her cubs.

Numerous women took their martial skills to a higher level. In 1301 a group of Italian women joined up to fight the crusade against the Turks. In 1348 at a tournament there were at least thirty women who participated, dressed as men.

This is not as unusual as you might think. In medieval times, all adults carried a knife at their belt for daily use in eating, chores, and defense. All knew how to use it. Being strong and safe was a necessary part of daily life.

Here is an interesting comparison. In modern times most women know how to drive, but few choose to invest themselves in the time and training to become race car drivers. In medieval times, most women knew how to defend themselves with a weapon. They had to. Few, though, actively sought the training to be swordswomen. Still, these women did exist, and did thrive as valued members of their communities.

So women in medieval times were far from shrinking violets. They were not mud-encrusted wretches huddling in straw huts. They were strong, sturdy, and well versed in the use of knives. Many ran taverns, and most handled the brewing of ale. Those who made it through childhood and childbirth could expect to enjoy long, rich lives.

I hope you enjoy my tales of authentic, inspiring heroines!

About the Author

Lisa Shea is a fervent fan of honor, loyalty, and chivalry. She brings to life worlds where men and women stand shoulder to shoulder, steady in their desire to make the world a better place for all.

While her heroines often wield a sword, they equally value the skilled use of their intelligence, wisdom, courage, and compassion.

Lisa has written ten medieval romance novels.

Please visit Lisa at LisaShea.com to learn more about her background and interests. Feedback is always appreciated!

Other medieval romance novels by Lisa Shea:

Seeking the Truth
Knowing Yourself
A Sense of Duty
Creating Memories
Looking Back
Badge of Honor
Lady in Red
Finding Peace
Believing your Eyes
Trusting in Faith

Each novel is a stand-alone story set in medieval England. These novels can be read in any order and have entirely separate casts of characters.

All proceeds from sales of these novels benefit battered women's shelters.